BATTLE FOR THE WOODLANDS

BOOK TWO OF MOTHERTREE

W.K. GREYLING

CONTENTS

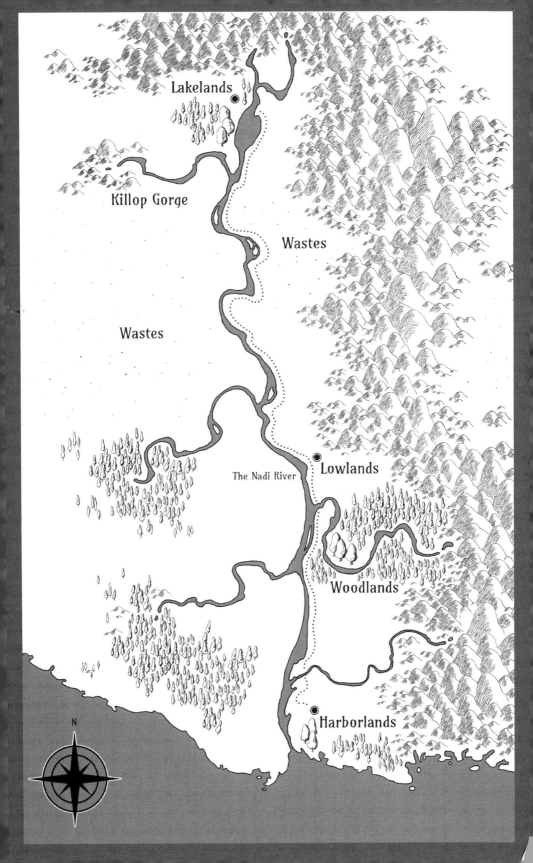

CHAPTER 1

"I have to piss."

Brite's reluctant whisper made Walde sit up in the darkness. He hadn't been asleep. Too much had happened this night to allow his mind to settle. His emotions clawed like chained animals at his carefully constructed calm. Fortunately, he had a measure of control over them. Singling one out and letting it rise to the surface was as easy as plucking a harp string.

Of course, he chose love. Who wouldn't? And the object of his affection was right beside him, unaware of his newfound feelings for her.

A shine of silvery Reacher light blossomed from his palms, and if he pushed his sleeves back, the entire underside of his arms. It illuminated the small space he and Brite were sheltering in.

His people called it the corpse darkness.

Many hundreds of years ago, a deep, rectangular hole had been excavated from a space between two massive Mothertree roots. Its four walls had been shored up with stone, and a door made from storm-felled Mothertree wood had been closed over its top. Holes carved out of the roots served as sockets for the door's wooden dowel joints. The pit's purpose was simple: to hold the bones of the dead. But after the Mothertrees were abandoned, the corpse darkness had been forgotten, its door concealed by vines and brush. Desperation had moved Walde to seek it out and use it as a hiding place.

He tried not to dwell on how many bodies lay under him. The bones were old and brittle and smelled faintly of ash.

Brite shifted to a kneeling position. She was tall, with dark auburn hair and a fey cast to her large eyes and wide lips. Walde's spare tunic hung on her slender frame like a night robe. She said, "I can't wait. I have to go now. And I'm not going in here. Do you think it'd be safe to go outside?"

They had been in hiding for at least an hour. Walde's face lifted to the shadowy door above. Curiosity nudged him. The muffled sounds that filtered into the pit offered little information about what was happening outside. "It should be, if you can manage it in the dark." He rose to his feet and grasped a handful of root hair. "I could go too."

"You mean..."

He grinned. "I mean to take a piss, not to stand around and watch you."

Brite returned his grin but then looked swiftly aside as if she'd been caught doing something embarrassing. She had been that way all night. Walde pinpointed it to the moment he'd agreed to stay with her rather than follow his father, Carrac, into the crack in the First Mothertree's trunk. Perhaps she was worried that she'd been too pushy.

The brightness in his hands and wrists had faded to a bare wisp. Only the strongest emotions produced Reacher light; maintaining such emotion required constant concentration. Gathering root hair around his wrists, he followed her up, and they shoved the door open together.

A cool wind, smelling of salt and oakum, brushed stray hairs from his forehead. A distant roar of agitated voices rose and fell with it. The sound was eerie in the darkness.

Brite whispered, "The crowd hasn't dispersed."

"No," he agreed. "In fact, it sounds like it's grown."

They stood under the boughs of an enormous dead Mothertree. Its bare, shadowy roots had once been covered by walkways. Now, only a few boards remained, many of them rotten. It was but one of twenty dead Mothertrees that ran alongside the harbor. Only one living Mothertree remained—the First—and it had become a doorway to some other place. Walde had unintentionally helped open the crack that now gaped enticingly at the base of its trunk. The sound of that crack opening had drawn both peacekeepers from the guardhouse and innocent partygoers from nearby harbor ships. Walde and Brite fled before they could witness what had happened, but from the angry clamor, it seemed the partygoers had spotted the glowing crack through the compound door and were subsequently prevented from entering it. Two huge trees now stood between Walde and the compound, preventing him from seeing what was happening.

He yearned to be closer to it, and not merely to satisfy his curiosity. His father had disappeared into that crack. Walde couldn't leave him. It would've been so easy to flee the Harborlands now, in the midst of such an uproar. Easy, and probably wise. He and Brite had killed several guards in order to free the wounded Reachers chained to the First's trunk. Indeed, they'd left a trail of death from the cell they'd escaped to the sentinel tower overlooking the compound. And while the city elders probably assumed he and Brite had entered the crack along with the other Reachers, there would doubtlessly be an investigation. Still, he'd come to the Harborlands to save his father, and he wouldn't abandon him now. Tomorrow he would have to leave Brite in the corpse darkness to investigate what had happened at the compound.

Thundering footsteps on boards made him shift his focus to the lamplit boardwalk at the harbor.

A group of men wearing unbelted jackets raced by, moving in the direction of the compound. Walde sensed purpose in their stance, and their unbelted jackets likely hid concealed weapons. He turned toward Brite, but she had drifted off into the darkness to relieve herself.

He refocused on the boardwalk. Would people be hurt or even killed because he had helped open that crack? He had hoped, perhaps naively, that the glowing hole in the Mothertree would have filled the elders with such awe that they would've allowed others into the compound to view it. The enticing glow had almost overcome Walde. Without Brite's restraining hand, he would have followed his father right in. The light must have stirred other people's curiosity, or onlookers would not have lingered at the compound. Perhaps if enough people joined the crowd, they could overcome the guards.

He refused to contemplate his worst fear—that the Reachers' physical needs weren't being met where they were, and when they finally had to leave, they'd walk straight into the drawn bows of their captors.

If their needs *were* being met, then they'd probably stay put for a while. Unfortunately, that meant Walde would have to remain in the Harborlands until the uproar subsided and he could return to the crack to retrieve them.

The uncertainty was frustrating.

Having relieved himself, he plodded back to the corpse darkness.

"Did you see anything?" Brite asked when they were safely inside, enfolded by blackness.

Walde used his Reacher light sparingly in the corpse darkness at night. A gap under the door's handle might leak a wisp of it onto the ground outside, alerting any nearby guards.

"No." He lay back into the hollow his body had made in the bone fragments. "I'm almost afraid to. People are going to be hurt tonight." And perhaps worse, he thought.

4

Brite said no more.

Walde tried to find sleep, but his eyes wouldn't close, even in the absolute darkness of the hole. A slow grimace pulled back the corners of his mouth. When one focuses on something they cannot do, the thing itself becomes so tempting as to be intolerable. That night, he simply wanted to feel.

He had been trained from the time he was a boy to stifle strong feelings, and until he'd become a Reacher, he'd believed he was good at it. Now that it was a matter of life or death, he'd come to realize how often he slipped up. When he had found his father alive and well at the compound, he had lost control. The blaze of his joy had been so powerful that he had unintentionally "reached," leaving Brite alone while he lay unconscious on the ground. When he finally woke up, dizzied and sensitized by all that had happened while reaching, it was to find a radiant Brite crouched like a sprite on the root. Once more, his emotions had run unchecked, and he'd been drowned by the realization that he loved her.

So much, so fast. For a short space of time, color and brightness had spilled into the grayness of his life.

And then he'd been forced to smother it.

He rubbed the unshaven scruff on his chin. This was foolish and indulgent. He ought to be getting sleep instead of yearning like a drunk for a few moments of gratification. It would do him no good to muddle over his relationship with Brite, to wonder if her affection for him could ever grow into something stronger. To consider all the reasons why he loved her and how wonderful her skin would feel under his hands—

He suppressed a groan and turned onto his side. When had he become so shallow and selfish?

"Walde…"

"Yes?" he replied, a little too quickly.

"Last night you asked me how I killed the guard after I escaped my cell. Do you still want the answer to that...or maybe the answer to another question?"

He grinned. "What do you want so badly to know?"

Brite's people were the descendants of tinkers and as such believed that everything came at a price, be it goats, favors, or information. Nothing, or almost nothing, was freely given. Brite still felt she owed him for helping her dispose of the body of a man she'd killed in self-defense, and nothing would convince her otherwise. To her, life was a pair of scales constantly tipping this way and that. Walde found it both frustrating and endearing.

He heard her sigh. "I want to know what happened while you were reaching. You told me you spoke to the tree god, to the one you call Thara, and that she used you as a–a—"

"A conduit."

"A conduit to help her open the crack. But I don't know why. I'd like to know what happened after you passed out."

He found himself nodding. He owed Brite this story, but he'd been holding it back for the simple reason that relating it would stir feelings in him he'd be forced to suppress. It was a poor excuse. "You remember me telling you about the tunnel?"

"Yes. It's your path to her. Your link."

"Link is the right word. The First's link was incredibly strained. In a healthy link, a Reacher only brushes Thara and is given knowledge. But this link was so damaged that I lost consciousness before I even got to her. When I did meet her, it was more than a brush—it was a collision. But I endured the pain and didn't let her go."

Brite must have sat up. The direction of her voice had changed. "Why?"

Why. He hadn't asked himself that question. "I don't know. Priorities change when you're reaching. It's like nothing else exists. Nothing else matters but communing with Thara." He swallowed tightly. "When the worst of it was over, a deep calm settled over me, and I sensed her there, all around me. I sensed her every emotion."

"Did she sense yours?"

"I thought she did, but I don't know. She told me I was the first to cling to her the way I did. She said that many have reached but never clung."

"I wonder what moved you to do it."

He snorted. "I don't know." He searched his mind for an answer. "When I left the Lakelands, it was to find and rescue my father. But then I learned about the dead Mothertrees and the children in the Woodlands who can't grow; I learned that elders here have been torturing Reachers in order to destroy the links, and that they did it openly. Because they could. Because they made people believe that Thara is really a parasite that fell from the stars..." His voice caught. He dragged in a painful breath. "I was so happy when I found my father. But I was also desperate. The two emotions twined and made me fire when I reached."

He sat up, felt the enticing warmth of her arm, and shifted subtly away.

Brite said, "Not everyone believes that lie about Thara. If they did, no one would be struggling with guards right now to be closer to the crack."

Walde wanted so much to agree with her, but there were too many other ways to view the situation. Perhaps the Harborlanders merely wished to satisfy their curiosity, and being deprived of the opportunity had sparked pent-up anger at the guards.

Brite asked, "Did you tell her about the lie being spread about her?"

"Yes."

"And...?"

"She didn't seem surprised. In fact, she told me it's the natural outcome of withdrawing from the Mothertrees, and, ultimately, from her. Her words were 'separation is the outcome of withdrawing.'"

Brite's hair flicked against her hand. Walde imagined her toying with it as her mind worked out the meaning of the words. "I see." She cleared her throat. "So what's the cost of separation?"

"Darkness and death. She said that Reachers must continue to learn from her and to pass on that knowledge, or people will cease to exist. Like sparks flung from a fire, we will cool and fade out."

Brite's voice sank to the barest whisper. "What else did she say?"

He pulled his knees up to his chin. She had told him not to despair. Given the opportunity, the Reachers could restore the First Mothertrees and plant others. Life could go on.

But that was before the Reachers had piled into the crack and disappeared. Walde had wanted so badly to go to the Woodlands with his father and Brite, restore the First there, and help the cursed children grow. Instead, he was trapped here, waiting. Was this what Thara meant to have happened? Or was Walde supposed to have followed Carrac and the other Reachers into the tree?

The thought startled a drift of light from him.

"What is it?" Brite's sleepy voice drifted up from the floor, where she had lain back down. He'd been so lost in thought that he'd forgotten to answer her question.

"I don't know. It's hard, not knowing where the Reachers are and how long they're going to be there."

"The tree god didn't tell you anything about the crack?"

"No." He shook his head roughly. "She just...said she would draw on people's sense of curiosity to work a change. When

I asked her if it would work, she said she hoped so. Nothing more." Sighing, he lay back down. "It's not that I don't trust her. I don't trust myself. And I don't trust that those in power here are going to respond the way she hopes they will. If the elders believe that the crack leads to Thara, they won't want anyone to go into it. If there's even a chance people will come back out knowing the truth, then the elders' power will be threatened."

"This might take a long time to settle." Brite tapped her fingers against something hard, probably a bone, he thought dryly. "I wonder if the First's new growth will make a difference to anyone. Before you reached, the tree looked dead. It still looks dead from a distance, but up close you can clearly see it has new shoots. When dawn comes, everyone else will see them too."

"But will they care? These same people abandoned their Mothertrees and seem to enjoy living like Lowlanders."

The Lowlands was a new settlement and until recently the only land where folk lived on the ground rather than in the treetops. The settlers had once been poor tinkers, but over time they had become wealthy and forgot what it was like to be of humble means. They paid the poor almost nothing to work their peat bogs and mines. Their corrupt legal system favored the wealthy, leaving the poor without rights. As a result, the place had become a hive of crime and injustice. Despite this fact, two of the three Mothertree lands had abandoned their dying trees and built new settlements patterned after the Lowlands.

He ran a weary hand across his eyes. The longer he considered the situation, the more complex it grew. And yet Thara had whittled it down to one word: curiosity. "What did you feel when *you* saw the crack?"

After a silence, she said, "Wonder. Simply wonder."

"Then others will feel the same. The glowing crack in the tree is compelling, and no matter what people have been led to believe, they'll be drawn to it. At the very least, they'll want someone to go in to get answers. Maybe the elders themselves will have to go in. Maybe that's what Thara foresaw."

Fabric rustled, and he felt the warm pressure of Brite's hand on his shoulder. "Do you wish you had gone in?"

"No." He touched her hand. Warmth filled his chest, and silver light sprouted around him. "I'm glad you pulled me back."

For several breaths, neither moved. The air seemed warmer, thicker, the darkness intimate. Walde didn't dare turn his head and look at her. He longed to discover if she returned his feelings, but this was the wrong place and time for it. If she did love him, then their relationship would change, and he didn't know if he could suppress the powerful emotions that would ensue. If he could, it would be painful.

More than that, it would be wrong.

He slid his hand away and turned onto his side. "I'm going to try to sleep. Sweet dreams, Brite."

***

When Walde finally succeeded in settling his thoughts, he slept like the dead. He woke gradually, blinking up at the smudge of light emanating from the gap under the door handle.

It was their second night in the corpse darkness, and they had grown comfortable there. The door was swathed in vine and moss. Walde had found it only because he'd been actively searching for it. The sea of bone fragments inside had been undisturbed, indicating that no one else had sheltered there. And who would? No sane person would want to open that door, never mind lie down on several centuries of human remains.

But Walde had discovered he could do many unthinkable things when he was pressed to do so. As could Brite.

He was amazed at how driven she was to help him. These were not her people. Until she'd met him in the Lowlands, she had never climbed an oak, never mind a Mothertree. "Reacher" and "Mothertree" were gossip words heard at Lowlander market stalls. They had little to do with the Lowlanders' lives.

But Brite had grown to believe in Walde's goal of restoring the Mothertrees. Comments she'd made hinted at a belief that folk needed Thara's guidance. She had cited her own land as an example of what would befall the world without it. Walde guessed that he had unintentionally blackened her land by his wistful descriptions of his Lakelands home. Well, so be it.

He shut his eyes and turned onto his side. For days he'd avoided thinking about his homeland. Before he had departed, only fourteen Reachers had been left to do their secret "maintenance" on the failing Mothertrees there. After the Lakelands elders had conspired with those in the Harborlands to drug and ship Reachers downriver, that number had likely dwindled to nothing. Without Reachers, the Lakelands Mothertrees would die.

Walde flinched from the thought.

He pushed his hands through his untidy brown hair. Brite might understand the severity of the situation, but she couldn't feel it in her bones like he did. She couldn't pine for a life she'd never had. For treelights and song rites. For living Mothertrees. The thought of it disappearing was beyond bearing.

His belly rumbled, and he swallowed back a stickiness in his throat. Soon, they would need to find a reliable source of food and water. They had already eaten half the mushrooms that carpeted the floor. If not for the food and drink they had nabbed from a guard's hut last night, they would've been in a bad way.

"Walde."

He jolted upright and found Brite's shadowy form standing over him. "I thought you were asleep."

"Listen. What do you hear?"

The tinge of fear in her voice unnerved him. He went still for several moments, hardly breathing. "I don't know. Birds."

"Those aren't birds."

The odd sound had grown louder. It was rough, toneless, and repetitive. It tickled his memory. Where had he heard it before?

When he remembered, his heart crashed painfully in his chest. "Dogs."

Reacher light flared, illuminating her wild eyes and pale face. "Guards will be close behind. What do we do?"

CHAPTER 2

The barking grew louder by the second. With an effort, Walde stilled his mounting anxiety. The guards wouldn't kill them outright. Walde knew too much, was too valuable, and Brite could be used as leverage to make him do whatever they wanted.

A shadow of the desperation he'd felt in the prison cell brushed him. No, he couldn't go back to that place. He couldn't allow them to poison his mind with their herbs, as they had done to the other Reachers. Most of all, he couldn't allow them to hurt Brite.

He snatched his bow and quiver.

"We fight them?" Brite whispered as he struggled to restring the bow in near darkness. His hands slowed. What chance did they have? The moment that door opened, several arrows would point down at them. Even if he and Brite managed to take out a guard, they couldn't avoid being punched down by arrows.

They were trapped.

He turned, letting a drift of Reacher light illuminate the pit's stone walls. Several feet of root hair hung down over the two longest walls, which stretched from the underside of the roots above to the floor. More than a foot of space lay between the hair and the stone wall. Could they try hiding in that space?

The barking was sharp and close. Muffled voices had joined it. Trackers, guards. Brite was trembling, a knife poised in her hand. Walde caught her forearm. "We'll hide."

"Where? Behind the hair? They'll see us."

"Not if we lie directly under the roots."

"What if the guards come in?"

"If they're in, they're in. We kill them."

Not long ago, Walde would have cringed at the thought of killing anyone. Now, he spoke about it with as much concern as he would give to hunting a rock deer. The change disturbed him.

Brite gave a stiff nod. Sheathing her knife, she turned toward the wall nearest her. Just then, a rustling and scraping filled the pit. Loose vines and debris were being removed from the door. Brite grabbed handfuls of root hair and dangled awkwardly as she struggled to get closer to the stone bricks. Walde hesitated and then hoisted her up until she was safely under the thick root. "Go!" she hissed.

At that moment, the door cracked open, dropping a white line of light onto the floor. Walde slid his bow into the quiver and clambered up into the root hair. The bow caught in the hair, forcing him to untangle it even as the crack of light widened. Panic roiled, threatening to overcome his desperate attempts to maintain calm. The hair under the root was damp and dirty, making his hands slide and his nose itch. He tried to wind the hair around his wrists and ankles so he wouldn't have to support his own weight using his grip alone, but when he did so, the hair stuck out into the middle of the pit. He found a slight ledge in the stone to rest a leg on and clung to the hair, his back against the wall.

The barking had risen to a fever pitch. The sound of the pin grinding in its holes was frighteningly close to his ear.

A deep male voice rose over the incessant barking. "I'd bet my grandfather's balls no one's down there."

"My dogs say they are," a woman retorted.

"Dogs like bones," a second man quipped, snorting at his own joke.

The first man ignored him and snapped, "Shut those dogs up, or I'll do it for you. Have some respect for the dead."

The woman shouted something, and the barking ceased. The pin resumed its grinding. Light flared into the pit. Brite was a still shadow behind the tangled root hair, her brown tunic blending well with her surroundings. Walde shut his eyes and waited, willing all thoughts from his mind. A tortured silence passed as several sets of eyes likely searched the small space.

"It's empty," the first man said, his casual tone ruined by an undercurrent of tension in his voice. "No sense going down."

"They were here," the woman insisted. "Look at the mashed mushrooms and the indentations on the floor. Not to mention the cut vines over the door. My dogs—"

"I don't care whether they were here or not. The place is empty now."

A third man who hadn't spoken yet said, "It's empty because they went into the Reacher tree. Think about it: the trail leads from here to the crack. It goes nowhere else. If they're not here, they're in the Reacher tree. Simple as that."

A kicking sound punctuated his words. The second man said, "Here's what's left of the lock. Looks like a shit smear."

"These pits should all be searched and locked. Yare, take…" The door slammed closed, muffling the rest of the man's words. After a little while, the muted voices silenced, leaving only the distant sounds from the harbor.

Brite dragged in a shaky breath and whispered, "Walde, we can't stay here. They could come back with a new lock at any time…"

"I know." He shoved aside the prospect of dying slowly in the corpse darkness.

"Where do we go? Up the Mothertree?"

He dropped softly to the floor and stared at the glimmer cast by the gap under the door handle. He had no idea what awaited them outside. The guards and dogs were nearby, and the harbor bustled with workers at this time of day. He and Brite would risk being sighted if they climbed the Mothertree in broad daylight. But what was the alternative? They couldn't just saunter down the boardwalk together. Brite had altered her only frock to make the compound's guard believe she was a harbor prostitute. The tactic had worked, but it had left Brite without suitable daytime garb. Walde's spare Woodlands tunic wasn't only too big for her, but it was also made from kessa. Harborlanders no longer wore the fabric spun from Mothertree pods. It would draw eyes and make them more vulnerable to capture.

He paced across the pit, sweeping shadows away with a glimmer of Reacher light. The inside of his mouth felt sticky. They needed water. There was a good chance they'd find a rain barrel in one of the abandoned huts in the upper branches.

Brite snapped an old bone as she landed. She swore under her breath and then stamped her foot, cracking another. "I'm beginning to hate this place."

He tried for some humor. "I don't know. Where else can you break human bones and get away with it?"

"In the Lowlands," she quipped, then amended, "if you're wealthy."

They both fell silent, peering up at the door. "This is a bad situation," he said. "If we open that door, we might find ourselves at the sharp end of an arrow. And the guard might not be in the hollow between roots. He could be standing *on* a root."

"I don't see why they'd station a guard here. They've already decided we went into the crack, so what would be the point of guarding this mortuary?"

It was a good point. But the mere chance of a guard stationed above unnerved him. He hated not knowing what lay on the other side of that door.

"Say there *is* a guard," Brite said. "He probably won't be staring at the door the whole time. If we're quiet, we could slip out and prepare a defense."

Walde offered a reluctant nod. "All right. We'll go up and take a look."

They waited a few more minutes before grabbing hold of root hair and scrambling to the top. Bracing himself against one of the two massive roots, Walde nudged the door open with a foot and peered outside. The weedy hollow came into view. It was empty.

He met Brite's eyes and mouthed, "I'll go first."

She nodded and propped the door open with her head and shoulders, allowing him to slide quietly out. His gaze fell at once on the tops of the two massive roots, but they were bare. A quick scan of the roots nearby revealed the same situation. For the moment, at least, he and Brite were safe.

Walde held the door open while she wriggled out. He threw one last wistful glance at their hiding place before gently closing the door. There'd be no going back now. For better or worse, they were stuck outside in broad daylight. Fortunately, the ground beneath the Mothertree was deeply shadowed. He crouched in the hollow beside Brite and took a closer look at their surroundings. The harbor was a different place than it had been the day before. Fewer merchant stalls lined the boardwalk, and no women walked together, chatting and enjoying the day. A group of men on a boat had stopped sorting fish and were speaking animatedly, probably about the crack in the First Mothertree.

The din from the compound had not dissipated. If anything, it had grown.

He shifted his gaze to the cart road, which ran parallel to the boardwalk but along the other side of the line of trees. Both the road and boardwalk were a good sixty yards from the trunk, far enough away that no one would notice someone climbing the tree unless they looked directly at the trunk. A path that cut across the space between this tree and its neighbor connected the boardwalk to the road, but it wasn't well used. He ran his hand over the back of his neck. They would climb, and climb fast. Hopefully they would find shelter in one of the abandoned huts.

He touched her shoulder, bringing her hazel eyes back to his. "Are you sure you want to do this?" He knew what it would cost her to go up the tree. He had never met anyone with such a fear of heights. She had pushed past it once, climbing halfway up a Mothertree alone in order to warn him that his life was in danger. Since then, she had gained a measure of confidence. But the fear lingered.

"If I wasn't, I wouldn't have suggested doing it."

He smiled. "You're a brave woman."

"I'm a desperate woman. There's a difference." She jerked her head to the road. "Let's go before the guards come to lock this place up."

They hopped onto one of the fat roots and ran along it toward the trunk.

Brite's time spent hunting with her uncle in the mountains had made her more agile than most Lowlanders. But her experience was limited to rocks and bogs. Trees were still foreign to her. Despite this, she was quickly growing accustomed to them. Every time she ventured out onto the roots, her steps were firmer, her gait more graceful. She didn't know it yet, but she was moving more and more like one of the treefolk. Walde had kept the fact to himself. Somehow, voicing it would've cheapened it. He could only hope that by the time she did feel at home in the trees, there would be living Mothertrees to dwell in.

They were only yards from the trunk when a wagon rumbled up the cart road, followed by two guards on horseback. The green stain of their garb, along with their unconcealed quivers, marked them as peacekeepers.

Brite ducked down into the nearest gap between roots. Walde, however, was too far from a gap and could only remain still where he was, balancing precariously on the hunched back of a root.

Several eternities passed before the wagon and horsemen went by. Thankfully, no one seemed to have looked his way. He and Brite reached the trunk at last and sagged against it.

Brite's face tilted up into the web of leafless branches and old paths. "Any chance we'll find water up there?"

Walde examined the tree. The bottom portion of the stairs had been removed in an attempt to deter Lowland workers—nicknamed Scats—from wintering in abandoned huts in the upper branches (the huts in the lower branches had all been dismantled). The poorest treefolk had always lived in the upper branches and collected rain in barrels rather than pay to have it lifted to them. It wasn't a bad existence. He replied, "If you don't mind drinking from a rain barrel."

"Sounds good to me." There was a false cheeriness in her voice. He wished she were more open with him about her fear.

The removal of the stairs had left a rising spiral of holes in the trunk's surface. Brite's lips compressed into a grimace of determination as she set her hands into holes and heaved herself up using the natural grooves in the bark as toeholds. Not wanting to get in her way, Walde waited until she disappeared around the trunk before following her up.

He climbed slowly, matching his pace to hers while ignoring a new clamor of voices and footsteps on the boardwalk. The sounds faded, and still he climbed. Brite never slowed, and the steadiness of her arms and legs reassured Walde. Only the small, tight sounds in her throat revealed her anxiety.

Finally, they came to the ragged edge of the winding staircase. Brite set her foot on the first step. "It seems sturdy, and the wood isn't rotten. At least from what I can see of it."

Walde descended a few feet and eyed the stairs' supporting beams. None had the tell-tale signs of rot and all appeared securely fastened to the tree. "It looks safe," he agreed.

Brite set her other foot on the step and began climbing, her hands trailing over the bark in case she needed to grasp it suddenly.

Up and around they went. The ground dropped away below, and the bright, sparkling harbor filled Walde's vision. Could the water be fresh? The harbor was at the wide end of a river that emptied into the sea. Even if it was a little salty, it might still be drinkable. If worst came to worst, he could sneak over to the dock when no one was around and fill his quiver.

He climbed on. The tempting sight disappeared, and the branches of neighboring Mothertrees replaced it, then the town—a grid of uneven streets broken by farm fields and a tree farm. Beyond it all lay the misty line of the mountains. The sights winked in and out through gaps in the branches.

Brite's tight voice cut through his reverie. "How much higher?"

He slowed and looked up. A platform jutted from the trunk above. It appeared to be the only platform remaining of the eight that had once hugged the tree. "Another two turns."

She nodded and went on climbing, but Walde thought he caught a muttered curse.

The sun brightened as they made a final turn. Just when Walde started to believe he would never see it, the First's blackened trunk came into view, peeking out between neighboring Mothertrees' branches. It was like glimpsing a strung-up corpse on a beautiful summer's day. Worse, because the tree was still alive. He paused, not wanting to see it but unable to tear his eyes away.

The First had been stripped of branches and the stubs slathered with pitch in an attempt to hinder their growth. Harborlanders called it "the Reacher tree" because it had come to be used as a prison pole for the chained Reachers. The herb forced on them had made them unable to control their emotions. In such a state, the undiluted strength of their torment had been relentless, causing them to withdraw violently into themselves. Such withdrawing caused damage to the First's link and had led to the decline of the Mothertree. Walde had restored the link by forcing himself through it, but it would take time for the tree to recover. Time, and the unceasing help of Reachers. He wondered if those in the crack might help it somehow.

He was about to take another step when a muffled snap from ahead made his heart lurch. *Brite!*

He charged up the winding steps, his palms whitened by Reacher light. As he neared the highest level, he halted, gasping at the sight that met his eyes. A step had cracked open, and Brite clung, white-faced, to the trunk while her legs kicked at the empty air. Walde lurched forward and grasped her under the arms.

She was hyperventilating. Her heart raced under his hands, and her breath was fast and sharp. If she fell, she'd probably slam through the stairs that spiraled beneath her, then through the next and the next until she hit the ground. It would be a horrible way to die. Leaning on the preceding step, he tried to haul her up, but her legs wouldn't stop working to find purchase. He held her tightly to him and whispered, "You're safe. I have you. Just stop moving and I'll bring you up. Please. Just for a moment."

At last, her legs went limp and he pulled her out of the broken step and onto the one above it. She came to life at once and scrambled up several steps until she reached the narrow platform. There she collapsed on her side against the tree.

Walde, having followed her up, touched her damp, trembling shoulder. "Are you hurt? Do you feel pain anywhere?"

Her answer was little more than a hiss of expelled air.

His own heart hammered as he searched for something to say. His brightened hands would have lit up the corpse darkness, but up here in the sunlight they were merely white, like fresh snow. "I'm sorry. I should've been there to catch you."

She found her voice. "It could've happened to you. Do you know that? And if it had, who would've had the strength to pull *you* up?"

The turn of her thoughts confused him. "I—I suppose I would've pulled myself up."

"I tried, but the way I fell made it impossible." She buried her face in her arm. "I don't know if I can take another step."

"Then don't. Just rest here. I'll see about finding water."

"No." She rose unsteadily to her feet and gripped his shoulders. "Don't. I was wrong about coming up here. It's too dangerous."

Walde's gaze flickered past her to the huts nearest him. Instead of the sturdy wooden paths of the lower levels, narrow, lightweight rope bridges spidered through the branches. The rope, made of linen reinforced by Mothertree pod silk, still looked intact. He spotted a rain barrel affixed to the side of a hut and swallowed longingly. It had rained hard two nights ago. The water would be fresh and cool, and the few remaining huts appeared intact. The rotten ones had probably been removed so they wouldn't come crashing down in a storm.

"Walde." Brite's stern voice pulled him back from his reverie. "If you risk your life to get that water, I'm not drinking it. I won't drink your life."

He sighed and forced a nod. Holding out his hand, he said gently, "Let's go back down."

An hour or a century later, they lay side by side in a wide gap between roots, a safe distance from the corpse darkness. Rough weeds and vines stuck into Walde, but they were no worse than the old bones he'd slept on. "I'm sorry," he said.

"That's the third time you've apologized."

"I mean it. I was scared to death at how close you came to falling."

She turned her head to face him. "Whose idea was it to climb that tree?"

"Yours, but—"

"Then why are you apologizing? It wasn't your fault. And if I'd fallen, you still wouldn't be to blame. You're not responsible for keeping me alive. *I* am."

If there was a logic to her words, his heart didn't agree with it. But he could find nothing to say in answer. Her hand brushed his, maybe by accident, maybe not. The unexpected contact sent a pleasant shiver through him, and he very nearly caught it and held it. *Not here.* Swallowing, he turned onto his back and gazed up at the web of branches. Gradually, his eyes closed and he drifted off.

He woke to the enticing smell of grilled fish. His stomach rumbled a response, and his mouth watered.

Brite groaned as he sat up and scanned the surroundings for danger. She said, "Gods, but that smells good. I'd wager the Scats have taken advantage of the crowd and are selling food and drink near the First."

The thought hadn't even occurred to him. But he saw no evidence of cooking fires nearby; all the activity did seem to emanate from farther down the boardwalk. "I'm going to head down there and take a look at what's going on."

Her mouth twitched up dryly. "Just to take a look."

He shrugged. "If you want something, I could make a stop on the way back…"

She shoved him playfully, dug out a coin from what was left in her pouch, and pleaded with him to be careful. In truth, Walde was less in danger of being recognized than she was. The Harborlands were riddled with her countrymen. And by an unlucky turn of events, several of them had recognized her at an inn shortly before she and Walde were arrested. Since then, her name had probably bounced around a few tables. She was now in constant danger, and there was nothing either of them could do about it.

He brushed himself off before picking his way over roots to the path between Mothertrees. From there, it was a short jog to the now busy boardwalk.

Folk were traveling in both directions. Those heading toward the First strode with the single-mindedness of a mother trying to fetch her unruly children. The others staggered drunkenly, nursing injuries and a blackness in their eyes that seemed a mix of resignation and anger. Walde put his hood up and walked as close to the harbor as he dared. He had removed his sheathed dagger and hoped he wouldn't miss it. His belted kriksa robe was common garb in the Harborlands, and his worn black boots spoke only of his economic standing. He tried not to meet anyone's gaze as he walked, least of all the occasional guard who strolled watchfully by.

Cooking smoke wafted toward him. He picked up his pace and soon glimpsed a row of braziers set up near the path leading to the compound at the First. Walde joined the crush of people gathered around the braziers. His silver coin bought him six fat fish wrapped in cloth and a large waterskin. He would have fought for a better price if he weren't so eager for the food and water. He filled the skin with water from a barrel beside a brazier and drained it. His thirst slaked, he filled it once more for Brite, then pushed the skin's cord over his wrist and left the boardwalk with the fish under one arm. As he turned up the path toward the compound, an aged man smelling strongly of liquor careened into him. Walde grasped his arm to keep him from falling.

"Think they can take it from us…" the man was muttering.

"Take what?"

He looked up at Walde, blinking as if surprised to see him there. "Our rights. That's our Mothertree, lad. Don't matter if she's dead or 'live. We've the right to go in her if we please."

Walde nodded. "We certainly do. Are the guards keeping people from going inside?"

The man snorted and swore. "Guards do nothin' but stand around and watch. It's those others—the seeders—who think they can control us." His wrinkled lips puckered, and Walde almost stepped back for fear of being spat upon. "I don't care what's in that tree, we've the right to go in 'er if we want. She don't belong to seeders or anyone else." He stumbled back from Walde and waved a crooked finger at him. "You tell 'em, lad. It's our right." He said more, but his drunken slur was lost in the roar of the crowd.

"Hey, friend!" Walde caught his arm before he wheeled away. "I heard that the Reachers went into her. Do you know if any came back out?"

"Come out!" He snorted and spit. "They wouldn't be stupid enough to come out. No, lad. Them that's gone in has stayed in. And the seeders can't do a damned thing about it." He wandered off, cursing and spitting.

Seeders. Back at the inn, a Scat sitting near Walde had used the word "starseed" when referring to the supposed parasite that had burrowed deep in the earth and attached itself to the Mothertrees. If Harborlanders had a word for people who held to such a belief, then there must be a word for those who did not. What did that other group call themselves?

The fish juices were bleeding through his robe, making him itch. Cradling the bundle under his arm, he clambered up onto the roots of the neighboring Mothertree and joined a group of onlookers.

The First Mothertree was a massive black column surrounded by a sturdy wattle fence. Three archers stood watch on a sentinel tower affixed to the trunk. Others were probably stationed at the neighboring tree's guard hut. Because the ground rose up around the First's trunk, Walde could just make out the top half of the crack that had opened at its base. The light emanating from inside was faint in the summer sun, but when night fell, it would become a beacon. He searched for the leaves that had sprouted and was disappointed by how small and inconspicuous they looked. Few in the crowd would even notice them.

The crowd. From a distance, the angry mass had seemed but a single beast, intent on breaking into the compound. The reality was far more disturbing.

Not one, but two groups had gathered at the gate. An uneasy space had formed between them, kept in place by peacekeeper guards. It must have broken a few times, for several injured people lingered at the fringes of both groups. As Walde looked on, the fence bent in, and he thought he heard a cracking sound. Shouts from the tower hushed the crowd, and Walde was horrified to see several archers draw their bows. The crowd shifted away from the fence, and the bows slowly lowered.

Despite what the old man had said, the guards were indeed preventing people from entering the compound. Their arrows weren't merely for show but would be used if needed. Walde feared that time would come soon.

He had seen enough. Cradling the fish, he slipped back down the path to the boardwalk.

He refused to think as he wound his way back to Brite. Thinking led to feeling, and he couldn't afford to slip up. Even so, he had lost much of his appetite by the time he reached the weedy hollow between two roots.

He was relieved to find Brite still waiting for him. But the feeling vanished when he considered the danger she was in. How could they stay here while the crowds grew and the fights intensified? Soon the whole area would be swarming with guards.

An answer came to him. For a few moments, he held it at a distance, turning it like a strange coin found on the road.

What if he sought out those who opposed the seeders and allied with them? Surely, someone in their ranks could shelter Brite. Once he gained their trust, he could tell them about his encounter with Thara. And then…

And then the story would spread and lead to a full-fledged rebellion against the elders.

He tugged worriedly on his chin and then shoved his whitening hands under his thighs. Doubt assailed him. Thara hadn't suggested he provoke a rebellion. His interference would disrupt the natural course of events that had begun unfolding the moment the crack had opened.

Brite said, "Are you going to eat, or are all these fish for me?"

He lifted his eyes wearily. She lay on her side, propped up on one elbow as she picked apart a fish. Walde dug his palms out from under him and smiled. "You can have three. I already ate one, so I'm not starving at the moment."

She turned the fish she had been working on and picked at the flesh. "I'll have to hunt down a prostitute tonight and see if she'll sell me a hooded cloak. Once I have that, you and I can take turns fetching food."

Prostitutes were the only women who strode the boardwalk at night. To blend in, Brite would have to take off the kessa tunic and wear only the soiled, mutilated frock underneath it. All so that she could balance a debt she felt she owed him for bringing him fish. He suppressed a sigh. "If you feel you must go, then I'd rather we went together."

"If you feel you must go with me, then you'll have to pretend to be my customer." Her gaze flicked to his and then away. Amusement glittered in her hazel eyes. Walde couldn't help but return the smile. Her lips and fingers were slick with juices. Auburn strands had come loose from her carefully braided hair and clung here and there to her face.

Suddenly he loosed a groan. "I just realized I haven't said a thing about what I saw at the compound."

"And I didn't thank you for the fish, so we're even."

He pointed out dryly, "We're never even."

"Eat first," she said, ignoring his jibe. "And then you can tell me what you saw."

When the fish were gone and an empty water skin lay between Brite's hands, he began his report of all he had seen and heard.

They squatted together against a root, propped up so they could watch the sun set over the harbor. The ever-present roar of the crowd had changed. There were gaps of near silence now, followed by angry bursts. When it went quiet, the world seemed almost at peace. Warm light limned the sailing masts and glinted on metal rings. Fishermen who hadn't joined the commotion at the compound repaired bad lengths of rope and torn netting.

"Seeders," Brite mused as Walde's quiet voice stilled. "I wonder if that's the man's pet name for them, or if that's what everyone calls them here."

"I never considered that. You think he might've made up that term on his own?"

"It's possible." She tugged on the water skin's leather carrying cord. "So. Not everyone believes the starseed story."

He gave a cautious nod. "It's an encouraging thought. And if they could learn to trust Reachers, there may be real hope for us."

"They'd trust you sooner if they went into the crack."

It was a big *if.* The whole world seemed suspended on it.

The orange sky darkened to violet and finally to indigo. A man came to light the boardwalk lamps.

Walde said, "It's nice, sitting together like this." The crowd roared again, and the sound lingered this time. He forced himself to ignore it and pressed on with what he wanted to say. Brite's gratitude for the fish had reminded him of his own unspoken gratitude for a much greater service. "I never thanked you for helping me free the Reachers. I still regret what you had to do, but things worked out in the end..." He trailed off.

Brite had gone still. He fancied that she was moved by his words, but one glance at her wide, restless eyes made him realize her thoughts were elsewhere. Suddenly, her back stiffened and she gripped the root. "Something's happening, Walde. Listen."

He cocked his head. The timbre of the roar had changed. Was it a touch higher now?

As he sat in silence, listening, a drift of smoke tickled his nostrils. He turned his head and peered through the Mothertrees toward the First.

The trunks and branches were outlined by a distant red glow.

CHAPTER 3

No, Walde thought, the First couldn't be on fire. It wasn't possible. Mothertrees didn't catch fire. Something in their bark made them almost impervious to flame.

The bark was smeared with pitch.

"Walde…"

He shook his head but couldn't look away from the terrible red glow. It was higher now, too high to have originated from a simple bonfire. Still, his mind refused to believe it.

Brite peeled off the spare tunic and stuffed it into her pouch. She stood and looked at him expectantly. "I can go and take a look."

The thought of her alone in the crowd jolted him out of his reverie. He shot to his feet and grasped her hand. "We'll go together."

Ignoring the naked fear in her eyes, he tugged her up onto the root toward the boardwalk. If it were safe, he would have brought along his bow and quiver, but too many guards swarmed the area. He would come back for them later.

The crowd had fallen almost silent again. A few men, fishermen by the look of their clothing, ran down the boardwalk ahead of Walde and Brite. The scent of smoke increased, and as they drew closer, a bright spear of fire shot through a gap in the branches of a neighboring tree.

It could be only one thing.

He didn't know he'd stopped walking until Brite tugged on his hand. She said something, but it was lost in the fire.

He took a step and stumbled. Desperately, he shoved his brightening hands into his robe. The world tilted dizzyingly. The First Mothertree was burning, and with it went his father's path back into the world; his path, and maybe his life, for when a Mothertree died, its connection to Thara died with it.

And who had helped bring about that end? A strangled sound clawed out of his throat.

"Walde!" Brite gripped his shoulders and shook him. "You can't save it. We have to go back."

Back. He shook his head. "No." Even as he said it, his legs were moving again, as if of their own accord. His despair was changing into something cold and hard. He let his arms fall, knowing the Reacher light would be gone. A new force had entered his body, driving him toward the burning spire.

They came to the path that led to the compound and slowed. People stood around everywhere, their eyes full of fire as they watched the inferno.

Inferno was the right word. Intense waves of heat pummeled the air around the First. The compound fence was a crumbling ring of fire. Guards had formed a tight line across the path between the two trees and were using their bows like prods to drive the stunned crowd toward the harbor.

The fire was worse than Walde's most vivid imaginings. The burning pillar rose two hundred feet into the sky. Centuries of ocean wind had bent the tree slightly. If it cracked, it would fall into the branches of the neighboring tree and set them ablaze. Not even a Mothertree's bark could resist the force of such an inferno. Once the neighboring tree caught, the fire would spread from one Mothertree to the next, until all twenty trees burned, taking the boardwalk with them and any nearby houses. The entire city might burn this night.

Suddenly a chunk of wood the size of a hut dropped off the First to the ground, spraying fire over its roots. The crowd surged back, their frightened cries blending with the terrible roar of the flames. Above them, the neighboring Mothertree's branches swayed in the hot wind. Walde gripped Brite's hand hard. She would not die here. He would not allow her to die.

His voice sounded oddly calm as he spoke into her ear. "We have to run now, and we can't stop until we're outside the city." As he spoke, another chunk of the First fell off and began its long plunge to the roots below.

The crowd was closing in around them. Without knowing if Brite had understood, he drove them both through the milling bodies until a space opened, then together they broke into a run. Others, perhaps suspecting the danger, ran with them down the boardwalk. As they neared the roots where they had taken shelter, Brite hissed, "Your bow!"

"No time."

The true peril of the situation seemed to hit her then. She picked up speed and they charged ahead, weaving around groups of people, ignoring shouted questions. If the fire spread, the people could save themselves by jumping into the harbor and swimming or sailing away. And if they refused to do that, then they were as foolish as the ones who'd started the fire.

His teeth clenched, and he bit back the anger he wanted so badly to feel. Instead, he focused on deciding the best way out of the Harborlands. His map was long gone, but he'd studied it enough to recall main streets and important buildings. At some point, he and Brite would have to leave the harbor and enter the city. If only he knew which were the wealthier parts. Rich Harborlanders kept dogs and weren't afraid of loosing them.

After passing four more Mothertrees, the boardwalk widened, and inns and market stalls spread out on platforms erected on the Mothertrees' roots. The paths connecting the harbor to the cart road were well lit and crowded with gawkers. Walde said, "Looks like they've closed off the road near the First. Good thing we didn't cross to it earlier."

They slowed to a jog and five Mothertrees later turned down a quieter path toward the road. By now, the scent of smoke had lessened, and only a brightness in the sky revealed something was amiss. A grassy hill swept up from the road. Several large new houses lay in a sedate chain atop it. Brite halted, slipped the spare tunic out of her pouch, and shrugged it on over top of her frock. The material was ambiguous in the darkness. He hoped no one would remark on the tunic's unusual cut.

He groaned and dragged a hand across his face. The First was burning, and he worried about how people would react to an oversized tunic. It was absurd. "I can't believe this is happening." He spoke the thought aloud, his voice hoarse.

Brite straightened and looked at him. Walde couldn't stand the pity in her eyes.

I hope, Thara had said. And Walde had acted, believing in that hope. What a fool he had been.

"Walde—"

He shook his head jerkily and started down the road.

They cut a jagged line through the Harborlands, Walde scarcely seeing what passed before his eyes. Stately houses turned to closed-up market stalls, empty plots of land dotted with tents, fenced-off farm fields, and animal pens. They saw no guards, and any people they crossed were hurrying toward the harbor.

They were on the outskirts of town, pushing through field grass and wiry heather, when Brite begged him to slow. The moment he stopped, she doubled over and struggled to get her breath.

"I'm sorry," he said, wincing. "You should have said something earlier."

Walde wasn't even winded. His years spent as a wasteland hunter had given him strength and endurance. If need be, he could have run another hour without pausing.

He wanted to. A terrible restlessness had welled in him the moment he'd stopped. He found himself kicking the ground to release tension. His gaze drifted past Brite to a distant orange smudge—the First, still burning. How the fire remained isolated was a mystery to him. He was sure it would have spread. But then how could he have known how Mothertrees burned? It had never happened before.

He kicked the ground again.

"All right," Brite said, straightening. "I can go on. But do we have to run?"

"Not if you're not up to it." His voice broke as he caught her staring at the orange glow.

"It didn't spread after all."

"No." The word had come out harsher than he'd meant. He wheeled away and started walking. The rustle of Brite's steps came to his ears soon after, and then she was at his side, jogging to keep pace. They both knew where they were heading. The Woodlands were their only refuge now, though Walde wondered what kind of welcome he would receive, considering how badly he had botched things.

The night deepened, tossing darkness over them. The field became a black pool full of hidden stones and biting insects. Gradually, Walde loosened his stranglehold on his emotions. Silvery light bloomed from the undersides of his wrists and palms, brightening the ground. He slowed so Brite could walk without stumbling but didn't offer to stop. He told himself it would be impractical. There was nowhere to shelter, and the recent rain had caused biting flies to multiply, making sleep impossible.

That was what he told himself. Deep down, he wondered if he *could* stop.

After a lengthy silence, Brite finally spoke again. "I wonder how the fire started."

"Seeders," he replied instantly, spitting the word. The elders wouldn't have been foolish enough to risk the Mothertrees. Each represented an enormous amount of coin. Doubtless they'd already chopped up the First's branches and begun selling the wood off to wealthy Lowland Barans. If the Mothertrees burned, the Harborlanders would lose a fortune.

He shook his head. The elders had never respected the Mothertrees as they should have. Least of all the Firsts.

Through the Firsts, all other Mothertrees had come into existence. They were ancient, still giants, full of wisdom if one listened for it. The idea of a First burning was incomprehensible. It didn't matter what Walde's eyes had seen; he would never come to grips with it. Never.

Once more, the unreality of the situation dizzied him. How had it come to this? He had trusted Thara. How could she have been so wrong?

He slapped hard at a fly and then rubbed his burning neck.

Brite asked, "You don't think it could've been an accident?"

He almost retorted that he didn't care. Instead, he said gently, "I'd rather not talk about it."

The night passed in silence. As they left the outskirts of the city, the biting flies lessened, leaving only field weeds and stones to deal with. The moon was a bright orb in the cloudless sky. The last time Walde had seen such a moon so clear, he had been hunting with his father.

Pain flared in his chest. The urge to stow it came and went. He didn't have the energy to force it back, and he'd lost the will to try.

How could he live with this? From the moment he had left the Lakelands, he'd never once given up Carrac for dead. Even in his bleakest moments, he had believed he'd see his father again. Now, even that hope was gone. His steps slowed, and he turned, shaking his head. What was he doing? In this frame of mind, he'd be useless in the Woodlands. He couldn't bring back their First while stricken by loss.

"Walde." Brite snatched his arms and made him look at her. "You think he's gone, don't you?"

He jerked away but couldn't find the energy to free himself from her grasp. "I said I didn't want to talk about it."

"He's *not* gone." She shook him a little, as if to force the words in. "You told me yourself you didn't know where the crack led. It's not a link. For all we know, it leads to a place that *all* the Mothertrees can access. And if that's the case, then you could open a crack in the Woodlands' First and beg Thara to release them. Through *that* crack."

Walde had ceased struggling. He wanted to tell her she was wrong, wrench himself away and return to his misery. Instead, he just stared at her, a breath half-drawn in his throat.

Was it possible? Could someone enter a crack in one Mothertree and come out dozens of miles away in another? Thara could be reached through any living Mothertree. Never physically, of course, but if the crack was just another way to her, then all the living trees were potential doorways.

Brite said, "You see, it *is* possible. You were just too upset to think of it." A beatific smile lit her face. "You can restore the Woodlands' First, open a new crack, and bring back the Reachers."

Not a hint of doubt lurked in her eyes. She believed he could do it, believed it right down to her bones. What had he done to awaken such faith in her? He brought a shaky hand to his forehead. He wished he could sit down in a chair and think.

"Well?"

He tried to form words. "It's possible. I can certainly try."

"Will you?" Her mouth straightened, and she eyed him expectantly.

"Yes." He hissed out a breath that turned into a startled laugh. "I will."

"Good." She let go of him and glanced away self-consciously.

Walde pulled her into his arms. For several breaths he said nothing, just held her to him as he had never done before. His restlessness eased, and a floating sensation settled over him. His breath hitched when he finally found words. "You just gave hope back to me. And that's worth something." He grinned. "Enough to cover all the debts you think you owe me."

"All but one," she agreed, her voice muffled by his shoulder. "I still owe you for disappearing that rapist."

He sighed but didn't let her go. She fit so perfectly against him. He ran his hand across her back, enjoying the warmth and closeness.

The gesture had a very different effect on Brite. Her warm breath on his neck deepened, and she drew subtly closer, molding herself to him until no space between them remained.

For an instant, Walde stood at a precipice of his own making. He was so used to numbing himself to passion that allowing it took a deliberate act. To make matters worse, he was still reeling from all that had happened. Still trying to make sense of it.

In the end, his body reacted before his heart did. A groan of long-accumulated desire shuddered out of him. He dragged his hands through her hair, loosing her messy braid, and tipped her head back so he could find her lips.

Her attempt to kiss him back was hesitant and clumsy. Could this be her first kiss? An unbearable sweetness pushed through him. He cupped the back of her head and kissed her face, tracing her jawbone, her cheeks, her eyelids. Her heated skin was soft as seed pod silk.

He found her lips again, silencing her small, hitched sounds. She had gained confidence and control this time, and Walde kissed her with abandon.

It was as fully a new experience as any he'd ever had. Although he'd kissed several women, he'd always held himself back, obeying the urge to avoid strong emotion. The body reacted anyway, but without love, desire was no more than an urge to satisfy a physical need.

This was an entirely different animal. His body and heart responded together. An ache built deep in his core, making his throat burn and his hands tremble. And all the while, he was acutely aware of her impassioned response.

Just when they were nearing the point of no return, he pulled away, leaving them to stare at each other breathlessly in the blaze of his Reacher light.

"I love you," he said when he'd found his voice again.

Her eyes closed briefly. "I love you too."

And there it was. Just as easy as that. He swallowed back a thickness in his throat. "I'll never leave you, not for anything or anyone. Never."

He expected her to return the words. Instead, she dropped her forehead against his shoulder and sighed. "I've been waiting for that since the Woodlands."

"The Woodlands." His brow furrowed. "What do you mean? What happened in the Woodlands?"

"Never mind. It seems foolish now." When he didn't speak, she went on. "Before you told the cursed children what happened to your father, I didn't know he'd been abducted. Had I known, I never would've let you cut through the Woodlands with me. It delayed your journey to the Harborlands by at least a day."

"You were being hunted," he reminded her.

"I know." She reached out and traced the curve of his jaw. "And you sacrificed valuable time trying to protect me. Do you know how that made me feel? I was already fond of you, but after that I was fully committed. I told myself I'd never leave you, not for anything or anyone. Never."

She gave the words back to him so gracefully. Walde's head was shaking. "I had no idea. When you came to my hut to talk about Carrac's abduction, I thought you were angry."

"But do you remember what I said before I left?"

He cast his mind back to that night. "I'd asked you about your destination in the Harborlands..."

"What you said was: where are you going anyway? And I answered—"

"I'm going with you." He remembered now. Her response hadn't struck him as important then. He had taken it as a refusal to answer rather than as an answer in itself. But the words had haunted him later, when she'd refused to leave his side. "I didn't realize that 'I'm going with you' was a declaration," he admitted. "But I suppose that's exactly what it was." It would be a frightful thing, he thought, to devote yourself to someone without knowing if they'd return your devotion. Worse still if they tried to push you away. Walde, fearing she would get hurt if they stayed together, had tried more than once to make her leave him. "I wish I'd known about it earlier."

"I wanted to tell you, but it didn't seem wise. I knew you had feelings for me, and I didn't want to loosen the tight lid you kept on them."

He snorted. "The lid couldn't have been that tight, if you noticed them."

"It was tight enough to keep your Reacher light down, and that's all that mattered." She swayed from one foot to another. "I'm so tired and thirsty."

As soon as she said it, weariness dropped over him, and he became aware of every ache in his body. "We'll come to the stream soon. Can you walk another hour?"

"If I must."

"We don't have to—" he began, but she was already charging ahead of him through the field.

The warm night was cooling as dawn approached, and dew gathered in the grass and wiry weeds. A new hole in his boot made his skin chafe and his toes slid in mud that had leaked through. He wondered how Brite's shoes had fared.

They walked side by side in the darkness, hands bumping now and then. The rustling grass and chirring crickets were all he could hear. His thoughts strayed to Brite's idea of opening a crack in the Woodlands' First. He considered it carefully from every angle and couldn't find a hole in her logic. There was only one flaw, and it didn't affect whether or not he would succeed.

Once he opened the crack, he could die. Thara had warned him of that when he'd agreed to help her open the crack in the Harborlands' First. Walde had expected the death to be instant. Instead, he had nearly lost himself in a strange, weightless space. Even thinking about that place threatened to lift the hairs on his arms.

He thrust the fear from his mind. If he dwelled on it too long, he wouldn't be able to reach. And he had to. Not only to reach, but to drive himself past caring to that place where no other Reacher had gone—into Thara's very presence, where he could actually speak to her. The prospect was tantalizing. And the fact that no other Reacher had managed it made it all the more alluring. When the time came, he couldn't let anything interfere with his task. Even his death. If he succeeded, the Reachers would be free, and the First's link would be restored. He could allow no thoughts of life beyond that.

CHAPTER 4

Dawn was magical. It began with a blush of violet behind the mountains. As the color gradually shifted to orange, the mists at the mountains' base remained a deep stormy blue. Walde clasped Brite's hand as they walked the final few yards to the stream.

"I stink," she said cheerfully. "My hair smells like fire and bones."

"I thought it smelled like fish juice."

"That too."

Suddenly, he pulled her to a stop and planted a swift but passionate kiss on her lips.

"What was that for?" she asked as he broke away and knelt by the stream to drink.

"I wanted to taste the mist on the mountains."

She snorted, but his glimpse of her smile told him he'd pleased her. They drank deeply but were too chilled to attempt washing in the icy water. The riverbanks were dry and sandy. Walde talked about making a fire, and Brite agreed it would be wise, but ultimately they both collapsed near the water's edge and didn't get back up.

He woke feeling uncomfortably warm. The midday sun bore down on him, heating the exposed side of his face. He crawled over to the stream and splashed himself with cool water. A glance at Brite told him she slept on, a clump of grass shading her cheek. He undressed and washed in the shallow stream, then scrubbed his robe against the flat side of a large rock. The unfamiliar material held together better than he'd expected. He wrung it out as best he could and pulled it back on. Between the hot sun and his own body heat, he judged it would be dry in under an hour.

Brite woke more slowly, wincing as if in pain. Her walk to the water's edge was stiff and halting. Truly, he had pushed her too hard the night before. But when he told her so, she wouldn't accept his apology. Her legs were her business, she said, and he should focus on his own aches and pains. She lent him a needle and thread from her belt pouch, and he repaired his boots while she washed, his back turned to give her privacy.

When the sun was still high, they set out hunting along the river. Brite's stiff gait loosened as she walked, and soon they ghosted along the bank, their footsteps muted by the trickling water. Brite had discarded her frock and wore only his spare tunic with the sleeves rolled up. Walde missed his bow. Although he'd made a show of drawing his dagger, he didn't plan to use it. Not when a practiced knife thrower walked beside him.

Half an hour might have passed before the nearby weeds shivered and the backside of a furry body came into view. They exchanged a glance. "Take it," he mouthed.

Brite crept closer, then closer still. When she was only a couple of yards from the beast, her knife flashed, catching it behind the neck.

It turned out to be a rather large groundhog. Walde gathered what kindling he could find and made a fire while Brite cleaned it. The fat stems of a hacked down bush served as their spit.

They sat in companionable silence while they watched it cook, Walde adding a constant stream of sticks to the fire. His gaze flicked regretfully to the heap of skin and entrails by the water's edge. The beast's fur would've made a warm neck scarf. It was a waste to leave it behind.

He said, "I could tan that hide if I had the tools for it. In the Lakelands, hunters skin and tan their kills. Some even finish the skins with dyes." He turned his hands, but the purplish stains he had become accustomed to seeing for years had faded from his fingers.

Brite nodded, but something in the careful way she held herself made him suspect her thoughts were elsewhere.

"What are you thinking?" he prodded.

She met his eyes then glanced quickly aside. "Is it true that treefolk hold off making love until marriage?"

The words had spilled out in a single breath. Walde just stared at her, hardly breathing as he carefully stowed his embarrassment. *Why embarrassment?* he asked himself. Was he ashamed of his people's culture? "It is," he replied firmly. "The rule stems from the reverence we have for our offspring. Just as a man nurtures and safeguards the seed pods on his branch, so he does for his children, including ones that come along by accident. That means staying with the mother of those children as her husband. That's quite a commitment to make if you aren't sure about the person. So we're taught to avoid the act that makes children until we're mature enough and in love enough to commit." He didn't add that couples did a whole host of other things. Lakelanders called it "messing around."

"I see." She cleared her throat. "So, you've never..."

"Never."

She turned the spit thoughtfully. "So treefolk feel it's essential to raise one's own children."

"That's right."

"Then what about the Reachers' children from the Harborlands? Weren't they fostered out to Woodlanders while their parents were still alive?"

Years ago, the elders had rounded up all the Reachers that still lurked in the Harborlands. While they awaited punishment, their children were sent away. Almost five years later, those children—now living in the Woodlands' abandoned Mothertrees—still held out hope that their parents lived. Walde shook his head. "I don't believe that the elders would have fostered out those children if they didn't plan on killing the parents."

"No?" She shot him a furtive look. "Then what about the Reachers we freed in the compound? What do you think happened to *their* children?"

Walde dragged a hand over his eyes. "I hadn't thought of that." He cast his mind back to the faces he'd recognized. Of the five Reachers he had seen closely, four had been from the Lakelands. The first was Idra. The older woman used to sell knives she'd made at the market. And quiet Ness had been there. Her father was a fisherman. And old Caln, Walde's reclusive great-uncle. The fourth was Walde's father. None of them had young children, but what of the others Walde hadn't seen? Those who'd been chained up around the other side of the tree? He shoved the stick into the flames. "Maybe the elders didn't test Reachers with young children." He tried to put confidence into his voice, but it sounded false.

His people were changing. Since the first purge more than a century ago, the tree-dwelling culture had suffered a slow and agonizing death. The Lakelands was the last outpost of that culture, and it would be the last to fall. If the Reachers failed to bring back the Woodlands' First...

He grimaced and shoved the thought firmly aside. "Let's change the subject."

"To...?"

"You choose."

She gave him a sidelong glance and then asked shyly, "How does one marry in the Lakelands?"

He turned the spit. "Young people usually exchange vows in front of family and friends and then celebrate with Ona. But it doesn't have to be that way. If the couple is older and wants a quiet arrangement, they speak their vows alone and go to the hut where they plan to live."

She gave a slow nod.

Walde watched her face closely. The knowledge that they had exchanged vows when they'd both said that they'd never leave the other for anything or anyone must be running through her mind now. Was she waiting for him to acknowledge it? He cleared his throat. "So how do people marry in the Lowlands?"

"Others must witness the exchange of vows, or a marriage isn't considered legitimate. As for unplanned children, well, I was one myself."

He nodded grimly.

In the Lowlands, crimes like rape were punished by set fines. Since the wealthy could afford to pay those fines, they did what they wanted to the poor, leaving a wake of destruction for others to clean up. Brite's young mother had likely been raped. Either unable or unwilling to raise the baby, she'd left it on an uncle's doorstep and joined a tinker wagon. Years later, the situation had threatened to repeat itself when Brite was attacked and almost raped herself.

Walde stabbed his dagger into the meat. Fat dripped and sizzled, bringing smoke into his eyes. "Meat's coming away from the bone," he muttered. He quickly sliced off a piece and offered it to her on the tip of his blade.

Brite had killed the rapist before Walde could, but not before she was hurt. The sight of her torn frock and bleeding forehead was forever seared into his mind. A part of him wished the man were still alive so Walde could give him the slow death he deserved.

It was a messy meal, fingers and chins glistening with fats and juices. They devoured the groundhog down to the bones and then rinsed their faces and hands in the river. It felt good to have a full belly. Walde lay back on the sand for a few moments and tried to clear his mind of the shadows that clung to it.

His eyes closed but then sprang open as a scratching sound came to his ears. He rose to his feet and turned.

The sound came from Brite. She was dragging a scorched stick along the ground, scoring a deep line into the sand. His mouth twitched up in an amused smile. "What are you doing?"

She didn't look up. "You'll see."

The first line skirted the water's edge for three yards. The second ran parallel to it, but four feet away and so near the grass and rocks that the stick jammed several times. She connected the two lines with two shorter ones, making a rectangle. Then she cast the stick away from her and stepped inside. "Well?"

He tilted his head and pursed his lips. "Is it some kind of Lowlands game?"

"No. It's our hut."

A silence fell as the meaning of her words crashed between them. Walde's lips parted dryly. "Our hut."

She gave a slow nod and lifted her hand, palms up, toward him.

Walde's fingers twitched. He wanted so badly to cross to her that his legs almost moved for him, but the part of his mind where logic still held sway warned him of the possible consequences. If Brite conceived now, and Walde died after opening the crack, then she would be left alone with his child, forced to repeat the same ugly circle again. But how could he explain that to her? If she knew Walde could die after opening the crack, then she would not want him to do it. Worse, she would blame herself for giving him the idea.

He didn't know what passed on his face, but it must have been terrible, for her arm fell to her side and her shoulders sank. Walde's heart beat hard in his throat.

Then a breath, like life itself, filled his lungs. *I won't die.*

As soon as he thought it, he believed it.

He went to her, picked her up, and swung her in his brightened arms. *His.* Of course she was his. Hadn't they exchanged vows?

His senses flooded with her as he pressed her to him, breathing in her sun-brightened hair, her soft, heated skin. She made a wild sound, something between a wail and a rapturous cry, before dragging him down with her onto the warm riverbank.

***

A while later, they lay in each other's arms inside the "hut," their clothing flung onto the bank. Walde's hand drifted over her thoughtlessly, tracing, smoothing. He felt at peace and... something more. He gazed up at the clouds scudding across the sky, at a bird wheeling, its wings tilted to catch the breeze, and something in him stretched to meet it. He felt...expansive and at the same time at one with everything—the rustling grass, the trickling water, the sighing wind—

"Walde," Brite sighed beside him and touched his arm. "You're blazing. What are you feeling?"

He shook his head and then regretted it as the world spun. When the dizziness had subsided, he was left feeling as if invisible tendrils radiated off him. He ran a hand over his damp forehead. "I think I was reaching."

"But there's no Mothertree here." She turned onto her side so she faced him.

"I guess there doesn't have to be."

A puzzled frown knitted her brows. "So what prompted it? I thought you had to feel something strong to reach."

"Usually that's true. But I've reached once before without strong emotion." He thought back to what he'd learned from Thara. "Strong, positive emotions make us expansive, and that expansiveness makes us reach. Negative emotions, on the other hand, cause us to withdraw into ourselves. That ebbing is what makes a link weaken and the power that enlivens a Mothertree to fail."

Brite gave a thoughtful nod. "So reaching is really about being open rather than closed."

"You could view it that way. But a Reacher's power isn't limited to the times we enter a link. Thara told me that we're always reaching a little, and that power is enough to maintain a healthy tree without us ever having to enter a link."

"But what about the normal ups and downs of life? It's natural to feel depressed sometimes. Wouldn't those lows weaken the link?"

"Not if things are as they should be. There used to be enough Reachers to cancel out those lows." *And now there are only a few,* Thara had said, *and until recently, most of them were suffering.*

After a silence, Brite cleared her throat and spoke again. "So making love made you want to reach."

He found a small smile. "To be honest, I didn't do it on purpose. It just happened." He lifted a hand to trace the flight path of the circling bird. "Reaching is a compulsion, as real as... as the craving to make love."

"I see. It must've been hard for Reachers to curb that craving while they hid all those years."

He snorted. "I couldn't have done it for long. In fact, I was already planning to leave the Lakelands before my father was arrested." He toyed with strands of her hair. "You know, my father doesn't even understand what reaching is. He thinks it's about pushing positive emotions into a Mothertree. He's never entered a link, even by accident."

"Do you think that's because he doesn't want to, or…"

"I don't know. It could be because he always held himself back. There's a tipping point for a Reacher, and when one goes over it, it's hard to pull back. I think he became very aware of that tipping point and never strayed past it, even unconsciously." He looked up from her hair and met her eyes. "Imagine living like that, without passion and joy. It changes you. Sometimes I wonder how much it's changed me." He sighed but then found a smile again. "I'm determined to be dark today."

"No." She trailed a finger down his jaw line. "You're like a fall day, bright and dark and breezy."

"Brite." He caught her finger and lowered it, all the while holding her gaze. "You're a gift I don't deserve."

Her lips compressed and quivered as she tried not to laugh.

"I'm serious," he said. "The more I know you, the more I wonder how you can say that no one misses you. You must have had friends in the Lowlands."

"I did have a friend, but after she married, we grew apart. I doubt she thinks of me at all now, she has so many children to feed."

"What about your uncle? He must care."

She turned abruptly onto her back. "He won't care."

Walde opened his mouth and then closed it. Brite's eyes had gone flat and distant.

It seemed a long time before she spoke again. "He used to carry me on his shoulders when I was little. I still remember the deep rumble of his voice against my leg. In my heart, I think of him as my father, though I never told him so. His wife was no mother to me. She took care of me the way she would sweep a floor. Just something to get done. But my uncle... He treated me like a real person."

"So what happened?"

"He wanted me to wed a friend of his, and it didn't matter how many times I told him no; he wouldn't give up. One day, I told him I'd rather work in the bog than marry his friend. I was almost relieved when he called my bluff. And at first it was good to be outside again under the open sky. But I missed him. And I wondered if he missed me.

"One day, a boy came with his father to help repair the roof. While I bundled the thatch, I told one of the stories my uncle taught me when I was a girl. I didn't know my uncle was listening until I turned the corner and saw him standing there, weeping." She swallowed and ran her arm across her eyes. "I went to him, and we just held each other, and I thought everything would be fine. But he worked too hard that day, and he...he had some sort of fit. After that, he lost the ability to speak and just lay in bed, staring up at the ceiling. My aunt's sister and her husband came to live with us then, and I became...a burden. Men from the bog kept sniffing around the place. I began to see why my uncle wanted to marry me off to his friend."

"And that's when you decided to move to the Harborlands."

She nodded. "There was so much work there for Scats. I thought I could be happy."

"Instead, you found me." He drew her arm off her face and kissed the underside of her wrist. "Your uncle loved you. He would care if he could."

"I know."

They lay in silence a while longer, then Walde drew himself reluctantly away from her and climbed to his feet. They had to be on their way again.

The rest of the journey was a blur. Walde refused to dwell on the possibility that he could fail to bring back the Reachers. As for the tragedy that had befallen the First, it was beyond his ability to grasp. Thara would make sense of it for him. With these cares set aside, he lost himself completely in Brite.

They didn't speak much on the way to the Woodlands, but every brush of her hand woke light from him. She made a joke of it, but often the jokes ended with them kissing passionately. Walde felt he could drink her. He'd never experienced such passion in his life, and he often felt on the brink of reaching. The fair weather and fresh mountain wind added to his euphoria, and the haunting notes of a song that he had once dreamed moved distantly through his mind. He had played that song the first time he'd reached. Now it seemed like he had always known it.

They came to the southern edge of the Woodlands in the middle of the night, tired, thirsty, and unwilling to take another step. Brite found a flat area under a pine tree, and Walde lay with his arms around her.

In the quiet darkness, with bodies curled together, every hitched breath and quickened heartbeat becomes as noticeable as flashes of lightning. The skin, separated by a thin layer of cloth, dampens and heats, and the slightest movement is like a step taken in a small boat.

With a groan, Brite dragged off her tunic and turned to face him.

Nothing could describe their lovemaking that night. The feeling of the pine needles under them, the slickness of their bodies in the lingering summer heat, Brite's soft, hungry lips. Walde completely let go. Time slowed, and the expansiveness returned. And it went on and on. Sensation lost its narrow focus and swelled until it felt as though the whole world throbbed with it. His thrusting became a reaching, a blinding rush of momentum toward some ragged, astonishing end. Brite's shuddering cry came to him as if from a distance.

He collapsed onto her a short time later, blacked out, then came to again. His blazing light held them like a star. "This is madness," he whispered after a time.

"Are you all right?"

"Yes. I'm just a bit dizzy."

"You were reaching."

"I'm sorry."

"Don't be," she said. "It was good. I didn't feel left out. It was more like...like you tried to take me somewhere..."

He grinned. "Who says I didn't?"

The dizziness was subsiding. He grabbed their clothing and draped her with the spare tunic.

"Feeling better?" she breathed as they lay curled together again.

"I feel as if invisible tendrils are seeping off me." He grazed her cheek with his lips. "I love you."

"I love you too. Sleep well."

***

The sound of a stick snapping jolted Walde awake. His tunic slid partly off him as he sat up and looked around. It was daytime, but the sun was well hidden behind heavy cloud cover. His gaze traveled from the field to the deep shadows in the forest.

At once, he saw them—a boy and a girl dressed in forest colors, each bearing a small bow and quiver sized for them. The girl, a dark-eyed brunette with sun-browned skin, held a broken stick in her hands. She had obviously used it to alert Walde and Brite to their presence.

Brite yawned and sat up. "What is it?"

The boy made a disgusted sound in his throat. "Adults are so gross. It makes me never want to become one."

"Shut it, Spit," the girl said.

Brite's eyes widened, and she hastily covered her naked breasts. *Spitfire*, Walde thought. That was the blonde boy's name. As for the girl's... He shook his head. Perhaps he'd never known it. The cursed children were not trusting.

Spitfire snickered. "Can you believe they slept naked on pine needles? Their backs must be a wreck."

"Can you turn around so we can dress?" Walde asked tightly.

They turned without a word. Only then did Walde notice the heavy pack by the girl's feet. Suddenly, he dropped his face into his hands and choked out a laugh. "Someone saw us last night, didn't they?"

At his words, Brite sucked in a breath.

The girl said, "A sentinel saw a light through the trees. When she got close enough, she recognized you and reported back to Albin."

Walde pulled on his robe. "And Albin sent you over to us with food and water." His eyes returned to the pack. Hunger was eating a hole through his stomach.

Spitfire asked, "Are you dressed now?"

Walde felt foolish as he and Brite devoured the dried venison and strawberries that Albin—or perhaps his sister, Frey—had packed so carefully. He imagined how the sentinel's report must have sounded to the young leader. Walde and Brite, bereft of the gear with which Albin had supplied them for their journey, had been spotted alone on the edge of the forest, making love without a care in the world. Had Albin concluded that they'd returned from their failed quest to beg off the children's charity?

Walde emptied the water skin and pressed it back into the pack. "Thank you. I know you were only following orders, but we're grateful all the same."

The girl flashed him a dimpled smile. She looked no older than nine, but Walde recalculated her age to thirteen. These cursed children of Reachers had ceased growing after their foster parents relocated from the Woodlands to the Lowlands four years ago. As the years passed, the former Woodlanders noticed this lack of change and developed a superstitious dread of them. One night seven months ago, Albin and his sister Frey gathered the children together and fled with them back to the Woodlands' Mothertrees. Albin had hoped that living in Mothertrees again would help them grow. He hadn't counted on the Mothertrees being dead.

Only the First still lived. Walde had sensed life in it—or more likely, its intact link—when he'd passed it on the way out of the Woodlands. And he'd promised Frey he would restore it if he could. Had Frey relayed this information to her brother? If so, then Albin wouldn't only be anticipating Walde's report of the Harborlands, but also the possible restoration of the Woodlands' First.

The thought lightened his heart, and he found he looked forward to seeing the young leader again.

The forest was dark and humid. A white mist lay like spider sacs in low-lying areas. Walde and Brite followed the children up a slope, picking their way around a dugout trap hidden under bits of bark and old leaves. The children took their safety seriously, and with good reason. They had been attacked more than once by groups of former Woodlanders who didn't like the cursed children living in their abandoned Mothertrees. Such attacks had come from the northeast side of the forest, though, and not the south. He wondered what had prompted Albin to set night watches on the Woodlands' southern side.

He peered at the lush foliage around him. The Woodlands' eighteen Mothertrees were tucked away in a low-lying area inside miles of dense forest. Walde had identified pine, cedar, beech, elm, poplar, maple, and willow oak in his travels through the Woodlands. Some trees were so young they could be stepped on, while others were large enough to have accommodated a hut or two. Walde wasn't used to the damp environment, and he walked carefully to avoid stepping on snails or slippery moss. His skin itched from bites he'd received during the night. Brite seemed equally uncomfortable, slapping at her skin even when it looked clear of bugs.

The children waited for them at the crest of the rise. The girl said, "I'd wager neither of you have been eating enough. That's why you're slow."

"We'll keep up," Brite promised with a cheerfulness that sounded false to Walde's ears.

"You'll have to. A bunch of people are waiting for you at the river."

Walde took a step and stopped. At times, one's tone conveyed meaning better than words did. This was one of those times. "By people, you mean strangers, don't you?"

Spitfire grinned. "They won't be strangers to you."

"But they will be to Brite," the girl pointed out.

Walde said, "You're both speaking in riddles. Who are they?"

"Lakelanders," the girl replied. "Hurry up, they're waiting."

CHAPTER 5

Spitfire shot a rabbit on the way to the river and gutted it with an ease that belied his small limbs. "Got a lot of mouths to feed," he remarked with a half-smile as he bound the rabbit's feet and attached it to a hook on his belt.

The rabbit was large, unbalancing his stride. Walde would've offered to carry it for him, but he doubted the boy would give up his trophy, especially when he had a chance to show it off to strangers.

They hiked in single file down a narrow but well trodden path, stopping three times to avoid traps. Several times, Walde questioned them about the Lakelanders. He'd learned that there were three adults and two children. Two of the adults—a woman and a man—were Reachers. Frey, together with a large contingent of archers, had met them on the east border of the Mothertrees and interrogated them. She had judged them to be harmless, and they had stayed the night. That morning, they'd left the two children in Frey's safekeeping and, depending on Walde and Brite's news, planned to journey on to the Harborlands.

Walde was unable to draw out any other facts, but his mind filled in the gaps. Somehow, two Reachers had escaped the Lakelands' purge. How they'd managed to survive the long journey to the Woodlands with children in tow was a mystery to him. They must have had help crossing the lake. After that, they would've been easy targets for tracker guards. The wastes were open and treeless, and the only source of water was the rushing Nadi River.

Walde doubted that Lakelands guards would pursue them all the way to the Woodlands, but the possibility must have moved Albin to set night watches on the forest's fringes.

Brite touched Walde's arm. Their gazes met, and he glimpsed his own worries reflected back at him. He said quietly, "We're safe here."

Spitfire had good ears. "Don't worry." He patted his bow with a small hand. "We'll protect you."

Walde might have laughed under different circumstances. Instead, he clasped Brite's hand and fell silent.

He ached for his bow. The dagger was a fine weapon in close quarters but useless for distance. As soon as he had time, he would hunt down a sturdy branch and fashion another.

Gradually, the forest brightened. The ground sloped steeply down toward the glittering river. The dirt path changed to lumpy stones, some of them feathered by dark moss. As the last of the trees parted, two moored rowboats came into view. One held folded blankets and a large basket, the other travel packs and a bow. A second basket lay open and empty on the shore. Three adults huddled nearby in intense conversation.

"Ho, Albin!" Spitfire called as he half-ran, half-skidded down the slope.

At the sound, the young leader stepped out from behind the huddle. "Spit. Lina." He grinned. "And rabbit."

"Isn't he a beaut?"

"He is indeed. Set him in one of the boats." The children nodded, and the young leader turned his gaze on Walde and Brite.

Albin was seventeen but trapped in a body that was more than four years younger. Despite that, he stood with a proud and regal bearing. His dark blond hair was combed back into a tail, baring a smooth, sun-browned jaw. A sheathed knife sat comfortably at his belt, its handle worn from use. He wore a purple kessa tunic and soft gray hosen that showed signs of being mended. "Walde, Brite, welcome back. I'd introduce you to my guests, but you may already know them."

He'd barely gotten the words out when a woman stepped away from the other adults she'd been speaking to and grasped Walde's hands.

Walde felt a wash of pleasure at seeing the Lakelanders. Although he didn't know the three well, these were faces from his homeland. Faces that, if he were honest, he'd never expected to see again.

The dark-haired man with heavy brows and a clean-shaven face was a Lakelands guard named Garen. Beside him was Shin, a middle-aged gardener with brown plaited hair and blue eyes that flicked here and there like a nervous hummingbird.

The woman who grasped Walde's hands was Elva. She had two young children with a lift mechanic named Bran. Like Shin, she had worked at the community garden. Walde had often seen her at market selling mint and valerian root. From the clean, fresh look of her tunic, Walde guessed that she'd paid a visit to Grella's spare clothing huts.

The barest ghost of a smile grazed her mouth as she greeted him. "Walde, Albin told us about your journey to find your father. Since you left, other Reachers have been down the river. My husband was among them." Her hands tightened on his. "Can you tell us what you found in the Harborlands?"

At her words, a deep stillness fell over the small group gathered on the beach.

Walde's throat went dry.

He couldn't tell them the truth. How could he say that after being tortured, their loved ones had walked into a Mothertree that had since burned to the ground? Had Walde been in their place, he wouldn't have accepted such a story.

There was really only one way to answer Elva's question, and that was to produce the Reachers.

"I can," he said slowly, "but there's something I have to do first. Can you delay your journey a few hours?"

"Why?" Garen interjected, stepping toward him. His voice was that of a guard's, friendly, while still retaining a note of authority. "Why can't you tell us *now*?"

Walde's gaze flicked to the short sword that hung at his side. "For my own reasons," he said firmly, then added, "Please, give me until this evening. We can exchange stories then."

Elva's hands pinched into his. "Can you at least tell me if Bran's alive? Please, just that."

Walde chewed his lip. Clearing his throat, he said, "I don't know. I'm sorry."

Elva's head lowered and her shoulders sank. Releasing his hands, she turned wearily, bumping into Garen as she did so. The action seemed accidental, but something in her face made Walde think otherwise. If Garen saw the look, he pretended not to notice it.

The former guard held Walde's gaze a moment longer and then muttered, "A few hours." After that, he wandered off to speak with Shin.

Brite leaned in and whispered, "I don't think they like each other."

In truth, all three Lakelanders looked tense and uneasy. Fear for themselves and their loved ones would've created some stress. But there was something more.

The thought frayed as Albin, now standing by the boats, waved him and Brite over.

"You must be hungry. Come and eat something."

Walde couldn't pass up the offer.

Lina shook out one of the blankets, and Albin unloaded a basket. When Walde protested that they could do it themselves, Albin shot him a meaningful look. Walde understood him at once. This was an invitation to talk quietly while the three Lakelanders huddled in conversation.

"I'm glad you're here," Albin whispered. "Those three have an ugly story to tell."

"Do you know if they were tracked?"

"They don't think so, but I've taken precautions anyway." He opened a wooden container, revealing toasted chestnuts drizzled with honey. "The Reachers are Garen and Shin."

"Garen was a peacekeeper guard."

"He's not a trusting person. He didn't want Elva to leave her children behind with Frey and me, so he tried to force her to stay behind. She refused. They're always at odds, those two."

There was a silence as Walde contemplated his words. Brite said nothing, but the way she tilted her head indicated she was listening.

Walde asked, "Did Frey tell you that the First isn't quite dead?"

"She did."

"And did she tell you I would try to revive it when I came back?"

A faint smile tugged on Albin lips. "Is that the *something* you wanted to do first?"

"It is."

His smile widened. "That's exciting news."

"I thought you would say so."

"Is there a reason you want to do it right away?"

"Of course."

Albin peered at him closely and then dug a spoon into the chestnuts. "Let me know if you need anything." Curiosity tinged his voice.

"I will."

***

The short paddle to the Woodlands' First seemed longer than it should have been. A light but steady rain fell, dotting the placid water with spreading silver coins. Ancient willow oaks grew along the riverbanks, leaning their wet leaves over the water. Walde and Albin rowed in the head boat with Brite and Lina between them. Walde hadn't stayed to find out how the others had sorted it out. He wasn't on the best terms with the Lakelanders. While they'd agreed to stop by the First and wait while he reached, they were clearly indulging him. Albin, on the other hand, was abuzz with excited energy. His paddle cut effortlessly through the water, and his back strained ahead. "Frey," he abruptly announced, "should be here to see this." Before Walde could open his mouth to reply, Albin had unhitched a horn from his belt and loosed several loud blasts.

The signal was answered in a few moments by another, and then yet another still, this one so far away that it was barely audible. Albin glanced back at him with a grin. "She'll come."

The boats drifted into brighter water. The willow oaks had given way to scruffy saplings. The Mothertrees towered beyond, their spreading boughs gray and misty against the white sky. As the boats neared the First, the riverbanks steepened and became stone walls. Thick wooden platforms capped the walls. The docks stretched along the river for at least a mile, wood slowly disintegrating as the years passed. If the rowboats had been fashioned from the same wood, they wouldn't have fared much better, but the color and grain revealed they were of Mothertree wood, probably from branches that had been damaged in a storm. Such wood was resistant to water and tended to crack rather than rot. The boats looked old beyond telling and appeared to have undergone many repairs. They wouldn't have been worth much to the

Woodlanders who had resettled in the Lowlands, but as the saying went, one man's trash was another man's treasure. Albin was lucky to have them.

The young leader steered the boat to the dock, and Spitfire leapt onto the platform to secure it. Walde sat very still in the boat, his eyes fixed on the towering Mothertree. As before, he sensed something from it, a surging presence that made his neck tingle and his breathing slow. Then, like a passing shadow, it vanished, and his eyes refocused on the thick, cluttered trunk that was at least sixty yards from the water.

And that was when it hit him: unlike the Mothertrees in the Harborlands, these had not been stripped of their lower stairs and lifts. How could he have forgotten that? Every piece of wood had been left and was slowly rotting away. Every step, every path, every hut. Even as he sat there, a faint creaking could be heard: loose, hanging planks shifting in the gentle breeze, dripping with rainwater.

What would happen if Walde disturbed that mess? He didn't have to guess. Even a small crack in the trunk would unsettle the already fragile stairs. If a portion of the stairs cracked and fell off, then whoever stood near the trunk would get crushed. Walde could avoid the threat by reaching from the top of the tree rather than from the bottom. But what of the Reachers who would come out?

The worst damage would happen right after the crack opened. If Walde were to explain the danger to Thara, perhaps she could convey it to the Reachers somehow, and they could wait a little while before coming out...?

The alternative was to dismantle the First's infrastructure—a task that would take weeks to accomplish. It would be a lot to ask of the children at a time when they felt threatened by outsiders. And what would happen to the trapped Reachers in the meantime? Only three days had passed since they went in. A person could live without food and water for such a time, but not for much longer. Walde suspected that they were being taken care of somehow, but it was just a feeling. He could be dead wrong.

Brite was calling his name.

Walde passed a hand over his forehead. His palms and wrists brightened for a few moments before he took control of his emotions.

"What's wrong?" she asked quietly, trapping his hand.

His words came out in a harsh whisper. "I'm an idiot, that's what's wrong."

"I don't understand."

"Look at all the shaky wood on that tree."

Brite leaned away from him as she looked up. Her sudden intake of breath let him know she understood. "Oh, Walde, how can you—"

"I can reach from the top instead of from the bottom." She winced, and he added, "I'll be careful."

"You'll have to be more than careful on the way down. If those stairs come loose..."

"I know. But if I take it slow, it shouldn't be a problem."

"And what about the..." She leaned in and breathed a word into his ear. "*Reachers?*"

"For that, I'll have to trust Thara." His mouth twisted as he spoke. But he didn't want to admit, even to himself, that he didn't trust her. He found a dry smile. "It'll be all right."

"I hope so."

They climbed out of the boat, Walde ignoring the curious stares of the adults and children alike. Once they all stood on the boardwalk, Walde announced that he was going on alone, and no one was to follow him.

Of course, everyone had to know why. Walde could have said that it was dangerous to stand under the Mothertree, but he knew Albin wouldn't accept that answer. The children often walked under the Mothertrees, and none had been killed yet by falling debris. The only explanation he could think of sounded preposterous. Yet it was probably true. "The new growth will disturb the rotting wood. That's why I'll be reaching from the top instead of from the bottom."

Garen snorted and turned aside to whisper to Shin. A few words drifted over. "...full of himself if he thinks he can..."

Walde gritted his teeth and steered himself to calmness. Albin made no response to the whispered words. He'd either pretended not to have heard them or was so deep in thought that they'd swept past his ears.

"I never thought of that," Albin mused, "but it makes sense. We'll go up with you, then."

Walde looked away from the huddled Lakelanders. "What?"

"If you think you'll be safe at the top, then so will we."

Walde pinched the space between his brows. "I'd rather you didn't. I don't want any of you to fall through a rotten step."

Lina said, "We've gone up those stairs before. If you test your weight on them first and stay close to the tree, there's no danger."

In the end, Walde couldn't dissuade the children from following him up, and he didn't think he had the right to stop them. They were mature enough to be cautious and experienced enough in this environment to recognize signs of danger and get out of harm's way. He loosed a weary sigh. As much as he disliked the situation, he had to accept it as it was. As he stood there, chewing his lip, yet another worrisome thought occurred to him. "Albin, will any part of the First be visible from outside the Woodlands?" Walde hadn't spied the Mothertrees from the north or south sides.

"Luckily, no. The tops of some of the other Mothertrees are visible from the cart road, if you know what to look for, but the

First and its neighbor are hidden behind a forested hill. I don't know what you'd see if you went into the mountains with a spyglass. Maybe not much, since they're so far away."

Another boat pulled up to the dock, and Frey leapt out of it. Walde thought that the rowers would join her on the boardwalk, but they pushed off at once, turned the boat around, and paddled back the way they'd come.

Like Albin, Frey was blonde and violet-eyed, with an open, sincere smile. Though she looked eleven, her true age was closer to sixteen, and she strove to look it by staining her lips red and darkening the space around her eyes with an oil and charcoal mixture. After assuring Elva that her children were safe with Grella, she greeted Walde and Brite with hugs and kisses and congratulations over their…marriage?

The awkwardness that followed might have been amusing if it weren't for the irritated Lakelanders. Without saying anything, their postures and expressions made it clear that Walde was straining their patience. He couldn't find it in him to care.

He spent a few moments alone with Brite before making the journey to the trunk. Rain had plastered her hair to her face. He kissed her wet lips, the drip on her chin, her warm cheek. "If it weren't for you, I wouldn't be doing this."

"I hope it doesn't kill you."

The irony, he thought, was that she probably worried about the stairs, while the greater danger lay elsewhere. He pushed that thought aside. "I won't let it."

"You'd better not. I still owe you, and I can't repay you when you're dead."

They both smiled at what had become a joke between them.

It wasn't easy parting from her. Only the prospect of being together again made it endurable.

It was a long, grueling trudge along the volatile paths and up the winding steps to the top of the tree. Walde went first, testing every step before trusting his weight to it. If a step could hold his weight, then it would hold the children's. Or so he reasoned. By the time he'd reached the top level, he'd been forced to skip over a score of steps. He marked each with a long scratch from his dagger before watching to make sure everyone came safely up behind him. The children's kessa tunics and hosen gave them better freedom of movement than Walde's kriksa robe. He stumbled onto the top level's platform, drenched in sweat and panting. The rain had let up, and he nearly choked on the warm, humid air that had crept in afterward. He circled the trunk until he found a spot that was right on top of a main branch and then lowered himself down on the platform's old planks. He felt safer knowing that a branch was under him instead of the open air.

The view before them was dizzying. From this height, he could see beyond the indigo hills to the far-off snow-capped peaks. The green carpet of the Woodlands' forest seemed to edge up to the mountain's feet. Mist hung over the trees, creating a sense of deep stillness.

"It's good to be home," Walde said without thinking.

"Home is a Mothertree," said Frey, who sat at his side.

Albin added, "Home is the life above and the earth far below."

Lina, beside Albin, stretched out her arms. "Home is a thousand blinking treelights."

"Home is sleeping in the sky," said Spitfire.

Walde leaned his head back against the trunk. A longing to reach filled him. And if he were honest, he knew he'd swept all other concerns aside just to plunge himself headlong into this link. But it was too late now. The children watched him, and the Lakelanders below waited while he indulged his whim.

❧

Walde thought of Brite. He called up memories and bathed in them, reliving feelings, sensations, simple words that turned his heart over in his chest. His love wasn't peaceful, but it was a door. He felt himself opening to it, expanding. Then his vision blackened, and he experienced a dizzying wave of vertigo.

When it receded, the gaping mouth of the link loomed before him. For an endless, tortuous moment he strove to get closer to it, but it was always just beyond his reach. Never before had he been stuck on the outside this way, unable to go through.

At last, he gave up, wrenched himself back into his body, and sat panting against the tree. Sweat trickled down his forehead. He cleared his throat but didn't speak. Nor would he turn and meet Albin's eyes.

What had just happened? He tried to consider the situation calmly. The link was intact, so the problem must lie with him. Something must be holding him back from fully surrendering to the link. He searched himself for an answer.

Could it be fear? He wasn't afraid for the children; they were safe with him at the top of the tree. As for the Reachers, he wouldn't open the crack until Thara assured him they would be safe. That left the danger to himself.

Back in the wastes, he'd convinced himself that he would live. Now...he couldn't be sure. There was a time when the answer wouldn't have mattered; it was a risk, and life was full of such dangers. But that had been before he'd met Brite. Had using his love of Brite as a means to reach been a mistake?

The thought had barely grazed his mind when something in the distance snagged his attention.

A crack had opened in the heavy cloud that hung over the forest, loosing a brilliant pillar of light. Where it landed, the curling mist shimmered and the trees blazed yellow green.

Wonder struck him. He seized on it at once and let it intensify. The brilliance of the light limned by dark clouds was more than beautiful; it was powerful. His heart answered to it, and it cared nothing about death.

The expansiveness returned, but he only sensed it for the length of a heartbeat, then all sensation vanished and he slipped sideways into the link.

A link was a lot like a tunnel. Though Walde couldn't see its walls, he sensed them instinctively, as one would sense a presence in the room. He had been frightened and disoriented the first time he'd found himself in this place. Now, it was but a pathway to home. All his worries vanished as if they'd never been, and he thrust himself toward Thara's receding presence. The very act of reaching for her was pleasurable. There was a rightness to it, a feeling comparable to when one knows their arrow flies true. But this was better still, for while an archer stands and waits for his arrow to hit its target, in this place, he didn't have to wait. He *was* the arrow, and he flew.

For a time, he imagined that the link was healthy and he would reach her soon. He could almost ignore his failing strength and loss of focus, but not the darkening of his mind. The link was frail and stretched. Walde's reaching would help it recover, but only at a cost to himself. And the worst was yet to come.

These were his last thoughts before he lost his desperate grip on awareness and slipped away.

He came to with a violent shock of pain. At once, he steeled himself to endure it, but it was like setting one's hand to a fire. He writhed. He screamed. His whole being buckled until it stiffened in place, like clawed fingers around a lifeline.

At long last, the terrible pressure lifted, and he collapsed, numb and oddly weightless, into a formless, lightless space.

A tentative sense of peace pushed into him.

This was where he most wanted to be. Where he belonged. Any feelings of mistrust could be put down to being away from Thara for too long.

"Walde." The voice entered his mind like his own thought-voice. But he knew it was not. His heart leapt to it. She went on, "I knew you would return. I was waiting."

"Then you know what happened to the Harborlands' First."

"Yes. Its link is no more."

The last time they had spoken, she had allowed him to feel her emotions. Now, she was completely opaque. It left him feeling stranded and worried that he had lost her esteem. "I did what you asked me to do. Did I do something wrong?"

"Of course not."

"Then…"

"We had a chance, Walde. But only a chance. Ultimately, people make their own decisions. I cannot force them to act as I wish, nor would I want to."

She sounded calm and distant. He wished he knew what she really felt. Surely she now regretted opening the crack in the Harborlands' First. He said, "I understand that. But it's hard for me to believe we did the right thing. I watched the tree burn."

"It is a loss," she agreed gently, "but not as great a loss as you perceive it to be. Your people could plant another twenty Mothertrees in a season, and in the span of one man's life, those trees would grow large enough to host twenty villages. *If* enough Reachers existed to tend them. Without Reachers, there can be no Mothertrees. And no way for people to gain wisdom from me. Those losses would lead your people down a dark and destructive path."

Walde was stunned by her words, his view of reality reordered by them. She spun a different view of the world, one in which Mothertrees held no real value in themselves but existed only as a way to guide people to peace and safety and to keep them from destroying themselves and everything around them.

Her view must become *my* view, he thought. Somehow, he had to change how he regarded the Mothertrees and focus instead on safeguarding the Reachers. He said, "Tell me what to do."

After a lengthy silence, he knew he'd asked the wrong question. "Forgive me. I should know by now that we have to make our own choices."

He expected her censure. Instead, she grazed him with the warmth of her affection. It felt like a reassuring hand on his shoulder. "I can give you this advice: stay true to who you are and what you are. If you do not, you will fail."

"Be who you are" was scarcely helpful, but he offered, "I'll do my best."

After a pause, she spoke again. "I am afraid for you, Walde. You came to help me open another crack. But the danger to yourself is greater than it was before. Every time I use you this way, you wear like an overused cloth. I wish there was another Reacher who could do this…"

She seemed to wait for him to offer another name. Did she realize how few Reachers were left? He strove to find words, but his mind felt pressed by the cold hand of fear. *I'll live,* he told himself fiercely. He had promised Brite he would. If he didn't, she would spend the rest of her life blaming herself for his death.

She asked, "Do you want time to think about it?"

"No. I'll do it."

"Very well." She paused again, and he thought he sensed the tingling of her buried emotion, like dulled sensation in a limb. "After we open the crack, I will speak to the Reachers. Not all of them will want to come out. Some have been grievously hurt in the deepest way a person can be. I will not force them to confront that pain if they do not wish to. They are safe where they are, their bodies suspended so they do not require sustenance."

"My father is there," Walde blurted. A vision of Carrac chained to the tree entered his mind. Though he'd looked sunken, his eyes had gleamed like two glowing coals. Surely, he couldn't have looked that way if his mind had been grievously hurt. But then Carrac had always excelled at hiding his feelings. "Can you tell him..." He searched for something Carrac would respond to, but everything he came up with sounded selfish. It was as she said. If he *were* truly hurt, then Walde had no right to demand that he come out. Still, the thought of leaving him behind was inconceivable. "Tell him he's needed."

"They will all hear that from me."

"And give him these words," Walde added hastily. "Remember what the tinker said, and how you answered him."

A tinker had once asked his father how he could stand living so high up off the ground. *A single slip,* he'd said, *and you're done.*

We get used to it, Carrac had responded. *And it's just another way to die.*

Carrac had said that knowing that his wife had died by falling.

One could get used to pain, Walde thought. Such a reminder would be painful, but Carrac had taught Walde that life could be so.

"I will tell him."

"Thank you."

He told her then about the danger the rotting planks and stairs posed to the Reachers. She replied that she was aware of it and would allow time for things to settle. Her response made Walde wonder just how much she knew of the world outside. But he didn't get the chance to ask. Like the previous time, she brought their discussion to an abrupt end, and Walde scrambled to prepare himself for what was about to happen.

She said, "I will miss speaking to you," then added, "Cling on to life. And remember your dream song. It will guide you back."

She brushed him then, as she had done once before, in warning. Walde's mind stiffened in response, and it took a great deal of effort to force himself to relax. To be the conduit she needed in order to work a change. Then she touched him again, this time with something akin to searing heat.

His whole being buckled. The intense pressure was more than pain; it was a mortal blow, one a person either lived or died from. He experienced an instant of sheer terror, then he almost lost consciousness. But she was with him still, holding him together as he became light. He knew what came next and steeled himself to it. *Stay with me,* he begged her.

Then he was hurtling away from her down the link. A terrible crack sounded, and his whole being shook with a juddering pressure.

Awareness slipped away from him.

CHAPTER 6

Walde shouted and woke with a stomach-wrenching lurch.

He almost wished he hadn't. The world spun sickeningly. He turned over and vomited. Voices were discordant notes around him. "Leave me," he mumbled. "Please."

He retched again, but nothing came up. He had never felt so ill. It was as though someone had violently shaken him until his brain rattled around like a seed in a pod. Someone held his spinning head and tried to force water into him. He managed a swallow before blacking out. He came to again, briefly, then let himself sink into blessed oblivion.

***

He woke feeling empty and deeply disoriented. He was lying on a straw mattress in a dim hut. Daylight peeked through cracks in the shutters. A blanket had been tucked around him. He slid his arm out of it and touched his forehead, feeling for an injury that wasn't there but ought to be. It was frightening to think he had remained unconscious while being hauled down the First, into a boat, and then up into another Mothertree. Yet that was precisely what had happened. He knew this hut, right down to the bird-shaped knot in the window frame. This was the hut he had guested in when he'd last visited the Woodlands.

A chair scraped the floor. "Walde."

He jerked upright at the familiar voice, his heart pounding and his hands and wrists brightening. His father sat on a chair beside the bed. They looked at one another for an endless moment. New lines had formed around his father's mouth, and there was a haunted look in his eyes. But he *had* returned. He hoped Carrac wouldn't regret it.

Walde pulled him into a fierce hug. "I've missed you."

"I've missed you too." After a pause, Carrac added meaningfully, "But we get used to it, don't we?"

Walde shook his head, then dropped his face into his father's shoulder and wept. Carrac held him tentatively, as a man would who'd spent long days in a sickbed. Walde didn't know what he felt. A part of him denied his father was even there. For too long, he'd had nothing but hope to keep him going. Now that he had Carrac back, he scarcely believed it was true. Yet here he was, solid in his hands and not going anywhere.

Truly, too much had happened.

Carrac slowly but gently drew away from him. "How do you feel?"

"Better." He wiped a blazing hand across his eyes. He was glad that his sleeve concealed the brightness along the inside of his arm. "How long have I been out?" He hoped it was still the same day.

"For the length of an afternoon. You aren't sick or in pain?"

"To be honest, I'm a little of both." He found a small smile. "How about *you?*"

Carrac drew in a noisy breath through his nostrils. "I'm alive."

Walde regarded him closely. He wore a clean brown tunic over gray hosen. His beard had been combed and his face washed, his graying brown hair swept back from his face. His bandages, too, were fresh and well secured to his hands. Had Carrac spent the time caring for himself this way, or had Brite or one of the children attended to him? He ran his hands over his thighs, searching for something to say. "So, what was it like inside the crack?"

A dry smile tugged on his father's lips. He leaned back. "There's not much to tell. Mostly, I just dreamed. Not normal dreams, mind you. In these, I was back in places I knew, like Killop Ravine, and the wastes. And everything felt real, the sun, the scents. I was alone but didn't feel lonely."

"Was Thara with you?"

"No. Not the way Brite says she was with you. She reached out and spoke to me sometimes. Asked questions I'd ponder for a while. Nothing dark, mind you. Her questions made me think beyond myself and my pain. It was like stepping out of a hole and into open skies. It was calming, peaceful." He sighed and looked down into his bandaged hands. "It's hard, being awake again, and remembering..." His mouth quivered, and he looked away.

A silence dragged between them. Walde was tongue-tied. He couldn't claim to understand how Carrac felt, nor could he apologize for drawing him back into the world. Most of all, he couldn't assure him that he would be fine now, that the memory of what was done to him would pass like a bad dream and he would go back to being the stout, good-humored hunter Walde had known all his life. Even if Carrac hadn't been tortured, he'd lost his home, his livelihood, his community. Walde had managed to thrust such things from his mind. Between Brite and the whirlwind of recent events, he'd had little time to dwell on them. But even if he'd had, he wouldn't have felt the loss as keenly as Carrac surely did. Unlike Walde, Carrac had spent decades developing his reputation and business. He'd had his own hunting trails, established buyers, a fixed routine. And he'd had his secret pastimes too. Carrac had planted an illegal Mothertree in a ravine in the wastes, and for thirty years he'd journeyed to it, giving it strength. What would become of that sapling now? Likely, it would die within the year.

"Things have changed," Carrac went on in barely a whisper, as if they'd been speaking together the whole time, "but I'm still your father. And a proud one, at that."

Tears threatened again. Walde set his hand on his father's stiff shoulder. "I learned from a good man."

"You didn't learn that sort of reaching from me. That was all you."

"Not true. Just because someone has the ability to do something doesn't mean they'll do it. You taught me endurance and stubbornness. Without those long days clinging to a windy boulder, I wouldn't have been able to break through to Thara and help open that crack."

Carrac snorted, but the ghost of an old smile touched his lips. Walde was tempted to tell him everything that had happened since he'd left the Lakelands. His old desire to gain his father's approval and esteem had returned full force, and having his attention only added to the attraction.

But just as he was sorting out where to begin, the latch rattled and the door swung open. Stark fear entered Carrac's eyes. The chair almost tipped over as he scrambled back into a dark corner.

Without thinking, Walde drew his dagger and rose unsteadily to his feet, ready to meet the attacker.

"Walde, what's wrong?" Brite stood in the doorway with a water pitcher, stunned and gazing nervously about.

Walde's eyes closed briefly. There had never been an attacker. He pushed back a wave of sadness and let a cold anger grow in its place. To think that someone could have hurt his father this badly. He slammed the dagger into its sheath.

Carrac spoke before Walde could, his shaky words punctuated by a cough of forced laughter. "Nothing. Just a fit of nerves. I'm fine now."

A question hung in Brite's eyes, but she let it pass. She smiled as she refocused on Walde. "I only stepped out for a moment, and here you are, awake and squirmy as a caught squirrel."

Walde grinned, despite himself. He cupped her cheek, then slid his hand down to her arm and guided her outside, mouthing "I'll be right back" to his father.

Closing the door, he kissed her. And just like that, the darkness fled. Shadows never survived around Brite. Perhaps she could help Carrac vanquish his. He drew a stray hair back from her forehead. "Does my father know that we're…?"

"Yes. I told him."

"And how did he react?"

She shrugged. "I think he'd assumed it. He certainly didn't seem surprised when he congratulated me."

Walde drew back with a puzzled frown. Brite's accent left no doubt that she was a Lowlander, and Lowlanders didn't marry Lakelanders. Not merely because they never met and mingled, but because they came from such disparate cultures. "He ought to be," he murmured but said no more.

Her breath tickled his ear. "When he begged you to follow him into the crack, you chose to stay with me instead. Think of what that told him."

"I never thought of that," he admitted. "And I suppose the fact that you were with me there told him something about *your* feelings."

"I'm certain it did."

There was a warm silence. Concerned about his father, Walde untangled himself from her and went back inside. Carrac was leaning against the far wall, his arms crossed against his chest.

Walde whispered to Brite, "I think he wants to be alone for a while."

"Should we go elsewhere? I want to tell you what happened at the First."

Carrac grumbled, "Don't leave on my account."

Walde almost asked if he was sure, but knowing his father, that would only make him irritable.

Brite latched the door and opened one of the shutters a crack. Walde guessed from the lowness of the light that evening had fallen. Albin and Frey would doubtlessly be preparing a feast for their guests. He fingered his queasy stomach.

Somehow, Brite's quick eyes caught the gesture. She scooped up a wooden pitcher she had left on the floor and pushed it into his hands. She spoke while he sipped. "After you left, Garen jumped on me like a kid on a berry bush. He seemed to think that just because I was a Lowlander, I'd give in to his pushy questioning."

Walde tapped a finger hard against his knee. "It wasn't you. He still thinks he can play the guard and get away with it."

"It was embarrassing. He kept asking the same questions, as if I were too slow to understand him. After a while, Elva came over and stared him down. I think they would've argued, but your reaching distracted them." Her mouth softened, and her gaze grew distant and wondering. "It happened shortly after the sun came out. There was a rustling sound, like wind. We all looked up at the branches, and they were hazed with green, just like trees in early spring. The Lakelanders were stunned. Then they all decided at once to cross to the trunk."

Walde's eyes widened. "No."

"Yes. And when I tried to stop them, they just ignored me. I didn't want to reveal what you were trying to do, but I didn't want them dead, either. So I told them the truth."

"And?" he prompted after a silence.

"Elva believed me. Garen and Shin did not. The three of them argued until it got so heated, I thought it would come to blows. But in the end, Garen stormed off on his own, and Shin stayed behind with Elva."

Walde asked tightly, "Is he hurt?" He couldn't be dead. Brite wouldn't have greeted Walde so cheerfully if Garen had died.

"No. He made it to the river before the crack opened." She shook her head slowly. "I'll never get used to that horrible sound."

"Did it cause much damage?"

"Hardly any. Some wood fell from the steps, but the stairs didn't come off. Right after the crack opened, the forest was full of horn calls. Albin answered them from the top of the tree. I don't know what message he gave them, but the calls stopped..." She trailed off. He offered her the pitcher, and she accepted it gratefully. "When everything settled, I hiked toward the trunk. Elva and Shin followed me without speaking. They seemed to accept that I knew what was going on." She took a long pull and then passed the pitcher back. "We were all so focused on the uneven ground that we almost bumped into a strange man. I saw the crack then. It couldn't have been wider than two feet, and it didn't give off much light. In moments, another four men had stepped out of it. For some reason, they all dropped to the ground in front of Shin when they saw her Reacher light, as if they were in the presence of the Berg himself."

The Berg was the Lowlands' illustrious leader. Walde tugged on his fledgeling beard, mystified by the Reachers' reaction to Shin.

Brite went on, "Elva and Shin began trembling. When I asked them if they knew any of the men, they said they didn't. But when a sixth man stepped out of the crack, Elva shrieked like someone who'd just seen bog light for the first time. The man walked straight over to her and caught her in his arms. Shin joined them, and they huddled together, weeping and mumbling while the other Reachers stepped out of the crack. Your father was last, and by then it was clear to me that the five on the ground weren't Reachers at all, but Harborlanders who'd managed to get into the crack somehow before the guards closed in."

Walde's eyes bulged. "It can't be. Thara said nothing about non-Reachers."

She shrugged. "But it's true. There are five here from the Harborlands. No, make that six. One of the Reachers is from there. His name is Zon."

He set the pitcher down slowly. This wasn't good. The men likely had families and jobs. They wouldn't be content remaining in the Woodlands with the Reachers. But if they went back to the Harborlands, they would inevitably carry their tale with them. How would that affect the vulnerable Reachers? The men couldn't ensure that their secret wouldn't spread, even if they only divulged it to their families. Their time in the crack had evidently given them a better view of the Reachers, but it wouldn't stop their tongues.

At the same time, though, it wouldn't be right to hold them in the Woodlands. He asked, "Where are they now?"

"With the children on the third level. The men didn't feel comfortable sleeping on the same level with the Reachers, so Albin separated the groups onto different levels. None of this has been easy for him. It's been hard enough, arranging to feed and shelter the children. Now, he has sixteen adults to feed and house—"

"Sixteen." Walde did a quick calculation. "Are you saying that only six Reachers came out of the crack?"

"Only six," she confirmed. "But that was all that were chained to the Harborlands tree."

Walde scrubbed his brightened hands over his face. Including himself, there had been fourteen Reachers in the Lakelands. Where had the others gone? Were they imprisoned in the Harborlands? Or floating down the river on a raft?

Brite touched his arm. "You'll get answers tonight. After supper, the different groups will tell their stories in the hall."

"I suppose I'm expected there too."

"You're expected," she agreed.

He grimaced, dreading the thought of walking into that room and being stared at by Reachers and non-Reachers alike. Everyone must know what he had done by now, and not all of them would be pleased by it. Albin must be annoyed at Walde for inviting strangers into his home without warning.

She said, "But Albin and Frey won't be the ones asking the questions. A Reacher named Idra has all but taken over this place. She even has Garen under her thumb. Albin has seen to the guests, but he acts more like a second-in-command now than a leader."

Idra. An image formed in his mind of a gray-haired but vigorous woman who sold stone knives and arrowheads at the market. Yes, he could imagine her in a place of authority. And the children would've been easily won over by her kindness and motherly ways.

A smattering of raised voices outside cut into his thoughts.

"That must be Elva and Shin," Brite said just as a soft knock fell on the door. "They wanted to talk to you."

Walde paused to look at his father before lifting the latch. Carrac's eyes were fixed to the floor, but there was a reassuring alertness in his face. Walde judged he wouldn't be startled this time.

Elva seemed taken aback when Walde answered the door. "You're up and about," she said.

He shrugged. "I'm feeling better. Come in."

As they stepped inside, Walde glimpsed Albin loitering at the mouth of the walkway leading up to the hut. Waiting, it seemed, for his turn to speak with Walde. Heaving a sigh, Walde closed the door and sat on the mattress.

Elva and Shin sat on the clothes chest that stood across from the bed. They both looked distinctly uncomfortable. Shin picked at the stubs of her fingernails while Elva crossed and uncrossed her legs. Shin flinched when Walde cleared his throat.

Elva chose that moment to speak. "Walde, I—*we* wanted to apologize for the way we treated you today. We didn't know that—that you could do what you did."

"Of course you didn't," he reassured her. "Why would you, when I kept you so completely in the dark?"

Elva blinked, seemingly flustered by his answer.

"Go on," he said.

"I also wanted to thank you for bringing my husband back to me. Bran has been hurt, but..." She paused, swallowing as if something sharp had lodged in her throat. "But he's alive and he'll recover."

Walde basked in the warmth of her gratitude. It was tempting to accept her thanks, and by doing so take full credit for bringing back the Reachers.

He thrust the urge aside and searched for something to say. "Your husband was a lift mechanic, wasn't he?"

She nodded, smiling faintly.

Walde said, "He always stopped and chatted with me when he came to repair the First's lift. He has a mouth made for smiling."

"Yes. That's him."

"I'm glad he came back. He didn't have to, you know. None of them had to."

"I know." She wiped at an eye with her sleeve. "He told me that." After a pause, she looked expectantly at Shin.

Walde had never heard Shin speak. And he soon understood why. He found himself fixed on her lipless mouth as she struggled to form words. "I thank you for—for—for bringing back m-m-my brother." She smiled swiftly and looked down at her restless fingers.

Walde looked from Elva to Shin. "I don't know what to say. To either of you. While it's true that I helped free the Reachers, if it weren't for Brite, it wouldn't have happened. She had her hand in every part of this, from beginning to end." He halted, waiting for them to speak, but they just went on looking uncomfortable. And all the while Brite sat, unthanked, on the bed.

With a small sigh, he got up and went to the door. "Thank you for coming by." He tried not to sound annoyed, but a stiff note crept into his voice anyway.

After they left, Walde glanced at Brite. She stood at the window with her back to him. Could he hope that she'd been so lost in thought that she hadn't listened to the conversation? With an effort, he pushed it all from his mind and waved Albin in.

Albin walked heavily through the door. His gaze slid past Brite without concern, but when it landed on Carrac, he turned abruptly as if to leave. Somehow, he regained his resolve. He stepped close to Walde, trapping him against the latched door. Their gazes locked and held.

The silence stretched, and it suddenly occurred to Walde that Albin was waiting for him to speak. They both knew what Walde had done. There was little point in restating it. Walde looked down and fiddled with a tear in his cuff. "I didn't go about things the right way today. I should have told you what I was really doing. You had the right to know."

Albin gave an almost imperceptible nod. "Yes. You should have. Had I known, I could have prepared for it. Instead, I was trapped at the top of the tree with a sick Reacher while strangers made decisions about my home. I thank you for restoring the First. If we aren't driven out of this place, maybe we'll get to live in it. Maybe we'll even start growing again. Or maybe this mistake will be the pebble that brings a rock slide down on us all."

The floor creaked under Carrac's step. "The pebble fell a long time ago, lad." His deep, calm voice settled over the room like a blanket. Walde glanced at him, startled. It was unlike his father to intrude on a conversation. "As for the Harborlanders,"

Carrac went on, "blindfolds wouldn't have kept them from knowing they were in the Woodlands with Reachers. This way at least they'll hear the stories and get a clearer picture of what's going on. After that, they'll be in a better position to decide what to do."

A stiffness formed around Albin's mouth and eyes. Walde guessed this wasn't the first time he had heard these arguments and rejected them.

It was all becoming clear to Walde. Albin's will to send back the non-Reachers had been overruled by Idra, and tonight he'd be forced to endure their presence while secrets tumbled out.

Albin said, "I guess time will tell."

"Albin." Walde caught his shoulder as he went to unlatch the door. "I didn't know that non-Reachers would come out of that crack. I'm as surprised about it as you are."

The youth paused, his fingers dragging on the latch. "I wonder if your knowing would've made a difference."

Walde could find nothing to say to that. He suspected that the answer was no, he wouldn't have delayed reaching in order to give Albin time to prepare. But Albin would never understand why. The compulsion to reach could only be grasped by another Reacher.

Perhaps Albin saw the answer in his face. Or perhaps he simply gave up caring. His stiff shoulders slumped, and Walde moved aside so he could unlatch the door and stalk out.

Walde paced across the room, kicked the chest, and paced back. "I've made an enemy of him."

"Let it be," Carrac said. "He's angry now because he's lost control, and I'm guessing that brings back some bad memories. But once things settle down, he'll come around."

Brite said, "It's more than that." She turned from the window, scooped up the empty pitcher, and went to the door.

"This morning, he still had hope that he would see his parents again. Now that hope is dashed."

Walde, noticing the puzzled look on Carrac's face, asked him if he knew the story of the Reachers' orphaned children.

Carrac nodded. "Elva told us after we came out of the crack. She wanted Bran to know that she hadn't left their children with…other young children. But I didn't know that Albin still believed his parents were alive."

"It was a cautious hope," Walde said. "And one that was shared by more than just him. The older children won't be celebrating tonight."

CHAPTER 7

The sun was beginning to set as Walde, Brite, and Carrac walked down the main path toward the spiral stairs. A smattering of small, enclosed lamps hung on hooks around the trunk. Normally the paths would be lit too, creating a sea of "treelights," but lamp oil was hard to come by, and the children found it more economical to carry lamps with them if they needed to travel at night. Walde patted the sheathed dagger that still hung from his belt. It felt good to be armed, even if it wasn't with his weapon of choice.

It also felt good to be clean again. Soon after Albin left, a couple of cursed children had brought a bucket of soapy water and some fresh clothes into the hut. After his overzealous scrubbing, some old wounds stung and itched. But the discomfort would pass.

Carrac said with a note of suspicion, "I'm amazed at how well kept these paths are. There's not a spot of rot anywhere."

"The children were lucky," Walde said. "Not all the Woodlanders abandoned this place. One old carpenter stayed behind with his dying wife and continued to make repairs on the stairs and paths. When the children came, he taught them how to cut and fit the wood and pegs. He died late last spring."

Carrac nodded thoughtfully as his bandaged hand grazed the guide rope running along the path. A scent of smoke and roasted fish drifted up from the riverbank, making Walde's mouth water. Brite bumped his shoulder and flashed a secret smile.

"What?" Walde asked.

"Nothing. Just you." After he shot her a quizzical look, she lowered her pitch and strove to imitate Walde's Lakelander accent. "If it weren't for Brite, none of this would've been possible."

So she *had* heard. But she didn't seem troubled by Elva and Shin's lack of gratitude. If she wasn't bothered by it, then he wouldn't be either. He grinned and swung her arm.

"Congratulations," Carrac murmured behind him, and the warmth in his voice left no doubt as to what he meant. Then he chuckled and added to himself, "A Lowlander. Imagine that."

They reached the stairs and began climbing. For the rest of the way, Brite chatted to Carrac about her foster father and what had led up to her leaving the Lowlands. Perhaps it helped distract her from her fear of heights. The elders' meeting hut was several levels up, and despite the good condition of the stairs, she never took her eyes off them. A swift glance at Carrac told Walde he'd noticed. Walde wished his father could've seen just how awkward she was the first time she'd walked on a Mothertree. It would've given him perspective.

Walde looked at the paths that spidered out from the trunk, at the numerous huts secured to branches. The tree was dead, its link obliterated. Walde sensed no life in it. And yet there was a warmth and vitality here that the dead Harborlands trees didn't possess.

It was still a home.

Voices drifted toward them as they mounted the middle level's platform and edged around the bulge of the meeting hut. Carrac halted in front of a life-sized statue of a guard and chuckled. At the sound, a child armed with a stout knife stepped out from behind it, gave them a quick once-over, then opened the hut door and waved them through.

The meeting hut was a high-ceilinged hall that followed the curve of the trunk for about thirty feet. Inside, eight pine beams carved with intricate knotwork lined the two longest walls. The Woodlanders had stripped the hall of its chandeliers and scrolls, leaving only the woodstove and a few empty cubbyholes behind. While scouring the Mothertrees for goods, the children had happened on several scorched scroll fragments. These Albin had tucked away into the cubbyholes, hoping to make sense of them one day.

The last time Walde had been here, he'd stood alone with Albin, poring over a map Frey had made of the Harborlands. The youth had been jittery with fear and excitement, still entertaining the hope that Walde would find the children's parents. Now he was little more than a shadow drifting at the periphery of the larger, commanding adults.

All energy in the room seemed to swirl around one adult in particular, a tall, willowy woman with a kind, open face and silver-gray eyes. Her skin was as weathered as an old fisherman's, but it fit smoothly over her bones, none of it sagging, despite her age. Her thick gray hair fell in a single braid down her back. The youngest of the cursed children gathered around her hip, vying for her attention.

This was Idra, the woman who made stone knives and arrowheads with her own callused hands. Her fingers were bandaged now, but the ease with which she moved them suggested that they weren't gravely damaged. Something eased in Walde as he looked at her.

She met his eyes. "Walde. You look well. Are you feeling better?"

"Much better, thank you."

She nodded, and her gaze traveled over the nearby Reachers, inviting Walde to look at them. Shin quietly picked her chewed nails. Beside her was Garen. The former guard met Walde's stare with an outwardly pleasant expression, but a stiffness around his eyes and jaw suggested the look was feigned. No surprise there, Walde thought. He recognized stocky, sandy-haired Bran, and short, slender Nessa. Both eyed Walde with open admiration. Walde's hunched great-uncle Caln leaned on a stick and grinned at his nephew. He had a bad leg from a fall many years before. Walde suspected he would take to his bed soon.

The last Reacher was a complete stranger to Walde, a tall, broad-shouldered man in his middle years with a full black beard that edged up almost to his eyes. His brows were long and bushy, and his thick black hair was smoothed behind him in a fat braid. Just as Walde noticed it, a little girl he recognized as Bran and Elva's daughter clambered up onto a table behind the stranger and lifted the braid, smoothing it with her tiny hands. She said, "I braited it. See? It's soft and nice now."

The man made no response. His black eyes, much like his beard, were wild and roaming, as if in constant search of enemies. Despite his rugged looks, however, he did not seem threatening.

Walde judged from the bulge of his muscled left shoulder that he was an archer. Probably a hunter. He clasped the man's shoulder in a hunter's greeting. "Well met, my friend. What's your name?"

"Zon." The man's voice was little more than a grumble. "I'm going to the mountains tomorrow."

"Ah. Will you be gone long?" The news surprised Walde, but he managed to keep his face impassive.

Zon shrugged. "However long it takes." His attention drifted away then, and the little girl went on playing with his hair.

"I'll brait your eyebrows too." She reached her arms around Zon's head and smoothed out his bristly black brows.

Elva said, "Kee, leave the man alone and get down from there." When Kee didn't move, her mother scooped her up and set her on the floor with her brother.

Frey swept into the hall carrying a chair. She placed it behind Caln, and the old man settled into it with a relieved sigh. "Dinner will be here soon," she announced cheerfully as she pushed three mismatched chairs together. Walde caught her gaze, and she returned it with a friendly smile. So, Walde thought, Frey didn't bear her brother's resentment. The fact lightened his heart.

She said, "You brought the First back to life."

"The link has been restored," he agreed.

Her brow puckered. "Link?"

"Its connection to Thara."

"I see. So if the link dies, the tree dies?"

"That's right."

Frey nodded gravely. "Before you reached, the First was the only tree that still had a bit of color left to it. I guess that means the rest are done in."

"Very likely. I'm sure that this tree's link is no more."

"How can you tell?"

He paused, uncomfortably aware of the other Reachers looking on. "It's like a presence in a dark room. You can feel when it's there. And you can feel when it's not." He didn't add that he'd only just started sensing these differences a week ago.

Frey exchanged a furtive glance with her brother. "Well, we still have one living tree, and that's more than we thought we'd have. Thank you for that."

Walde inclined his head.

The door swung open again, and two men bearing a wooden platter heaped with grilled fish entered the hall. Walde, Carrac, and Brite shifted out of their way. Moments later, another three followed behind, carrying stacked wooden chairs. The men set the platter on the makeshift feasting table, arranged the chairs around it, and then retreated to the far wall, where they sat cross-legged on the floor.

Not one of them had met the Reachers' eyes or even acknowledged their thanks.

It was too much for Walde to bear. He crossed the room in a few strides and crouched down in front of the non-Reachers.

The men looked to be in their late teens—too young to recall a time before Lowlands culture had seeped into the Harborlands. They had shed the kriksa robes they'd doubtlessly worn when they'd entered the crack. The kessa tunics and hosen they wore now didn't fit well, and Walde guessed that Grella's stock of men's clothing was running low. It was telling that they'd chosen to wear kessa, even when it didn't fit them. Kriksa was a Lowlands material that had become popular in the Harborlands. Were they trying to shave away all vestiges of that culture?

If so, then they had a long way to go.

Walde asked them, "Why do you keep away from us?"

After a pause, the man closest to him licked his lips and spoke. "Are you a Reacher?"

"I am."

His head sank lower. He spoke slowly and gravely, as if Thara listened to every word. "The tree god gave us knowledge. One of the things she taught us was the importance of Reachers. So we thought we should treat you…important-like."

Walde ran a hand across the back of his neck. He suspected that nothing he said would make a difference, but he had to try. "It's true that Reachers are important. Children are important too. Without them, there'd be no future for us. But we don't worship them. The treefolk worship no one. We meet one another's eyes when we speak, and we don't act like servants to a Lowlands Berg."

The chamber had grown silent. Watching the men's faces, Walde could almost feel their minds working, sorting through his words and deciding if they were true. At last, a man who looked slightly older than the others raised his eyes to the Reachers at the table.

Idra smiled at him. "What he says is true. Treefolk have no masters. We respect those in authority as long as they respect the Mothertrees. But we never lower our eyes to them. That is a Lowlands custom."

Walde glanced worriedly at Brite. More rocks would be thrown at the Lowlands before the night was through, and while she disliked her people's culture, that wouldn't stop her from feeling the blows.

The man sighed. "It's hard to change how we feel."

"I know," Idra said gently. "But you'll have to try. There are only few of us here, and that means we'll have to work together in order to succeed. We can't do that if you distance yourselves from us."

Wise words. Walde offered the man his hand. "My name is Walde. I was a hunter back in the Lakelands."

"Walde. You're the one who…" His head fell, and he drew a shaky breath. It seemed to cost him a great deal of effort to lift his eyes again. "My name is Tir. And these men are Lerin, Fin, Cadar, and Hess. Fin is my brother, and Cadar, Lerin, and Hess are our cousins. We built a boat together—" He managed a nervous smile. "Not a very good one. But that's where we were when we heard the crack that night."

Walde could have guessed they were related. They all had high cheekbones, large, beaky noses, and receding chins. The combination made them look distinctively bird-like.

Tir's last words were drowned by a childish squeal. Bran and Elva's children were wrestling under the table. Their mother scooped them up and held them apart as they wriggled.

Idra said, "We want to hear the rest of the story. But let's eat now—all of us—and we'll tell our stories afterward."

If anyone had doubted the cursed children's tale, Bran and Elva's young ones resolved the uncertainty. No one could deny the differences between their six- and seven-year-olds and the cursed children who'd remained frozen at that age for nearly five years.

Soon after the Reachers began eating, Spitfire strode in, proudly bearing three cooked rabbits. When he offered meat to the Harborlander men, they revealed that they'd eaten fish at the cook fire on the boardwalk and were not hungry. The children gladly took the extra portion, and before long, the platter on the table held only bones.

The hut had grown warm and stuffy. Frey opened the shutters, revealing a spray of lamplight on bare, shadowy branches. An earthy scent wafted toward him, reminding him of the nearby forest. There was a meaningful silence. Despite the cheerful, hearty meal, Walde hadn't forgotten what danger lurked outside the Woodlands.

He glanced around at the other Reachers. Several had gone still as they stared out at the darkening night. He wondered if they shared his thoughts.

A girl stood up in the midst of that silence, removed a lyra from a wooden box, and retreated quietly to an empty space along the wall opposite the windows. After a bit of tuning, she plucked out a gentle song that softened the shadows and made the flame in the lamps grow and blur. Watching her tiny hands over the strings, Walde had a sudden, powerful urge to take the instrument from her and draw a song from it. He had not touched a lyra in many days, and while he preferred to play it with a bow, he could pluck out a melody just as easily. His fingers twitched as he reluctantly stilled the longing.

He blinked and suppressed a yawn. Grella, a neatly dressed girl with tightly braided brown hair and an easy smile, prodded the youngest away from Idra and led them in a sleepy line to the door. Elva and Bran followed behind her with their own children, Bran promising to come back if he could. Walde's great-uncle stood up then and offered to stay with the children so the parents could return. Bran took his arm to help him down the winding stairs.

The lyra sang on. Frey opened a jar of honey and berries and spooned some into wooden bowls. "I wish we had Ona," she sighed as she worked. "I've heard it's just the thing when adults get together in the evenings and tell tales."

Carrac muttered, "It's probably better that we don't have it."

Zon loosed a snort of laughter, drawing many surprised faces. "Ona," he said wonderingly, then drifted off again into his own world.

Idra cleared her throat. "Thank you for your hospitality, Albin, Frey. I'm sure we're all grateful for your kindness."

There was a general murmur of agreement. Frey's cheeks reddened. She glanced at her brother's downturned face.

Albin's mouth twitched up in a small smile. "Well, we all chipped in, didn't we?"

Bran and Elva eventually returned. Idra decided that since there weren't enough chairs, they should push the makeshift table into a corner and sit together with the non-Reachers on the floor. No one argued. Idra was oldest, and if she didn't mind sitting cross-legged on hard wooden slats, who else would dare to complain? Frey fetched spare blankets, and everyone huddled in a circle. Albin spaced himself and the remaining three children on either side of the non-Reachers like a buffer. Idra smiled appreciatively at that decision. Despite their efforts, the five men were still nervous around the Reachers. Idra sat directly across from the wall, lamplight dancing in her crinkled silver-gray eyes.

Fifteen adults and four children watched her. Of the four, Walde knew Albin, Spitfire, and Frey. The lyra player, a dark-haired girl who looked to be ten or eleven, hadn't divulged her name yet. Many others were on sentinel duty. Walde hoped Albin would reward them somehow, considering what they had given up.

The lyra player sat next to Frey, her fingers still over the gut strings. As Idra began to speak, she struck a low note, making a rumble like thunder.

"I am a Lakelander and can only speak as a Lakelander." Idra opened her bandaged hands in a shrug. "For years, we've been isolated from other communities. Our only news came from the tinkers, and they had good reason to keep us ignorant. If we'd found out that ours were the only living Mothertrees left, we could've demanded more for our pod goods. So they kept us in the dark or told us outright lies. We knew that the Woodlanders had left their Mothertrees and that Harborlanders were slowly doing the same, but we didn't know that the Mothertrees in both lands were dead—or all but dead," she added hastily. "We'd heard that the Harborlanders had done a purge, but we knew nothing about the cursed children. Most of all, we didn't know about the ugly lie that the Harborlands' elders had spread about Thara."

She paused, and the lyra loosed another soft, low note. Walde could tell from the faces around him who knew of the lie and who did not. He dreaded the moment they all learned the truth.

Idra continued, "Tonight, more gaps in our knowledge will be filled, but it won't be easy to sit here and listen. If any of you need to leave, then do so. No one will think less of you for it."

She looked pointedly at the children as she spoke. Though their true ages probably ranged from fourteen to seventeen, Idra clearly regarded them as younglings who ought to be in their beds rather than listening to disturbing tales. But no one was about to drag them away. Albin met her eyes squarely, his mouth a tight line. Frey looked down into her folded hands. The lyra player's head was cocked, and her finger hovered over a string.

"Very well," Idra said stiffly. "I think we should start with Walde. Nessa will speak on behalf of the seven Reachers next, then Garen will speak, and finally the non-Reachers from the Harborlands. After that, I hope we'll have a better idea of what's going on and how we ought to move forward."

Walde looked around at the nervous, avid faces. Then, gathering breath, he plunged them all into the icy current of the Nadi River.

Once more, he relived the moment he'd realized that Carrac still lived and that the Harborlands elders had conspired with the Lakelands elders to ship Reachers on rafts downriver. Then he dragged them through the rapids and onto shore. Left without supplies, he was forced to live off hunters' root as he made his way toward the Harborlands.

Carrac murmured beside him, "What was your plan?"

"I didn't have one beyond reaching the Harborlands. I couldn't make a plan without knowing what was going on there."

"That's fair," Idra said. "So how did you meet your new wife?"

Brite, who had been leaning on Walde's shoulder, stiffened. Walde said, "I happened on her in the Lowlands hills. At the time, she was on her way to the Harborlands to find work, so we chose to travel together." He spoke lightly, hoping not to draw further interest.

Idra seemed to accept his explanation. "And then?" she prompted.

Walde took them through the Woodlands to the wastes that lay beyond, then on into the Harborlands. His account of getting chased by a dog for stealing clothes off a line drew chuckles from the non-Reachers and looks of horror from Elva, Shin, Garen, and the cursed children.

Elva exclaimed, "The Harborlanders keep dogs?"

"Not only dogs, but all sorts of penned animals. Wealthy Harborlanders also own huge plots of land."

"Who w-w-works them?" Shin asked, her head still bent so that no one could meet her eyes. She was a gardener, Walde remembered. This would interest her.

He said, "Probably the Scats—I mean, the poor Lowlanders who came to the Harborlands for work."

A non-Reacher Walde recognized as Cadar muttered, "Scats aren't the only ones that're poor." Everyone waited for him to elaborate, but he said no more.

Albin was staring sightlessly at the shuttered window. The Harborlands had once been his home. It must trouble him to hear about how much it had changed.

When no one else spoke, Walde pressed on, guiding them into an inn where he had first heard the starseed story. Haltingly, he explained the tale that had been told to him by a Scat there.

He had scarcely finished before the lyra grumbled and the room descended into a chaos of confused voices. Idra tried and failed to bring back order. In the end, she and Walde simply let the storm ride out. By the time it was over, Garen, Shin, Elva, and the cursed children seemed to have come to grips with the horrible truth: many Harborlanders believed that Thara was an ancient parasite that had fallen to the earth inside a star. Freed, she had burrowed deep and attached herself to the

Mothertrees. Having granted the Reachers power to commune with her, she had striven to influence others, twisting them to her sinister will.

This was the tale, and on the surface it seemed convincing. Even Walde had lost his balance when he first heard it. He glimpsed that same torment now in Albin's gloomy face.

The non-Reachers were flushed and restless. Walde caught snatches of whispered words, "Never really believed that," and, "Seeders don't think, they just do."

When everyone had run out of words, the lyre grumbled again, and Walde went on, taking them from the inn to the guardhouse. Shoving aside his anxiety over what Carrac might think of him, he revealed that he and Brite had both killed in order to escape their prison cells. With nowhere else to go, they had sheltered in the corpse darkness.

"No!" Carrac exclaimed, his face a picture of shock.

Walde paused, startled by the brightening of several palms. "Yes. In fact, we stayed down there for two nights and a day."

Bran's deep voice rumbled, "How did you sleep and eat?"

"We slept on the bones, and when we grew hungry, we ate the mushrooms that grew on them." It sounded so much worse than it was.

Idra said, "I suppose you had no choice." Her mouth quirked. "I hope you didn't...*do anything else* that would've dishonored them."

"No," Walde and Brite both said together.

Spitfire snorted. "Imagine what their backs would've looked like."

Walde shouldn't have found the remark so funny, but he did, and not only him; everyone in the circle either grinned or chuckled.

Frey got to her feet, filled some water cups, and distributed them to her guests. With the tension eased, the rest of Walde's story bubbled out of him.

The only interruption came when he revealed that Brite had killed a sentinel stationed in the tree next to the Harborlands' First. Zon demanded to know what she had looked like. Once Brite gave that description, he scrambled to his feet and stalked out of the hut. The others who had been chained to the tree reacted differently, but with no less intensity. Carrac lowered his face into a bandaged hand. Nessa turned away so no one could see her face. Even Idra retreated into herself for a while.

Walde wanted to kick himself for even mentioning the female guard. He had forgotten his hunch that she had been the Reachers' torturer. Evidently, that hunch had been correct.

Walde leaned over Brite to Idra. "Should we postpone—?"

"No," Idra said tightly. "Let's go on." And after a few nods from the Reachers, Walde forced himself to speak. Gradually, the Reachers recovered and even leaned in as he made known the considerable part that Brite had played in their release. A creak in the shutters told him that Zon probably hovered outside, listening in solitude.

Absolute silence reigned as he spoke of his reaching and the conversation he'd had with Thara. "Darkness and death" hung like a heaviness in the air. The crack slammed open in the Harborlands' First then, and his audience found their breath. Walde gave them a light-hearted reprieve before dragging them all down toward the First's terrible end—an end that all in the audience already seemed to know about.

Unable to go on after that, he let Brite carry the tale for a while.

Brite was a storyteller. Her uncle, who had been both bard and hunter, had taught her the use of words better than a bow. She made Walde's breakdown seem fitting rather than pathetic, and her idea of fetching the Reachers from the Woodlands' First a happy accident rather than her own brilliant plan. He didn't think she would tell them about her "hut," but once she had begun, she couldn't stop, and she made it sound so dreadfully romantic that it brought Frey and Nessa close to tears.

Walde, fearing that she would go on to detail their lovemaking, picked up the story from there, pressing on to his most recent encounter with Thara. Several heads bobbed as he spoke of how she had reordered his view of reality. A Reacher was more important than a single Mothertree. The idea sounded preposterous, and yet she had made it true. Her logic was irrefutable. He held back her advice about staying true to who he was and what he was. It felt too personal, and he hadn't had time to analyze it properly. He also kept secret the chance that he might have died. Brite and Carrac didn't need to hear that.

At last, his words ran out, and he was relieved when Idra spoke again.

She paused first, looking around at the other Reachers before refocusing on Walde. "What can we say? You and Brite spent days in danger and discomfort in order to help us. We owe you a debt for that."

Walde kept his face smooth of expression, but inside, a bubble of nervous laughter threatened to burst out. As wise as she was, Idra was probably clueless about a Lowlander's sense of justice. If she declared that the Reachers owed Walde and Brite a debt, and Brite weighed that statement and found it to be true, then she would expect the payment of that debt.

He was about to assure her that they owed him nothing when Nessa spoke, her voice quiet and halting. "I was supposed to go next, but I don't think—that is, I'm not quite in the right frame of mind to talk about what happened." She clenched and unclenched her hands over her knees. Walde's heart went out to her.

"I'll go next," Garen offered, his straight mouth not quite hiding the eagerness in his face.

Idra and Nessa agreed. Garen cleared his throat and began.

CHAPTER 8

"As many of you know," Garen said, "I was a Lakelands guard. Normally, you can't become a guard if you have Reachers in your family's history, but the few sprinkled through my mother's line weren't caught, so I went through the training, thinking that I might be of service to other Reachers someday." Garen looked mainly at Walde, Brite, and the non-Reachers as he spoke, and it occurred to Walde that the others already knew this tale, or at least a part of it. "A few days after Carrac's false execution—"

"Did you know," Idra cut in, "that it was a false execution?"

"No." His mouth twitched. "And I wasn't one of the archers who sent him on his way."

"Of course not."

He paused, as if deciding whether she mocked him or not. Then his shoulders lifted in a jerky shrug and he went on, "A few days after his false execution, the elders of every village held a community meeting at the base of their respective Mothertrees…"

While the darkness outside deepened and the wind stilled, Garen's horrible story unfolded.

The village meetings had been held simultaneously just as the sun sank beneath the horizon. Folk, having heard that a new Harborlands tea would be served, brought their own cups and stood in line to receive the brew. Then they sat, sipping and listening to the elders' jabbering. Garen and the other guards had been told to stand by in case there was a disturbance. It was a strangely worded order, but he thought nothing of it until the villagers began blinking and swaying like drunks. He assumed the elders would end the meeting then. Instead, they announced that a purge would be done, and all the Reachers would be rooted out and executed.

Garen was hard pressed to contain his emotion over that frightful announcement, and he began to suspect that the tea contained a drug meant to dull the villagers' wits so that Reachers wouldn't be able to control their light. As the night wore on, he learned that his theory was true. Although no Reachers but him lived in that particular village, several in neighboring villages were arrested and led off to the prison at the north end of the lake. Garen tried to take a night watch either at or near the prison, but the best he could do was one two nights later.

The Reachers were sent down the river the next morning. Elva found Garen a few hours after, and they reconvened in her hut along with Bran's sister, Shin. Shin, fearing crowds, had been out gardening during the fateful meetings. Besides her, two other Reachers had survived, but both were aged and bed-ridden. Several others had died fighting arrest, including five who'd been unknown to them. Among the known were Garen's cousin, Gus, Idra's cousin, Quinn…

"And old Tam," Idra cut in with a sigh. "He used to make monthly visits to trees that had no Reachers. He would reach at night, with gloves on. He was the only reason they stayed alive."

Walde had spied Tam in a pub once in the Lakelands' First. He was a short, stocky man who lived alone and played the pipes. The thought of him quietly reaching in the dark, heedless of nearby guards, was heart-wrenching.

Garen went on to detail their escape. He and Shin knew that if the elders were intent on rooting out Reachers, it would only be a matter of time before they were caught and killed. As for Elva, she couldn't stand to live in the Lakelands anymore, looking on the faces of those who'd murdered her husband. They decided to flee to the abandoned Woodlands.

The next day, Elva packed some travel supplies and headed off with her children to the community garden. When darkness fell, she, Shin, and the children left the garden and hiked to the tree farm where Garen was stationed. The tree farm edged up to the twin rivers that flowed into the lake. Garen led them through an oak grove and alongside the rivers until he came to a place where they could cross safely. With the children on their backs, they forded the rivers and edged around the northern shoreline of the lake. They walked all night, Elva and Garen carrying the children while Shin hefted the packs. By dawn, they were well away from the lake and took shelter against an embankment along the Nadi River.

The rest of the story was uneventful. Halfway through their journey, it poured rain and they were forced to hike on the Nadi's rocky shore until the muddy road dried. They traveled swiftly by night and slept against the embankment by day. Their food supply held out until they reached the Woodlands. They hadn't traveled long before they encountered the cursed children and learned from Albin that the Reachers might still be alive.

Elva's eyes seized on Walde's. "We were surprised that you still lived. Rumor had it that you jumped into the rapids. It was considered a suicide."

Walde's lips tugged up in a dry smile. "I suppose it's better that way."

There was a space of silence, then Idra straightened as if she had been asleep, and the worrying questions tumbled out. "Garen, could guards have tracked you from your post near the tree farm?"

"I don't think so. It was a windy night. The ground was hard and full of old, dry leaves."

"And the banks of the twin rivers are rocky," Idra added, almost to herself. Walde met her eyes and saw relief there. If the guards hadn't tracked them, then the danger to the Woodlands might be postponed. The additional time would allow them to muster a better defense. Idra went on, "And what of your wife, Garen? You haven't mentioned her yet."

The former guard flinched at the question. "Well, she isn't here, is she?"

"No. And I don't suppose you left her without a word."

Walde hadn't known that Garen was married. Had his wife simply refused to go with him? Or had it been even worse than that? Either way, the revelation put Garen's disagreeable behavior in a whole new light.

Garen's voice was tight and clipped as he answered. "I told her I was a Reacher. She didn't take it well, but she promised to keep it to herself, and she won't break her word."

"Words don't break." Zon's gruff voice drifted to them through the open window. "People do."

Idra asked, ignoring the intrusion, "Did she know you were leaving?"

"Yes. But I didn't tell her when or where." His shoulders jerked, and this time Walde identified it as a tic rather than a shrug. Despite himself, Walde felt a twinge of pity for the guard. He couldn't imagine how difficult it would have been to part from Brite, not knowing if he'd ever see her again. But in that case, at least Walde would've carried the knowledge that she still loved him. Did Garen have even that? If his wife had truly loved him, surely she would've accompanied him to the Woodlands.

He hadn't realized he'd been staring at the former guard until their gazes met. Garen's jaw stiffened, and an anger akin to jealousy flared briefly in his eyes. Suddenly he stood, refilled his water cup, and strode out the door.

Idra watched until the door closed and then turned back to everyone with a sigh. "I think we've found Garen's sore spot. I wish I hadn't needed to press on it. Shin, what about you? Who will notice your absence?"

Shin sucked on a fingernail she must have torn. "N-n-no one."

"No one," Bran agreed. "Shin often wanders off. She likes sleeping on the ground in the summer, and alone. She's been known to disappear for days on end. And after what happened to me..." He shrugged. "No one would be surprised if she vanished for a whole summer."

Idra gave a slow nod. "And Elva, how long before *your* absence will be noticed?"

"I'm not sure. I told my neighbors we'd be spending some time with Bran's mother, who lives two trees down. They knew how hard Bran's death was on me and offered to look in on my blooms." She chewed her lip. "And that's something Garen forgot to mention. Soon after the meetings, the blooms on two Mothertrees wilted. And those were the only ones that came out this year. The people blamed the Reachers for it. It's as if they think the Reachers wilted the blooms on purpose, out of vengeance or something."

Her words gusted through the circle like a chill breeze. Walde tipped his cup and stared at a reflection of lamplight in the water. The incident would've reminded Lakelanders of the pods that had dropped off after the first purge a century ago. The Mothertrees had recovered, nursed in secret by the few Reachers who had escaped the purge. That would not be the case this time. Little did the Lakelanders know how dire their situation now was.

Carrac said, "The blooms wilted because Reachers fought for their lives while unable to control their emotions. Hard to believe the elders would've been so stupid."

"Or not stupid," Albin murmured, and several adults perked up at the rare sound of his voice. "The Lakelands elders conspired with the Harborlands elders. Think about what that means."

It might mean many things, Walde thought, vaguely amused by the question. But Frey understood her brother's mind and answered almost at once. "It means that the Lakelands elders believe the lie about Thara."

Albin shot her a grateful smile. "Indeed. And if that's true, then they won't want to continue as tree dwellers. First they'll let the Mothertrees fail, and then they'll slide the lie in, just as the Harborlands elders did."

The other Reachers looked pained. Idra shook her head while staring at the ceiling. "But where would they go, and how would they live?"

Walde said, "They could do what the Woodlanders did and relocate to the Lowlands. As for their living," he lowered his voice, "they might sell off Mothertree wood to wealthy Lowlanders."

There was a stunned silence. Idra pursed her lips. "Have you heard that Lowlanders want that wood?"

"They want it," Brite confirmed grimly. "The Barans want it, and because the former Woodlanders won't sell it to them, they're having to look elsewhere."

Elbows on his knees, Walde cupped his jaw in his hand. "The river flows past the Lowlands. If the Lakelanders prepared the banks, then they could drive the wood downriver."

Brite mused, "But if the Barans are willing to pay good coin for that wood, why would the Harborlands elders create competition by bringing in the Lakelands?"

A Harborlander named Tir answered, "Maybe 'cause it'd be too hard for 'em to ship that wood." When no one spoke, he went on, "Think of it. Even by horse-drawn wagon, it'd take two days to cart a few chopped logs from the Harborlands to the Lowlands. But that river would push 'em hard and fast. Might be that the Harborlands elders offered to help them Lakelanders fix up the river like and even help drive the wood in exchange for a cut of the profit."

Albin was nodding glumly. He seemed about to speak when Idra pleaded, "Enough, please." A sheen of sweat stood on her brow, making Walde wonder if she'd been working to suppress her emotions. The thought gave him a twinge of guilt. He should have considered how his speculation would have affected her before so thoughtlessly tossing it out.

She glanced around at everyone in the circle. "Does anyone have evidence that Harborlanders have either sold Mothertree wood or are considering selling it?" After a concert of shaking heads, she went on, "Then we've ventured far into the wastes of conjecture. The situation is bad as it is. We don't need to make it worse. Let's take a break, shall we? When we return, we'll continue the stories."

Little by little, people rose and dispersed. Walde, wanting a breath of fresh air, left his father with Brite and wandered outside. Garen had gone back in. As for Zon … Walde saw no sign of him, but that didn't mean he wasn't lurking nearby.

Walde leaned on a railing built around the platform and gazed at the paths and huts, now wreathed in shadow. A handful of stars peeked out in the gaps between bare branches. They seemed cold and lonely.

Frey crept up on him so quietly that he almost jumped when he found her at his elbow. Lamplight spilled on the pale moon of her cheek.

She said in a tight, quiet voice, "I'm afraid."

Walde placed a hand tentatively on her narrow back. "We're all a bit afraid."

"Albin is afraid, too, though he'll never let you see it. And both of us are grieving for our parents. Idra told us she never saw any other Reacher prisoners, either at the guardhouse or at the compound. So they're dead. Plain and simple. While you were asleep, Al and I had to tell the children that. A few of them cried, but most didn't seem to care. Perhaps they are beyond caring." Her shoulders trembled, and she ran her wrists over her face. "It was always a dream anyway. But you know what's strange?"

He dropped his arm and met her wet eyes. "What?"

"I'm almost glad they're not here. Because then they'd be in trouble with the rest of us. And they'd be afraid too. It's like we're on a sinking boat, all of us together, and there's no shore to swim to. Nothing but dark water."

Walde shuddered, and his Reacher light glimmered before he hastily stilled it. He drew in a long breath of cool night air. "It's not over yet. I get the feeling that the non-Reachers want to stay here. If they do, then they'll want to invite their close friends and families. With more bodies and a strong enough defense, there's a good chance we'll survive."

"Albin won't like that idea much."

No, Walde thought dryly, *he won't.* "What do *you* think?"

She shrugged. After a long pause, she said, "Have you ever tried drinking a cup of butterflies?"

He kept his lips tight to keep from smiling. "No, can't say I have."

"That was my father's saying. When things got tricky, he'd say it's like drinking a cup of butterflies. He'd say that if he were here now."

He touched her shoulder. "You should get some sleep. It's been a long, hard day and you don't need to feel worse than you already do."

She shrugged his hand away and wiped her face with her sleeve. "You wouldn't say that to Elva."

"Elva isn't mourning her parents."

"I'm staying." She turned on her heel and marched back inside. Walde followed behind her with a sad smile.

The circle closed again on the floor. Zon and Garen had rejoined them, but two of the children—Spitfire and the lyra player—had disappeared. Albin and Frey sat on one side of the five Harborlanders, Elva on the other. But the separation was hardly needed. The men didn't seem nervous of the Reachers anymore. Tir and Fin even managed to engage Zon in conversation. The wild man was a Harborlander like them but had spent most of his years in the mountains. He became a Reacher when he was well into his twenties and far away from any Mothertree. When Bran asked how that could have happened, his face stiffened and he would say no more.

Idra had regained her composure and wore a grim, determined look. When everyone had quieted, she drew them into the warm fire of her voice. With courage, she took Nessa's place and told their tale.

The Reachers had drifted on the Nadi for two days and two nights, conscious for most of that time and trapped. Some had been bound so tightly to their narrow rafts that they could scarcely breathe. They slipped in and out of consciousness, the movement of the river making some so nauseous that they retched while gasping for air.

Walde listened with mounting horror. He had never considered the discomfort Carrac must have endured on his raft. The river was swift, and his father had been unconscious when Walde had left him. He had seemed safe on the vessel. Now Walde wondered at his own stupidity.

With an effort, he stowed his unease and refocused on Idra.

On a clear, windy night, their journey finally ended. A patrol ship hauled them in, one by one, until all four lay bound but freed of their rafts on the rough deck. Gagged, they were unable to communicate, even to beg for water. The ship glided into the harbor, and guards met them. The prisoners were escorted to cells in the guardhouse, where they remained for two days, perhaps longer.

Idra said, "It was hard to tell the passage of time in those dark cells." She was bent forward, her hands buried in her lap as if hiding from a memory of pain. "They fed us very little, and the only drink they offered was that wretched tea. But we drank it. And then we plunged into what seemed a long and terrible nightmare. The elders came into the darkness of our cells and tried to convince us of their lie. I suppose they wanted to break our spirits. Make us feel dirty and evil. I felt every surge of anger, hatred, sadness, and fear. The emotions rode through me freely, and my Reacher light was a cold reminder of my failure. The others wept and raged as much as I did, and their torment fed into my own. But as bad as that was, it would get worse. Much worse."

She drew a shaky breath. Walde glanced nervously at his father. Carrac was as still as the statue that stood guard over the hut. Idra continued, "I was heavily drugged when they led me off to the Harborlands' First. As I drew close to it, I sensed its sinking life and knew I would make it worse. I think we all knew we were knives lancing it with pain, and that fed into our own pain.

"I won't go into detail about what happened to us there. You've seen our bandaged fingers and can guess what sort of tool caused the damage. It's enough to say that the pain was unendurable.

"Although it seemed like an eternity, the four of us were only bound to the tree for a few hours before Walde came and the crack opened. As for the others," She peered sideways at Zon, noted his hunched shoulders and brittle face, and shifted her gaze to Walde's father.

"I can't talk about it now," Carrac said, quietly but firmly.

Idra gave a slow nod and then seized her water cup jerkily and drained it. "So there it is," she said as she set it down. She looked at Walde. Her eyes were tight and haunted. "You've tied yourself into knots trying to figure out what's happening and why, but it's all very simple. The Harborlands elders want the links and the Reachers gone. It doesn't matter whether they want it because they believe their own lie or because they think everyone should live like Lowlanders. If they win, the outcome will be the same."

After a heavy silence, Tir cleared his throat and said haltingly, "Only the seeders hold to the lie. The rest of us, well, we've gone on with our lives, or with what's left of 'em."

"Seeders?" Idra's weathered lips parted, and her forehead sprouted lines.

Tir said, "The ones who believe the starseed story. Most of 'em are wealthy and don't care 'bout the trees no more. But the fishermen care. Every night they lie on their decks and stare up at the old huts and branches. And they get drunk and talk about the way it used to be. For the older ones, it's all talk. But the younger ones would give their lives to see somethin' change." The other Harborlanders nodded at his words.

Idra leaned forward and fixed him with a hunter's gaze. "I think it's time you told us your story."

CHAPTER 9

Tir lowered his head and picked at a stray thread on his tunic. "There's not much to tell. Me and my lads were half-drunk when we heard the crack. It was a tree sound. Like when lightnin' splits a branch. But the sky was clear, so we thought, can't be that. Must be somethin' goin' on at the Reacher tree.

"We sobered up pretty quick-like and ran as fast as we could." His mouth quirked. "It seemed like an adventure, with the horns blastin' and folk standin' around in chaos as we ran by. We got to the gate before the guards did and charged through."

"Why?" Walde asked.

Tir glanced at the other four Harborlanders, and they either shrugged or shook their heads. "Don't know. Sometimes you just do somethin', and there's no reason for it. Just a feelin'. I remember that my heart pounded, and I knew somethin' 'portant was happenin'. When I saw the crack, and the light in it, I didn't pause, not even for an instant. None of us did. We just ran right on in." His finger jerked on the loose thread. "I wish they hadn't closed off the gate. My girl would've come in with me. And my da and sisters." He dropped the thread and his weathered fingers clenched. "Now it's been days, and no one knows where we are. They probably think we're in prison, or worse." His face lifted, and he met Walde's eyes with a passionate, pleading stare. "Let us go back and fetch our loved ones. We'll be quiet and careful like, and—"

"That can never happen." Albin had spoken, and his voice was as chill as a winter wind.

Tir ignored him and kept his eyes fixed on Walde's. Why, Walde asked himself, did the man plead with *him*? Why not with Idra, who was clearly the leader of this group? Walde glanced at her, expecting an irritated frown. Instead, she looked vaguely amused.

"Idra?" Walde queried.

Her mouth straightened, and she found her firmness again. "I think we should discuss this *after* we've formed a council. And we should form one soon. Perhaps even tonight."

She had managed to surprise everyone. Even Carrac lifted his perpetually bent head and stared at her.

A council was made up of elders who had been elected to that position by other elders. Ancient tradition held that Reachers couldn't join a council. In times past, Reachers held the position of spiritual guides and storytellers. The two groups had shared power, the elders governing, the Reachers teaching and guiding. It had been a delicate and often uncomfortable balance of power that the elders had ultimately found a way to break. Now, Idra was about to turn it all on its head.

And maybe that was for the best. Maybe a council should've always been a mix of Reachers and non-Reachers from the very beginning. If it had been, then the purges might never have happened.

A council. A dry smile came and went on his face. Such a solemn, formal arrangement in order to govern a few wild children in a dead Mothertree. It might have been a joke if it weren't for the terrible fact that every decision made would affect the future in ways that no other council had or probably ever would. This was the last holdout for the Reachers. They could not afford to misstep now.

Idra went on, "We're a small group here in the Woodlands, and not everyone will want to be on the council. Conversely, not everyone who'll want to be on it can be. Although Albin is young, I think he has earned his place, if he wishes it." She looked around, perhaps to see if anyone would argue. No one did.

"What about my sister?" Albin demanded. "If I deserve to be on the council, then so does she."

At his words, Frey rose and brushed the wrinkles out of her tunic. "I don't wish to be on the council."

"Frey." Albin grasped her hand, and they looked at one another silently. Walde couldn't guess what Albin saw in her face, but whatever it was seemed to weaken his resolve. She drew her hand away.

Walde pitied Albin. Few here knew, as Walde did, that these two had led as a unit, Albin often turning to his sister for advice before speaking. Without her at his side, he would likely feel lost and alone, unsure of his choices.

Albin's head sank, as if accepting a punishment. "Very well."

"Frey," Idra said after the girl bade them farewell, "could you go to Elva and Bran's hut and relieve Caln? Please tell him that we need him here."

"I'll go," Elva offered. "I don't wish to be on the council either."

There was a rustle of whispering from the five Harborlanders, then three stood up, leaving Tir and Fin on the floor. Bowing their heads to the broken circle, they exited the hut. Walde was sure that Zon and Shin would join them, but no one else took their leave. Walde clasped Brite's hand in both of his, holding her to him like a netted bird.

Idra asked with a hint of annoyance, "Does anyone else wish to leave?"

Brite leaned forward. "If you don't mind, could you tell me more about how this 'council' functions? We have nothing like it in the Lowlands."

"Of course. A council is usually made up of several experienced men and women from a single village. One member—called the chairman—leads the meetings and introduces proposals. After some debate, the other members vote on the proposals."

Walde drew a finger over his lip to hide a smile. Idra had managed to describe a council without using the word "elder." He wondered if she merely disliked the term or if there was a deeper reason for avoiding it.

Brite said, "What about family members on a council? Say that a father, son, and grandson all sit on it, along with a wife or two. In that case, wouldn't a vote be more likely to go their way?"

Without knowing it, Brite had touched on the very sore spot that treefolk had regarding councils. "I'm asking this," she went on, "because Walde and I would likely vote the same way. That would give Walde two votes instead of one."

"That's true," Garen muttered. "And there's Walde's father and perhaps even his great-uncle. Too many family members for too small a council."

Walde reluctantly agreed with Garen. Though he did not wish for either Brite or Carrac to leave, he understood the importance of having a balanced council.

Elva returned to say that Caln was weary and didn't wish to be an elder. Brite slipped her hand out of Walde's then and stood up. "Thanks for offering me this chance, but I think I'll decline," she said, and ducked out with Elva before Walde could think of what to say.

After they were gone, it was decided that a council member could have one family member sit on the council with them.

Garen had Shin. Tir had Fin. Walde had Carrac. That left Nessa, Albin, Zon, and Idra to sit alone. A fair council in comparison with many. The irony that a Lowlander had shaped that fairness was not lost on him.

Walde glanced at the window, imagining Brite plodding down the stairs to the bottom level. Love for her filled him. Such an intelligent, deep thinker. By all rights, she should've won a place on the council. He'd have to find a way to make it up to her. He could promise her reports after every meeting; beg her advice on future proposals…

"I hope," Carrac whispered, jolting him back to reality, "those are pleasant thoughts."

Walde refocused on the table they were now seated around and almost groaned. His palms and the undersides of his wrists glimmered, and he knew that if he pulled his sleeves back, the light would also issue from the underside of his arms.

Fortunately, it seemed no one else had noticed. Albin was hunched over the table, tearing a worn, scorched sheet of paper into ten squares. Nessa had left to clean out the honey pot, which would serve as a makeshift voting jar, and everyone else was trying to figure out a way to moisten some old, dry ink that Albin had scrounged from a cubbyhole. They were preparing to vote for the chairman.

Walde suppressed a yawn.

While he understood the need to follow protocol, he deemed this an utter waste of time. Everyone would vote for Idra, including himself. So why bother with charred bits of paper and dried ink?

Carrac was still waiting for an answer. Walde admitted, "I was thinking about Brite."

His father nodded, perhaps expecting that reply. "It's probably better she's not here. When she's with you, you're very focused on each other, whether you realize it or not.

That's not a bad thing, but on a council you don't want that sort of distraction."

Walde couldn't agree with him, and he was glad when Idra snatched everyone's attention back to her. She proposed that since everyone's name began with a different letter, only the first letter in a candidate's name need be put down.

And so the wetted ink was passed around along with a sharpened feather pen. The papers settled like leaves into the jar, and as Walde had suspected, no one needed time to think about who they would vote for.

Who would Idra vote for? The thought made him sit up straighter and stare at the jar with interest.

Zon, being unconnected to anyone on the council, was asked to read the votes.

When Walde heard his name read first, he immediately glanced at Idra. But his assumption that the first ballot must be hers was instantly quashed when Zon read the second ballot, and then the third. Walde stared at the table, forcing back shock and discomfort as his name was read out, again and again. All but two had voted for him. And one of those votes had been his own.

He could not look up. He did not want to meet Idra's eyes and see the hurt in them.

"Walde..." Idra's voice tugged on him. She did not sound wounded. "You have been voted chairman."

He wanted to demand why. Why choose him over wise Idra? It seemed an extraordinary act of stupidity.

"You look surprised," Idra said.

"That's putting it mildly."

Nessa said, "You shouldn't be. Thara used you to help us. If she trusts you, then *we* trust you."

As she spoke, Garen's jaw stiffened and his head dipped down. A small reaction, Walde thought, but telling. Garen hadn't voted for him.

Walde reluctantly got to his feet. Had he said the wrong thing while telling his story? Made it seem as though he had Thara's favor? He sorted through the words he had used and couldn't think of anything that might've come across the wrong way. "What am I supposed to do?" he asked dully to no one in particular.

They settled him at the end of the table, leaving four seated on one side and five on the other. Walde ran his hands under the edge of the table. *Just play the part*, he told himself. He was good at pretending. He'd done well at it when he'd been forced into a confrontation with the Lakelands elders.

To buy time, he reiterated how a council worked. Several nodded. He searched for something to say. Should he postpone an official meeting until tomorrow?

No. After such a long and depressing night, something needed to be said. "It's been a tiring day," he began haltingly. "I think we should make this short and meet again tomorrow after we're better rested."

The others nodded in relief, and he went on more confidently. Security was still uppermost in his mind. If those on the council didn't feel safe this night, then none of them would sleep soundly. "Albin, what steps did you take after the Lakelanders came in order to secure the Woodlands?"

The youth gave a thorough report. Walde had already known about the armed sentinels but was surprised to learn that Albin had also sent a tracker to scout the full length of the cart road from the Woodlands to the Lowlands. She was to leave no trail or be visible to any traveler.

The news sparked an outburst of annoyance from the others, especially from Garen. Why had Albin kept this from them? How could Albin be sure that the tracker would remain hidden? And what would she do if she were captured?

Albin answered these questions calmly and thoroughly. Only the way he folded his arms tight to his chest revealed his nervousness.

The moment he finished talking, Walde snatched back the council. "Thank you, Albin." He leaned in and cupped his chin in his hands. *Be optimistic.* "We may be safe for the moment. Even if the guards found the trail and followed it, I doubt they would travel as far as the Woodlands. It's as Idra said, Lakelanders rarely leave the Lakelands. Maybe some of you remember Drem, the murderer who escaped his cell and fled to the Lowlands?"

"No one pursued him," Idra said, her head cocked thoughtfully. "I suppose they considered him banished."

Walde was nodding. Banishment was how murderers and rapists had been dealt with in the past. Some traditions never truly disappeared. He said, "So, Garen and the others may be treated the same way. However, that doesn't shield us from the Harborlands. When the officials visit the Lakelands again, they'll find out that three potential Reachers and two children escaped. I don't know when that visit will take place. It could be next week or it could be next month, but when it does, we could be in danger. Everyone knows that the Woodlanders abandoned these trees. They're an obvious haven for runaway Reachers." He paused, drawing in a tight breath. "I recommend that we prepare now for a future attack. That means doing an inventory of our weapons, finding out who can use a bow, and training the others. The newcomers will need to learn the horn signals. And with more bodies available, we should also consider adding more sentinels, and perhaps more traps." *And if, while doing all this,* he thought dryly, *we have any time left to spare, we should work on repairing the First's stairs, paths, and huts so everyone could move into it. Too much to do, and too little time.*

He paused and glanced around. The change in those seated at the table was palpable. All sat straighter, and a few seemed to tingle with suppressed energy. Albin's eyes gleamed as they fixed on Walde. Walde nodded to him faintly, and the youth found a small smile.

Carrac was the only one who looked troubled. Walde frowned. He hated his father's shyness. It wasn't like him to hold back words. If anything, Carrac was usually too blunt, too free with his speech. He had always been an imposing, gruff bear of a man. Now, he was hunched and reticent.

"What are you thinking, Father?" Walde said at last, trying to keep his voice even.

Carrac flicked him an uneasy glance. "Something you said. About preparing ourselves for an attack. I might have this wrong, but are you suggesting that if a force of guards comes against us, we should meet them?"

Did he mean that? He pictured a force of guards entering the Woodlands, intent on killing. "Yes, I suppose I do. In the face of such an attack, I don't think any of us would willingly lay down our weapons and die."

Tir and Fin's beaky noses were pecking a nod. Fin said, "The Reachers are important. They must be protected at all costs."

"No, not at all costs." Carrac slapped the table emphatically. "There's always a limit, a moral limit to what we do. If we go beyond that, then we've changed like the Harborlanders have changed. Treefolk don't mass together to kill. That's not who we are."

Stay true to who you are and what you are. If you do not, you will fail. Thara's words breathed like a soft echo through Walde's mind before tattering away.

127

Garen snorted. "No disrespect, Carrac, but you're wrong. Think of the first purges. And the conflict that precipitated them. All done by treefolk."

"And all those events led to suffering."

Garen said, "An attack from the Harborlands would lead to suffering too. So choose your pains." Garen had Carrac's bluntness, Walde thought, but none of his kindness.

Albin said, "I'd prefer a bit of suffering to darkness and death."

Walde pushed his hands through his hair. "I don't think any of us want this sort of fight. But if it happens, it happens. We don't want to be like a man who brags that he's not afraid to die, but when death comes calling, he changes his mind. Better to be prepared than regret it after, when it's too late."

Several heads bobbed in unison. Carrac remained still, his eyes bleak with some unspoken fear.

Walde cleared his throat. "Well, we still have to vote on it. Later."

Walde's eyes felt sticky and his body heavy as he made his way down the spiral stairs with his father. Neither spoke. Walde feared that he'd offended him and that in the coming days that offence would only deepen. He didn't want to think about how painful that would be. He'd only just regained his father, and he wanted the time they spent together to be pleasant, not shadowed by disagreement.

And it was more than that. Walde thought back to the last full day they'd spent together, out in the wastes. Carrac had taken pride in Walde's strength and control as a Reacher, and Walde had silently absorbed that praise, never revealing the fact that Carrac himself couldn't properly reach. But now that Carrac knew the truth, it would be yet another shadow between them.

They stepped off onto the bottom level and walked as silently as two hunters could up the narrow path.

Carrac glanced back at Walde. "My hut's across from yours. Could you step in for a moment?"

Walde's eyes closed briefly. "Of course." Better to resolve matters than let them fester.

Carrac's hut had no chair or bed frame. A thin mattress lay on the floor, layered with more blankets than was necessary on a warm summer's night. Beside it was a blackened wood stove and a small chest with a scorched corner.

"It suits me fine," Carrac said, guessing Walde's thoughts and settling them. He strode across the room slowly, paused, then turned and looked Walde square in the face. "I voted for you, lad. Not because Thara trusts you, but because *I* do. Even when we disagree. Do you understand?"

Walde swallowed; his Reacher light glimmered as gratitude rose in him. "I do. Thank you."

His father shot him a crooked smile and walked to the shuttered window. A bandaged hand rose, grazed the sill, and fell. "I know I've changed. I've seen how you look at me, like I'm an injured animal."

"Father—"

"I am," he admitted woodenly. "Of course I am. But so are you. You've been hurt in a different way, but no less dangerous."

Walde's eyes fell. He nudged the toe of his boot into an empty knot in the floorboards. "I don't know what you mean."

"Yes, you do."

He shook his head. No, nothing could match being chained to a Mothertree and tortured. How could Carrac even suggest that Walde's experience had left him as scarred?

The question moved uncomfortably through him.

As he shifted from one foot to the other, he became aware of a foreign object in his right hand. It was only the lamp handle, but it sat just where he'd once grasped a knife hilt. Suddenly he could feel the wetness of blood again, the resistance of the guard's body to the blade. The hours that followed had been terrible as he tried to come to grips with that death. And yet he had moved on. Killed again. And after the second time, he'd felt nothing. He hadn't gone on to worry about the sentinel's loved ones, or about the pain the man must have experienced before he expired. He'd simply pushed it from his mind.

What did that mean? What kind of monster had he become?

And what right did he have to ask others who had never killed before to do the same? He turned away from his father's knowing eyes and lifted the door latch. "I'm tired. It's been a long day."

"Yes, it has. But this is something we need to talk about."

"I don't think so."

"Walde—"

"Will you talk about what happened to *you*?"

There was a harsh breath, then silence. Walde opened the door. He paused on the threshold. "I'll think about what you said," he offered. "And about how it might affect my judgment."

Carrac made no response. Walde closed the door firmly and almost ran down the walkway toward his faintly glowing hut and Brite's waiting arms.

CHAPTER 10

The next morning came with a wash of warm summer light and gentle laughter. The children who had spent the early hours on sentinel duty breakfasted by the river, along with Elva's children. The five Harborlanders had fished again using worn, mended nets left by the Woodlanders.

Walde and Brite sat cross-legged on the boardwalk, waving smoke away, when the wind changed direction. She wore a green kessa tunic and soft gray hosen. Her long auburn hair hung over one shoulder, soft and glossy after being washed. She shot him a sideways smile as she bit into a roasted chestnut.

The sentinels had settled down nearby with wrapped fish on their laps and bows and quivers at their sides. Walde opened an ear to their chatter.

"I saw Nothin' again," a sandy-haired boy began with a smile in his voice.

The fellow beside him said, "Nothin' likes to be seen. What did he do this time?"

"Pissed on my tree."

"Nothin' pisses." A giggle. It was obviously an old joke.

A girl asked, "How do you know Nothing's a boy?"

The sandy-haired boy answered, "Because girls don't piss on trees."

"Girl squirrels do."

"I've never seen a squirrel pee. How do you know they pee?"

The girl said, "Nothing told me."

On and on it went, until they had tired themselves out laughing. Gradually, talk turned to the First Mothertree. The crack in the trunk had darkened, and at Albin's urging, a couple of children had filled the hole in the ground at the bottom of the crack with rocks and dirt so animals wouldn't burrow into it. Some dirt must've already fallen into it, for the crack hadn't been very deep. Their voices lowered as they spoke excitedly about how they planned to return to the First and begin repairing the steps and paths. A living Mothertree. With real buds. They sighed, and Walde knew well what they were feeling.

Just as he knew that he couldn't keep them from it. Listening to their excitement, he felt his own unfolding, great and unwieldy as a wave. It was a Reacher's yearning. And if he felt it, then the other Reachers must feel it too.

Everyone swooned toward the First. Yet they didn't have enough people to repair it. The night sentinels couldn't sacrifice sleep in order to work on the stairs and paths. And the adults hadn't been trained on how to lay boards and fit pegs. The village needed more hands, and soon. Tir's suggestion to bring family and friends to the Woodlands was looking more and more attractive. As much as Albin feared the idea, Walde would have to propose it to the council. He was considering how he might approach the subject when Brite flicked him with water.

She had just rinsed her hands in the river and was squatting beside him with a wry smile. Guilt assailed him. Had she been speaking? He'd been so lost in thought that the chatter around him had disappeared. He bit his lip.

Brite was alone in this place, a stranger among strangers. Before, they had both been exiles, leaning on each other as they lived from one moment to the next. Now that Walde was back with his own people, that situation was at an end. But it wasn't over for her. And if he wasn't fully with her in the moments they spent together, she would begin to feel stranded. He caught her wet hands. "We should go hunting together."

Eagerness lit her eyes. "When? Now?"

He had opened his mouth to answer when a loud rumble of footsteps sounded on the boards. Glancing back, he saw Albin leading a train of Reachers down the boardwalk. "Now what?" he muttered.

The reason for the gathering was swiftly explained. Albin had decided to show the newcomers some of the sentinel posts, but as he gathered them together, he discovered that Zon was missing. Not only was the hunter's hut empty, but the boy who had prepared his mattress swore that it had never been slept on.

Walde suppressed a curse. He had completely forgotten Zon's whimsical remark about the mountains. But if the hunter's bed hadn't been slept in, then he was probably long gone.

But how had he slipped away without anyone noticing? Wouldn't the sentinels have sighted him? And if they hadn't, what did that say about their effectiveness? As he considered how he might phrase that question, Garen jumped in with his usual lack of grace and laid it out like someone slamming down a carcass.

Albin's jaw tightened in response. "The sentinels only guard the main paths leading to the Mothertrees. If someone pushed through the dense forest, they could evade the sentinels."

"But not," Carrac murmured behind him, "without leaving a trail to follow. And not without making a whole lot of noise."

Walde asked Albin, "Have you checked the traps?" He'd never forget the experience of falling into one of Albin's dugouts. And he had succumbed while it was daytime. At night, he wouldn't have stood a chance.

"They weren't disturbed," Albin assured him. "The sentinels always check them when they're done their shifts."

Idra said, "We're getting ahead of ourselves. How do we know that he's gone at all? Zon is an odd bird. Maybe he didn't like his hut and sought out another."

Albin stared down at his feet. "I think we should look for him. If he did sneak away, it would be good to know how."

In the end, the group split off and went their separate ways, Albin, Idra, and Carrac to track the area across the river from the inhabited tree, Garen and Shin to search the huts, Walde and Brite the forest's edge behind the tree. The rest stayed to breakfast with the children.

Walde doubted that Zon was asleep in another hut. "If he's still in the tree, it's because he's hurt or sick," he said to Brite as they trailed behind Shin and Garen up a path toward the trunk. The front of the tree was a vast space of roots and paths that became a tangled, rotting mess as it merged with the neighboring trees' fronts. Zon could not have ventured over that chaos in the dark without making a sound.

They left Garen and Shin at the stairs and took the only maintained path that stretched across the space behind the tree toward a wooded slope beyond. The path, which was built atop a thick, low root, ran alongside a tidy shade garden the children had lovingly weeded. The rest of the space was overgrown with vine and weeds. The forest was creeping in. Scarcely fifty yards yawned between the trunk and the wilderness.

He and Brite scoured the forest's edge. Her eyes were as sharp as his, spotting small things he'd observed but hadn't given voice to: evidence of buried structures, overgrown trails. Everything but signs of Zon's passage.

They returned to the trunk and peered up the winding stairs. Walde mused, "Do you think Garen and Shin are finished?"

"I don't see them at the boardwalk, so they're probably still up there. We could work our way up to meet them. I overheard Garen say they would work from the top down."

Walde shrugged and followed her up. They each took a level, searching every hut that didn't have a string of chestnuts on the door. (The chestnuts indicated the hut was occupied.)

The tree was quiet and seemingly empty. All the children who could be spared were either on sentinel duty or by the river with Caln and Elva. Walde reached the third level alone. He listened for Garen and Shin but still heard nothing. He had lifted his hand to a door latch when a soft moan made him pause. Silence, then a deep-throated chuckle. The sound drifted through a gap in the hut's closed shutters.

"W-w-we should go." The worried whisper was unmistakably Shin's.

Garen answered, "Yes, we should." Another moan, and a sound like kissing. Walde shook his head at him. Garen had only just left his wife and was obviously still hurt by her rejection. To leap from that sort of relationship into another in a short time was unhealthy.

A floorboard inside the hut creaked. Walde, worried they would come out and find him eavesdropping, slipped around to the side of the hut and crouched under the window.

"Why did you vote for him?" Garen's whisper was barely audible.

"Because of what Ness-sa sss-said." She sounded guilty, like a child who had done wrong and was waiting for censure.

"Nessa jumped to her own conclusions. None of us knows what really happened while Walde was reaching. All we have is what he told us."

"But he—he opened the crack."

"No!" he hissed. "*Thara* opened the crack. She used him because he was there. That says nothing about how she views him personally."

A thin smile grazed Walde's lips. It was good to know that someone aside from himself viewed the matter clearly. It meant that he hadn't embroidered his tale.

"But he s-s-saved them."

"Only because they happened to be chained up with his father. Walde went to the Harborlands to save Carrac. Not them. Do you understand?"

A heavy sigh. "I n-need to think."

"There's nothing to think about."

"You don't believe that he—that he had that convers—?"

"No, I don't think he had a warm heart-to-heart with the tree god. I think he made it all up so you'd trust him." The floor creaked again, and someone—probably Garen—kicked something. "And then he had the gall to act surprised when he got voted in. One of these days, I'm going to break through to Thara myself and find out what really happened."

Good luck with that, Walde thought. But his amusement was dampened by the threat in Garen's tone. The man didn't merely dislike Walde; he hated him. It was baffling. Walde had done nothing to deserve it, and he could think of no way to mend it. If Garen didn't believe Walde's story, then nothing Walde could say would convince him. From now on, he'd have to keep a close eye on Garen and how others interacted with him. If Garen went out of his way to sow doubt in Shin's mind, he would do the same to others. But with what purpose? What did Garen really want?

The answer eluded him.

He slipped back to the pathway. He had just reached the stairs when Garen and Shin stepped out of the hut. The former guard flashed him an artless smile. "We found nothing. What about you?"

"The same."

Brite called up the stairs, "Nothing down here!"

"That's that then," Garen said. "He's gone."

And so he was. Before the morning was over, the Reachers gathered again by the river to discuss the Nothin' they had found. The five Harborlanders lingered shyly at the group's edges, listening with every pore.

The mystery of Zon's disappearance had grown. A more thorough search of his hut had revealed he'd taken a hand lamp to light his way—yet more proof that he'd planned to tackle the dense forest rather than the easy trails. But how had he left no signs of his passage? A forest hunter might've had that skill, but Zon had hunted in the mountains, not the Woodlands.

Tir offered an answer. "There's some forest in the mountains near the ocean. Even wolves, or so they say. If he's hunted there, then he'll know how to walk quiet-like through the forest."

A silence fell as everyone contemplated that.

Idra broke it with another of her loud sighs. "So he left. And now we know that Harborlands' hunters can slip through the forest unseen." Her gaze landed on the fishermen. "Do hunters side with the seeders?"

They looked at one another and shrugged. Tir said, "We haven't heard one way or the other, but between you and me, I doubt it. Hunters are a strange lot, rough and woolly-like. Most of 'em live half their lives in the mountains and don't care 'bout the goings on in town."

"Woolly?" Carrac queried with a hint of amusement.

"We're wasting time," Albin cut in before Tir could answer. "It's nearing noon, and I wanted to show you at least a couple of sentinel posts." He didn't add that he hoped some of the newcomers could man them in the near future, freeing up children either to work on the First or man additional posts. But Walde guessed that was his intention. He nodded, pleased that Albin was wise enough now to trust the newcomers with his secrets.

The group rallied, and in a short time Albin had distributed the newcomers into four boats. Caln and Idra stayed behind to care for Bran and Elva's two children.

Walde found himself in the second boat with Tir and Brite. The Harborlander was well muscled and matched him stroke for stroke. It was a good feeling, similar to how he used to feel when playing music with Jak back in the Lakelands.

Jak. Walde's oar broke the surface too hard, and he struggled to maintain his rhythm. Poor Jak. How would his former friend feel when his efforts to play for the Lakelands' First failed and the tree languished before his eyes? As he thought about Jak, other Lakelanders he had known and liked thrust themselves into Walde's mind. But his pleasant memories of them were soiled when he thought about how they had looked on the morning of Carrac's fake execution. He had found no remorse in their eyes. No compassion. Only Jak had shown any grief over the affair.

Since then, it appeared that the Lakelanders' hate for the Reachers had only grown. It was no use, Walde thought. Best to set them all from his thoughts.

The boats passed under a curved stone bridge. The river was flanked by towering Mothertrees, all set back far enough that the roots never reached the boardwalks. Had the branches been leafed, the river would doubtlessly have been shaded. Instead, it was draped by a shadowy web of branches. Walde's thoughts drifted to Zon. How far would the hunter venture into the mountains? And why, after joining the council and learning of the danger everyone faced, had he taken off that very night? Walde could think of only three reasons for his flight: he was mad, he was a coward, or he bore a secret that he wanted no one to learn about...

He jolted as someone touched the small of his back. "Walde."

Brite. His eyes closed briefly, wondering why he was so easily startled. "Yes?"

"You talked about us hunting together."

"Yes. We should. Soon."

She smiled. "Good. I want to learn archery. I'll need to shoot well if I'm going to man a post."

He forced a nod, though he hated the idea of her alone at a sentinel post. He comforted himself with the idea that he could arrange the schedule somehow so that she was never posted far from the Mothertrees.

They docked near the last Mothertree on the east side of the river, and Albin pointed out a post on the tree's fourth level, which afforded an excellent view of the river as it curved, heading toward the Woodlands' eighteen Mothertrees. A smattering of small, concealed dugouts along the boardwalk, Albin said, would foil an intruder's quiet approach and alert the sentinel. When Garen asked how the sentinels could see the river at night, Albin explained that no intruder could ford the river at night without a light source. "And there's the sounds, of course," the youth added with a grin. "The river amplifies them all, every tiny splash, every snapping stick."

They continued south until the docks ended, then they crossed at another stone bridge, followed the river as it bent around, and hiked up a steep wash.

Walde eyed his father furtively. Carrac had lost weight during his imprisonment, and while he still had muscle, he didn't move with the ease he'd once had. Walde vowed to keep a close eye on him. If he was fatigued, he probably wouldn't show it until he was on the verge of collapse. Thankfully, Albin had promised that their destination wasn't far away.

The land leveled off, and they hiked through what must have been an old tree farm. Then, without warning, the lines of young trees vanished and jagged rocks took their place, thrusting up out of the earth like the points of giant arrowheads. Ancient, crooked trees bowed over them, all greened by moss and trailing vines. Walde couldn't have imagined such a landscape.

But it would only get stranger.

As they traveled on, the forest brightened again, and a cliff came in to view, pocked by large holes and hung over by bright strings of vine. The cliff was at least fifty feet high and went on into the distance without any sign of ending. It was a long and shadowy wall.

Carrac leaned into Walde and said in a whisper usually reserved for times when he stalked prey, "This is an old hunting trail, and I'd wager that cliff is home to all sorts of animals."

Albin glanced back at him. "Animals…and perhaps men. If Harborlands guards ever came here, they could hide out in the largest of those caves without any of us knowing. Yesterday, I added two new posts so we can watch this place. One at God's Eye and another between there and the main trail."

"Smart idea," Bran said.

Albin made no reply, but his neck reddened.

They pushed on. The land dipped down at the cliff's base, and at its lowest point, a white mist pooled.

Brite slowed and stared at it with wide eyes and parted lips. She said to Walde, "Do you smell that?"

Now that she'd mentioned it, he did. A faint scent like rotting eggs. The last time he'd encountered that smell, he'd been helping Brite dispose of a corpse. He said, "It smells like a bog."

"Yes. It does. There's water under that mist. I'm sure of it."

They scrambled over a few jagged rocks, Albin charging ahead with child-like exuberance. When the land leveled off once more, the youth halted and pointed down toward the base of the cliff. "Have a look at that."

Walde refused until his father was safely off the rocks. Even so, he felt something warm brush his face, like a hot, stinking breath. When they all stood on the lip of the ditch, Walde steeled himself and looked down.

The low area at the base of the cliff had widened to about twenty feet before thinning again. White mist rose out of the gap like steam from a pot. Hair rose up on Walde's arms. He wasn't the only Reacher who leaked light as he stared down at the clouded eye.

Garen asked, "What is that thing?"

Albin grinned. "The Woodlanders called it 'God's eye.'"

"But what *is it?*"

"Hot water," Albin said. "I've heard there are other pits like this at the foot of the mountains, but they have no water, only steam."

Walde glanced at Brite. "You've been in the mountains. Have you heard of anything like this?"

The others fell silent at Walde's question and focused on Brite. She nodded. "My uncle called them steam cracks. He used to say that the mountains let off steam because they're hot. But there aren't many such cracks. I've only seen one, and it was small and dry."

"I've heard of steam cracks," Carrac said, and the five Harborlanders added that they'd also heard of them.

Garen shot Albin an irritated glance. "Did you bring us here just to show us this?"

"Of course not." Albin's face stiffened in annoyance. He'd obviously been hoping for a different reaction. "I told you. I added a couple of new posts. We're close to one now." He lifted two fingers to his mouth and whistled.

A horn blast answered him. The sound was loud and hollow, enhanced somehow by the cliff wall. In the nearby forest, a thicket rustled and a small animal bounded away.

As the blast faded, a hoarse panting sound became detectable. Walde turned to find Carrac hunched forward, breaths puffing out of him like a bellows. Reacher light peeked out from his bandages.

Walde grasped his arm. "Father."

Carrac jerked away, shaking off Walde's hand. For a long and terrible moment, everyone stood and stared at him. Little by little, his breathing slowed and he straightened. He ran a trembling hand over his forehead. "I'm fine," he said gruffly, still facing away from the group. "Go on and do what you were going to do."

Albin didn't move. He looked grim. "Did they make blasts like that in the Harborlands?"

When Carrac didn't answer, Bran said haltingly, "They did in the early morning when we were asleep in our cells. But it only happened to us twice. Carrac had been there longer."

Walde's jaw tightened. He wanted to be alone with his father, away from everyone's pitying eyes. He wanted to assure him that he could still be useful, not as a sentinel, perhaps, but as a weapons trainer. And he could hunt. In time, he would overcome this. He only needed time.

"I'm fine," Carrac repeated, impatience creeping into his hoarse voice.

Albin sighed. They didn't stay long after that. Albin showed them the sentinel post, which was up a tall tree only twenty yards or so from the trail. The sentinel was completely hidden by leafed branches. No one could have identified his location from the blast, giving him a measure of safety if he needed to alert others.

The sentinel—a grinning Spitfire—scurried down his tree and joined the others on their hike back. Normally, a sentinel would've relieved him, but Albin had only posted one watch to the God's Eye location. Walde doubted even that was necessary, and while they walked together, he told Albin so.

Walde learned then that the trail ran all the way to the edge of the Woodlands, where it merged into a wash. It was an opening, and one that led to caves where men could hide.

Once more, Walde regarded him with appreciation. The youth met his gaze, and in his eyes was a silent plea for trust. They could be allies. Vote together at meetings. Have each other's backs.

Walde dragged his gaze away. In the ensuing silence, he recalled the arm knife Albin had given him and reluctantly unfastened his dagger from his belt. "I should give you this, in exchange for the blade I lost."

Albin shook his head at once. "Thanks for the offer, but keep it. It sits better on you than it would on me."

Walde wasn't satisfied with the answer, but he could find nothing to say. No, he thought, that wasn't true. There was something he ought to say, and the longer he put it off, the less meaning it would have. He glanced behind him. Brite was keeping Carrac's mind occupied with friendly chatter. The others were farther behind. "I'm sorry I didn't find your parents. I know what you hoped for, and how painful it must be to have that hope crushed. If you ever want to talk about it…"

A pained expression darted across the youth's face. After an uncomfortable silence, he said tightly, "I won't. But thank you."

And that was that. Walde's offer was a thing between them now, for better or worse.

They crossed at a stone bridge and waited on the other side until the others had joined them. Once everyone had gathered together, Albin taught them a few horn calls. He made the sounds in his throat, repeating them again and again until everyone remembered them.

Walde watched Garen out of the corner of his eye. The former guard bore an outwardly pleasant expression, but he couldn't hide the tightness around his mouth and stiffened shoulders. He obviously didn't like being schooled by Albin. Even if the youth had looked his actual age, he was still several years Garen's junior.

Not that that should matter. A wise man recognized that almost everyone knew something he didn't, be it a child or a grandfather.

Garen's simmering discontent didn't ease after Albin finished the lesson. The moment they started back along the river, he strode up to Albin and paced him. His voice was deceptively pleasant. "How many cursed children are there, twenty?"

"Twenty-three."

"And all this time, half of you have been away, scattered throughout the wood on sentinel duty."

"Not half. We had nine posts, and only four of those had night watches."

"But still, most of the time only the youngest and a handful of others stayed at the tree to fend for themselves."

A tight silence, then, "Yes."

"So what would you have done if a large group invaded? How would your posts and calls have protected your home?"

Albin stopped abruptly and turned to look at him. Walde could see what it cost him to look up and meet the imposing guard's eyes. But he managed it. Just. He spoke clearly enough that everyone could hear him. "We didn't come here to protect a tree. We came here to protect ourselves. If there was such a group, a sentinel would've warned us so we could all slip away. We're good at hiding. We would've hidden for as long as it took for them to go away, and then we would have resumed our lives. The point is, we survive. No matter where we are. The posts and calls allow us to do that."

"I see." Garen cleared his throat, obviously taken aback by Albin's intelligent, impassioned response. "Well, I suppose that's worked for you. But things have changed. Now we *do* have a tree to protect. A living tree. How will these posts and calls shield it from danger?"

The fire went out of Albin's face. After a long pause, he said quietly, "I have no idea."

CHAPTER 11

They returned to the inhabited tree with a few hours to spare before supper. Brite went back to the hut to wash while Walde scrounged up some food to tide him over. He'd just decided to spend the last hour before supper gathering materials to make a bow when Brite came back with an eager smile.

She said, "Someone left a sack of things at our door. Come and look."

She was so adamant that he set his plans for the bow aside and followed her up the stairs, a cloth filled with strips of deer jerky in his hand. His curiosity grew as he watched her climb. Never had she taken the stairs with such abandon. She didn't even glance over the edge as she raced around the trunk.

He was grinning stupidly by the time they walked through the door.

The sack lay on top of the clothing chest. Walde set the jerky on a nearby chair. As he did so, his stomach rumbled, and he wondered if Brite would mind if he ate while she unloaded the sack. He was about to ask when his eyes snagged on a bow and quiver leaning against the chest.

He couldn't help himself.

He scooped up the bow at once and examined it. The bow hadn't been made from a stunted waste tree. In fact, he couldn't identify what wood it had been made from. Only that it was strong. The grip felt good in his hand, and the string dangling from it was new, probably the rawhide of a deer. He strung the string to the other end, plucked an arrow from the quiver, and drew it. A grin stole over his face. Yes. This fit him well. It was the right size, and it had been made with his strength in mind. Who had crafted this for him? Albin couldn't have found the time. Frey, perhaps?

While he was puzzling it out, Brite upended the sack onto the bed and sorted through the various items that had been inside. Walde glimpsed a set of cups, a scorched clay pot and spoon, a dented metal pan with a cracked handle, a chipped mirror. Brite set each aside carefully, as if they were wedding gifts instead of the Woodlanders' leavings. She had nearly gone through everything when a small, carved figurine made her gasp. Walde leaned in to get a closer look.

An old, hunched man stood in her cupped hands. He carried a sack over one shoulder, and something knobby protruded from it.

She whispered, "It's the bone man." Her finger traced the sack and bone, the old boots and ragged tunic. All had been delicately painted in shades of yellow and brown.

Walde didn't realize she was crying until a small hiccup of sound escaped her throat. He thought she might wipe away a few tears and move on; instead, her shoulders trembled and her head sank into her chest. Without a word, he knelt beside her and drew her into his arms. She made no sound as she wept, the tears wetting his shoulder. The wooden figurine was a hard lump between them. He tried not to think as he held her. She'd tell him what had brought this on. Until then, it was useless to worry.

At last, she pulled away, running an arm over her eyes. "That was stupid."

"You must have felt something more than gratitude."

"I can't explain it." She let out a harsh breath. Her face, tilted to the light from the shutters, was reddened and patchy, her eyes bird bright. "No, I can, but it makes no sense."

"Try."

She nodded as she stared down at her closed hands. "I'm a Lowlander, and everyone knows it. They respect me because I'm your wife, and because of how I helped free the Reachers. But they don't look at me like they do everyone else. I've told myself that I don't care. I have you, and Carrac doesn't mind being around me. But this…" She opened her hands. "This is a piece of me. A piece of the Lowlands. A little girl carved it because she liked the tale I told her about it. And she wanted me to know that."

Walde didn't know what to say. He couldn't force people to look at her differently, and he couldn't lie to her about how they viewed her. He wanted to hunt down the girl and shower her with praise.

Brite stood and set the carving on the chest. She walked aimlessly around the room for a few moments before stopping by the window. "I have to get used to this place."

"We can find a larger hut, if you like."

"I'm not talking about this hut. I'm talking about the trees. All my life, I've lived in an open space. The Woodlands feel closed in and dark. It makes me feel…edgy. Not myself." She sighed and looked at Walde. "I'm sorry. I'm sorry about all this."

"Don't be." Was that all he could find to say? His tongue felt clumsy in his mouth.

She went to him, her slender body maneuvering gracefully around the bed until they stood together in the lowering sunlight. For an instant, she looked at him as she had looked at the figurine. Like he was a lifeline. Then the expression passed like a chill wind. She sighed it out and smiled.

He kissed her.

Sometime later, as they lay tangled in blankets, gnawing on deer jerky, Brite rolled onto her side and dragged her fingers through his overgrown facial hair. "I've never seen you without all this fur."

He nuzzled her palm. "Do you want to?"

"Yes."

"Then you will."

There was only one man Walde was sure carried a proper razor. So, with some trepidation, he made his way to Garen's hut and knocked lightly on the door. Most of the newcomers were in their huts, readying for supper and the long meeting to follow.

Garen swung open the door and started at the sight of Walde. His face was damp, and he smelled of soap. On a chest nearby lay his gleaming short sword and a whetstone.

Walde tried to find a friendly smile. "Would you mind very much if I borrowed your razor?"

Irritation flickered in Garen's eyes before he managed to contain it. "You may, if you bring it back as soon as you're done with it."

"Of course."

Garen retreated into his shadowy hut and returned with the razor tucked into a cloth. He made a show of wiping it until the blade gleamed, sharp as the edge of a new leaf in spring.

Few things were as unsettling as standing close to an armed man who hated you. Walde managed to keep his expression neutral as Garen tucked the blade into its sheath and handed it to him. "I'll see you at supper," he said brusquely. Before Walde could answer, he had already shut the door.

Garen's razor was a dream. Peacekeeper guards shaved regularly, so possessing a well-made razor wasn't an extravagance for them; it was a must. Brite held up the chipped mirror while he methodically removed the beard, cutting the length first before going in tighter. He managed it all with only a couple of nicks to his face.

Brite watched with a half-smile as he cleaned the blade. He thought of trimming his hair and decided against it. Easier when it was long to tie it back in a tail.

She pointed out, almost shyly, "You have a little dimple in your chin."

And that was all she said. They had to leave or be late for supper. But he grinned as he caught her hand on the way to the meeting hut. She liked it.

It was enough to endure the odd looks he got when he strode into the meeting hut.

Garen chuckled as Walde returned the razor. He stood just inside the hut, as if waiting for Walde to walk in. "You should have kept the beard. Without it, you scarcely look older than Albin."

It was quite the exaggeration, Walde thought sourly. "Brite likes it."

"Brite likes it a lot," she said and walked on, tugging Walde gently along with her.

The sentinels had seen nothing again that afternoon. For some reason, the news eased the fear and tension that had plagued everyone the evening before. Walde found his own relief in the bow and quiver stowed in his hut. After some inquiries, he learned that Idra had made the bow with her own bandaged fingers. The children had fetched her tools and supplies, and she had crafted it by the river's edge. Walde wanted to offer her something in gratitude, but he had scarcely touched the dagger before her hand stopped his. "It was a gift," she said. Walde glanced at Brite, worried that she may be feeling slighted. But Brite's smile had no shadow in it. After supper, she knelt down beside a little girl who sat cross-legged on the floor with other cursed children. They spoke together for some time, and the girl flushed more than once before Brite left her to return to Walde.

The evening's lightheartedness didn't linger past supper. The nine remaining members of the council sat glumly at the cleared table, four to each side, with Walde at one end. He lifted a hand idly to his chin and then dropped it. No beard. He hadn't realized how much of a habit tugging on it had been until it was gone.

Clearing his throat, he waded into the conundrum they faced. The council couldn't vote on a plan to secure the Woodlands, because it would preclude work on the First. At the same time, they couldn't discuss work on the First without tackling the problem of security.

As Walde had anticipated, Tir and Fin offered a solution to the problem at once: let them return to the Harborlands and invite their friends and family. That way, there would be more workers.

Walde glanced at Albin, expecting a fiery retort, but the youth remained quiet and brooding.

Instead, it was Garen who spoke first.

"We need more than that. Bring in the ones who oppose the seeders, then we might have enough people, and hopefully some who know how to fight."

Albin's back snapped straight. He regarded Garen with wide eyes. "You can't be serious."

Garen shrugged and looked aside, as though Albin wasn't worth talking to.

Albin went on, "Just because someone doubts the starseed story doesn't mean they sympathize with Reachers."

"They would, once they heard the truth from Tir and Fin."

"Some would," Albin allowed, "but not all. And it would only take one flapping mouth to bring us all down."

When Garen took too long to respond, Idra leaned in and addressed Tir and Fin as if the others hadn't spoken at all. "You want to live here with your close friends and families."

"Yes," Tir said quietly, then added, "If they wish to."

Idra said, "I don't think we have the right to naysay that. None of us own this forest. Am I right, Albin?"

Albin's mouth twitched, but he managed a tight nod.

And just like that, Idra had bypassed a council vote. Did she realize that? Walde bit his fist to keep from grinning in amusement.

They went on to iron out the details. Fin and Cadar would go, wearing their old fishing garb (which Grella had wisely kept). They would arrive at the Harborlands at night and remain concealed until departure, only speaking to friends and family members they could trust. The departures would be staggered, with one group going one day and another the next. They would sell their most valuable possessions and take only what they could carry on their backs. Metal tools would be welcome, as would certain seeds. Albin listed off what he could use with growing enthusiasm. If their neighbors inquired, they would simply say that they were moving. Evidently, many poor Harborlanders talked about "moving to the Lakelands one day." It would be assumed that these families were doing that very thing.

The groups would travel on the cart road that ran along the Nadi. When they arrived at the Woodlands, they would make a campfire at the forest's edge and wait until a sentinel arrived to escort them in. Disobeying this request might result in embarrassment and injury.

Throughout all this, Walde was silent and thoughtful. It was by no means a perfect plan. Even if Fin and Cadar arrived at the Harborlands in the dead of night, there was a chance they'd be recognized by someone who had noted their sudden disappearance. There was also a chance that the "moving to the Lakelands" idea would backfire. A nosy elder might pull a family aside and question them. Or worse, the elders might decide to send officials to the Lakelands earlier than they had intended to.

He tugged again on his bare chin. Danger would come to the Woodlands one way or another. He just hoped that this new plan wouldn't hurry it along before they were ready for it. Before he adjourned the council, he proposed that, while waiting for the Harborlanders, all who were able should train to use a bow and take turns on sentinel duty.

To his surprise, the vote was unanimous.

***

He should have slept soundly that night. The meeting had gone well, and he had drifted to sleep with Brite curled contentedly against him. But at once, an old nightmare he'd hoped never to have again assailed him. He stood on some sort of precipice, and while the wind battered him, he screamed, again and again. Something essential was falling away from him into a dark void, and with each passing moment, the ache of its loss grew keener. He wavered on the edge, powerless to stop it, while threading away to nothing.

He woke just as he felt himself fall.

He was panting. Sweating. Burning with Reacher light. It was a miracle that Brite hadn't wakened. He drew the blanket back over them both and sought to control his wild panic. He couldn't let this sort of thing happen once he moved into the First. While the tree itself wouldn't be damaged from his repeated nightmares, the branch beneath his hut would suffer. He had only to recall the damage he'd done to Carrac's branch in the Lakelands to know how destructive his nightmares could be. His father had recommended taking daleroot to help him sleep without dreaming. He hoped the herb grew in the Woodlands. If not…

If not, then he'd have to ask Fin to bring some back from the Harborlands. Daleroot would certainly grow there. The Harborlands grew every sort of herb imaginable.

He shut his eyes and tried to sleep.

A breeze slid through a crack in the shutters, cooling his damp face. The tree was so quiet that his ears rang. As he lay there, feeling the emptiness in the tree, a hideous urge to reach stole over him. It truly was like real hunger. Not thinking about it didn't drive it away. He untangled himself from Brite and turned over. Worse. A slow ache was building in his core, and there was a dull pressure behind his eyes.

He was stronger than this. He would push it back as he pushed back strong emotion.

It was a long and trying night. He slept intermittently and rose at the first blush of dawn. While Brite slept on, he dressed quietly and hurried out.

He needed to reach.

The air was cool and hazy with mist. He got to the river just as a new group of sentinels were piling into a boat. A girl Walde remembered as Lina sat at the stern. It was her job that morning to ferry sentinels up and down the river. Walde offered to row with her as far as the First. He was relieved when she didn't ask why.

"Get in," she said simply. The others shifted to the center, and they shoved off.

They rowed into a deepening mist. The Mothertrees on either side of the river were shrouded in white. The docks were shadowy lines. Even sound seemed dampened by the heavy air. What, he wondered, was the point of posting sentinels in this situation? Walde asked, "How do you find your posts?"

"We just do," a boy answered.

Lina said, "The mist never lasts. You'll see."

Walde had no idea how Lina knew when to pull to shore to let sentinels off, but she did it twice before letting Walde off at a dock. The mist was still too thick for him to see the First, but he sensed the familiar hum of its link.

"Don't walk on those boards," Lina warned as Walde scrambled up. "Crawl."

Could Zon have *crawled* along the boardwalk in an early morning mist? The question moved uncomfortably through him as he crossed the walk and scrambled over roots toward a path. His elbows and knees skated on the slippery old boards. The mist was like a cold tongue on his skin, and the wet ground quickly drenched his clothing. Thrice, he caught splinters in his skin. It was enough to reassure him that Zon couldn't have traveled far like this. He would have left a blood trail.

Should he try reaching on the roots? At dinner last night, Idra had told him privately that he could've saved himself the trouble of climbing the First if he'd just reached from its roots. Evidently, unlike the branches, both the roots and trunk connected directly to the link.

He shook his head. There was still so much to learn.

He hadn't traveled much farther when the shadowy pillar of the First's trunk resolved in front of his eyes. The path he'd been following widened into a courtyard that encircled the tree on all sides. He came to the stairs and, rising to his feet, circled them until he passed the bottom step and approached a bare space of the trunk where song rites would have taken place.

Except that it wasn't bare.

Shin sat cross-legged inside the crack that he had helped create. She was far from the tidy, cowering mouse he was used to seeing. Only her lipless mouth and small, upturned nose identified her. A gray blanket draped her body and partially hid her glowing palms. Her hair, normally brushed back into a severe braid, lay across her narrow shoulders in an inky spray. She had been unconscious when he approached, but as he stood there, her eyes opened and she leaned away from the wall of the crack. Her sightless gaze seemed to look straight through him before it focused, and she gave a violent start.

"Sorry," Walde said at once. "I didn't know you were here. How did you come here?"

When she had collected herself, she slid a hand out of the blanket and reached for something at her side that the shadows had concealed. A lamp. "I w-walked here before the mist came. I flashed the light to w-w-warn the sss-sentinels."

"I see." He kept his face impassive. His feelings were mixed about her being here. While it was certainly a relief to know he wasn't the only one with a burning desire to reach, he had wanted to be alone. Now he wondered if he'd be able to reach at all.

Shin set the lamp aside and stared glumly at the fading light in her palms. "I can't. N-n-never could."

"Can't what?"

"Get into the tunnel."

Walde pressed his lips together to keep from frowning. So, his father wasn't the only one who had never entered a link. He wondered how many others had the same problem, and if there was a polite way to find out. It was becoming clear to him that the Reachers had never met together in the Lakelands to discuss reaching, either because they'd been in fear of being caught or because they'd considered reaching too personal. He wished he knew what Reachers had done in the past.

He sat down by the edge of the crack. "I can try to help you."

"Yes. Do."

Shin didn't like eye contact, so he spoke to her from where he crouched at the edge of the crack. He had no idea if his hunch about why some might fail to reach was correct. But he didn't let her hear uncertainty in his voice. He said, "While we're awake, we keep our emotions in tight check. We do it so often that it becomes automatic. So automatic that even when we're reaching, we might hold back without realizing it." He told her then about the time he'd failed to reach when he was at the top of the tree, and why. Shin listened without a word. And when he fell silent, she said she would try again. And this time completely let go.

Walde waited, hugging his cold limbs and thinking about how foolish he had been not to bring a blanket. His kessa jacket was so damp that it scarcely added any warmth.

Shin came to after a short time, and her little whimper told him she had failed once more.

The sky was brightening, the mist thinning as the sun warmed the air. Walde leaned his head back and stared up at the hazy boughs. He said, "Stop thinking and just listen. Do you hear the thudding of drips falling from the branches? The distant birdsong? Look out of the crack. Do you see how the mist shifts and eddies as the breeze touches it? Watch the mist and forget everything." After a silence, he began to hum his dream song. Carrac had called it a passage song. Reachers used to make songs like that, he had said, because they opened a way into the Mothertrees.

Now, the song was starting to work on him in a predictable way. He was growing expansive. In another breath, he would reach. But he couldn't do that. Not while Shin was reaching. It felt rude to enter a link while someone else was inside it.

He stopped humming and forced the expansiveness back. Doing so was painful. He hunched forward and held his head. Gradually, the world steadied, and he dropped back against the tree.

He glanced around the edge at Shin. She was deeply unconscious and as tightly wrapped in the blanket as an unopened bud. He sighed and looked away with a weary smile. It was good. He wasn't reaching, but that didn't seem to matter anymore now that he knew Shin was. He sat and waited, his hand running over the familiar grooves of the Mothertree's bark. The mist cleared, and birdsong filled the space at such a volume that he imagined their flapping wings. He stared at the swollen buds on the branch above him. The initial green had changed to a deep purple. They would bloom late, but bloom they would.

Shin made a small sound. Walde allowed her a few moments of privacy before crouching in front of her.

All shyness had drained out of her, replaced by triumph and wonder. She didn't look away from him as she spoke. "I did it." She loosed a happy sigh. "I w-want to again."

"I know." He grinned. "Did you graze her?"

"Yes!" She banged her little fists on her knees. "But I don't remember the w-w-wisdom she gave me."

"I didn't either, the first time I reached."

He stood up and stamped to get the blood flowing again in his cold feet.

Shin grabbed her lamp and crept out of the crack. She set her hand on his shoulder. "Thank you."

This was almost as good as reaching, he decided as he made his way carefully back to the others. He vividly remembered what it had felt like to truly reach for the first time. It had been life-changing. To help someone do that...

He suddenly knew that this experience would always be something between him and Shin. And it would be the same for every Reacher he helped. He shook his head and smiled.

As he neared the dock at the inhabited tree, though, his cheerful mood evaporated. Fin and Cadar were readying to leave. He'd known they were going today, and last night their departure had made perfect sense. It still made sense. But knowing that didn't ease his lingering fear that something would go wrong.

The daleroot, he reminded himself, and increased his pace.

CHAPTER 12

Walde sat alone on the back porch of a repaired hut and watched the gentle curve of the river far below. While he waited for his sentinel shift to end, he played what the children called "the alphabet game." It was more a puzzle than a game. Fifteen wooden tiles lay in a frame that could hold sixteen. The tiles were marked with the first fifteen letters in the alphabet. By moving them around on the frame (using the missing space), one could spell out words or try to get the letters in order from A to O. To make the game more suited to sentinel duty, the letters protruded on the tiles, allowing one to distinguish each letter without seeing it. Playing it this way hurt Walde's head, but he found it strangely addictive. The game and the metal horn were the only two objects he kept on his person while watching the river.

Both, he had learned, had been gifts from the old man. He had purchased them from tinker wagons which lumbered up and down the cart road by the Nadi River.

Walde set down the game on his lap and stretched.

Two weeks had passed since Fin and Cadar left for the Harborlands. Before they'd gone, Walde had requested the daleroot. To his surprise and dismay, he'd learned that several others had already requested some. Either those people weren't sleeping well, or, like Walde, they worried that their nightmares would affect the First. Neither possibility was good. Walde ought to have raised the issue at council but couldn't bring himself to do it. It felt too personal.

Two weeks later, he still couldn't.

It had been a busy two weeks. He'd spent the first couple of days following Albin around to learn the locations of posts and traps. During those hikes, he'd managed to have private conversations with several Reachers. Shin had revealed that Garen could enter a link. But her brother, Bran, could not. That had left Nessa, Idra, and Caln as question marks.

And Zon. If the hunter ever came back.

Walde hadn't enjoyed the prospect of asking the women if they'd ever entered a link. For a whole day, he'd pondered how he would do it. In the end, though, it had been simple: admit he had trouble recalling the wisdom that Thara passed to him while reaching and see if they'd own up to the same difficulty.

As he had hoped, they both did, indicating that they could enter a link.

Caln could not. And worse, he didn't think that was a problem. Like Carrac, he was proud of how he reached and believed he could do no better. And even if he could, he was too old to change.

That left Bran.

Fortunately, the lift mechanic had been eager to talk. Shin had made her training session with Walde sound magical, and he wanted to begin, as soon as possible. So they'd met at the First early one morning, and Walde encouraged him to sit in the crack. What had worked for Shin, he'd reasoned, would work for Bran. But it didn't. Instead, Bran grew agitated and even fearful. Sitting at the base of a Mothertree with Walde hovering nearby triggered painful memories of his torment. Bran couldn't reach again that day, either up the tree or on its roots.

So, that night, Walde hunted down the lyra player and asked to borrow her instrument. Though he assured her that he would treat it as if it were his own, he still felt the weight of her worried eyes as he walked off with it under his arm. In truth, he hadn't expected her to part with it at all. Lending out one's instrument wasn't like lending out a razor. He knew from his own experience that she wouldn't sleep well until she had it back.

Walde still missed his own lyra. It had been many weeks since he'd so much as held one. Although the girl preferred to pluck the strings, a worn bow lay in the case, waiting for Walde to touch it. With Bran calm again and settled against a root and the instrument tuned and tightened, he drew out the haunting melody of his dream song.

He didn't know where Bran went after that. If, indeed, he went anywhere. Nothing else existed for Walde but the music. When one song ended, he slid into another, and then another. Every song he'd ever played drained out of him, screaming of the Lakelands. Walde had never been an emotional player. Song rite music tended to be dry and formulaic, and he'd always played it that way.

Until recently.

Now, what was meant to mimic gentle growth became tumultuous waves, drowning and washing over. He didn't weep with them. This wasn't sadness he played, but something more akin to joy. The power of the emotion made his Reacher light blaze. Yet somehow he was beyond reaching as he wrung himself dry of the Lakelands.

At last, he ran out of songs. He lowered the bow with damp, burning hands and set it in its box. He started at the sound of clapping. Bran stood over him, shaking his head and smiling, and a few yards away, four children jumped and hooted. They had come, as they had every day lately, to work on the First. So far, they'd stripped the main path of rotten boards and were working their way toward the stairs.

With a twinge of guilt, Walde set the lyra back in its case and snapped the lid shut. He'd intended to help Bran reach. Instead, he had indulged himself and wasted precious time.

"I did it," Bran said abruptly, scattering Walde's thoughts and making him stare. "Thank you."

***

A distant murmur of voices over the water told Walde his sentinel shift was done. He left the game and horn by the chair and scooped up his bow and quiver.

The sun had disappeared behind the trees. In the Lakelands, it would linger long over the wastes, brushing the horizon with every color imaginable, but here both sunrise and sunset were concealed by mountains and trees.

The Woodlands would never feel like home. He had come to grips with that now. Home was a memory, a place of safety that began to die the moment he became a Reacher. He would never get it back. And, he told himself, he didn't want it back. The passion he'd glimpsed in a sunset had never been his in the Lakelands. He'd never played the lyra with feeling until now. Never loved a woman until he met Brite. His life burned now on a knife's edge of danger, but at least it burned.

Brite had long finished supper and was home when he strode through the door. She cried out in pain as he pulled her into his arms. "Don't," she warned, "touch my back. Or my shoulder. Or my arms."

He grinned. "Did you train with Carrac again?"

"No. With Idra." She gestured to a cloth-covered plate on the chest. "It was fried fish coated in chestnut flour today. I saved you a few strawberries, but they look overripe."

"Thank you."

She spoke as he ate. "Carrac seemed strange today. He was off on his own a lot this afternoon, moving about like a squirrel readying for winter. He told me he wants to talk to you."

Walde swallowed his bite a touch too sharply. "Did he say why?"

"No." Her lips compressed. She picked a strawberry off his plate and turned it. Light from the lamp glittered on its tiny seeds. "But I think you should go to him soon."

Walde hated that he now dreaded speaking with his father alone. Their last private conversation still throbbed painfully at the back of his mind. He didn't know what he'd do if Carrac was determined to bring it up again.

Still, he finished his food quickly and hurried over to Carrac's hut.

He had scarcely knocked before the large man opened the door and tugged him inside.

At once, Walde knew that something was wrong. The shutters were tightly shut, though the summer air was cool and pleasant. Light from a single lamp shone on a stuffed leather pack on the floor. Walde hadn't seen that pack before. He asked in a strangled voice, "Are you leaving?"

Carrac stepped close to him. "Yes. But I'll be back. I promise you that."

"Where? Why?"

An odd patience touched his father's eyes, and for some reason, Walde was transported back twelve years to the moment Carrac had given him a square-shaped medallion and told him to stow his strongest emotions inside it. The medallion and its leather chain were lost to him now, confiscated by Harborlands guards. But the memory of how he'd come by it was as strong as the memory of wearing it.

Carrac said, "I'm going to Killop Ravine." When Walde didn't immediately reply, he added, "I have to, lad. I can't leave her to die there. I can't."

A vision of his father's sapling entered Walde's mind. It grew by a glittering river, with the curved wall of a ravine encircling it like a shield. All of it was so far away, it was like a dream. He sank bonelessly into a chair and ran a hand over his forehead. He couldn't believe what he was hearing. Was Carrac losing his mind? Walde said, "That doesn't make sense. You say you'll be back, but it's going to take you a week to get there and a week to get back. By the time you're back here, it'll be time to go again."

"That's not so, lad. The sapling doesn't need me every week. And I'm planning to linger a few days. Reach as much as I can before heading back."

"Reach." Walde dropped his arm and just stared at him.

Carrac looked down at his tightly folded hands. The bandages were off them now, revealing the darkened ends of fingers where nails had been. He spoke in a low, husky voice. "I know that you and I reach differently. But my way still works. I've seen it work on my tree."

Walde stopped himself from shaking his head. He wanted to help Carrac reach, had even looked forward to it. It had never occurred to him that his father wouldn't want that help. "I don't care," he heard himself say. "The only thing I care about is your life. And I can't see why you'd risk it for a sapling."

Carrac's eyes hardened. "I knew that you wouldn't understand. You've never grown a Mothertree from the seed up. I've spent thirty years raising that tree, going down into that ravine time and again to reach. I can't let it die now. I can't."

Walde rose unsteadily to his feet and crossed the room. Wretched jealousy rose in him. But fear was even stronger. He struggled to stow them both. "Reachers," Walde reminded him, "are more important than Mothertrees."

"Well, I'm not," his father said matter-of-factly, then went on before Walde could frame a response, "Let it go, lad. This is something I can do, and safely. I know all the paths. I know when to travel and when to lie low. I could find Killop Ravine in the dark."

"You could, if you were on the other side of the Nadi. But you're not. And you can't cross it. You'd have to go back to the Lakelands and edge around the lake."

"Yes."

"How do you know that the north end of the lake isn't being guarded? By now, the elders might suspect that Garen and the others left that way."

Carrac's mouth quirked. "Albin's scout returned while you were on sentinel duty today. She went as far as the twin rivers and didn't see any sign of guards there. Nor any sign that the Reachers were followed. It seems that you were right when you said they wouldn't leave the Lakelands."

Once more, Walde found the chair under him. This was good news. He ought to celebrate it. Instead, he wished the opposite were true. He groped for an argument. "That doesn't mean you'll be safe. You'll still have to pass near the guardhouse—"

"I plan to cut a wide path around it."

"If a hunter sees you, it's over. The guards will follow your trail. And after they have you, they'll send you back to the Harborlands. After that..." After that, he would be drugged and forced to talk. Then they would all be in danger.

"They won't get me alive."

The words fell like heavy stones. Walde dragged his hands over his thighs. It seemed a terrible jest that his father would make the same effort to save a sapling that Walde had made to save him. It diminished all that he and Brite had done, while at the same time jeopardizing it. But what could Walde do to stop him? Warn the others so they could arrest Carrac and put him under guard? He couldn't do that. "I suppose," Walde said tightly, "that you want me to keep all this a secret."

"I do."

Yet another burden to bear. He almost wished Carrac had just slipped away and told him nothing. Walde's voice sounded hollow when he spoke again. "How do you plan to get into the ravine?"

Carrac rummaged through his pack. "Albin has a store of tools and supplies in a hut on this level. I snuck in there today and found rope and a hook. One of the prongs is damaged, but it'll do." He held it up to the light.

"And you have a knife?"

He nodded curtly. "A stone one I made." The firmness in his tone told Walde he would not accept the dagger, just as he wouldn't accept help reaching.

Walde sighed and stood up. Suddenly, he didn't know why he was there. He turned toward the door.

Carrac grasped his arm. "Don't go away angry."

Anger didn't begin to describe what Walde felt, but it would have been pointless to tell him that. Walde asked, "When are you going?"

"Before dawn."

This was it then. Walde might never see his father again. He turned aimlessly, his throat tightening. Reacher light sprayed across the hut. He wanted to tear into his father for leaving. Make him feel guilty. Selfish. A fool for ignoring Thara's advice. Instead, he pulled him into a fierce hug.

Carrac whispered, "I wish you could join me. We were going to go back there together."

"Yes. We were. Come back to us."

"I will. I promise."

CHAPTER 13

Walde woke to a faint scraping sound. He lay still for a moment, caught up in an unfinished dream. The bed was empty. Brite had left during the night for a sentinel shift. Warm light pooled on the mattress by his outflung arm. He stared at it, wondering why he'd been so anxious the night before. His father would be fine. He had sneaked off to Killop Ravine countless times, and no one had ever caught him at it. That said something, didn't it?

The scraping resumed and then a faint creak as one of the shutters opened. A goldfinch poked its neck into the room. Walde lay still as it hopped from the sill to the edge of the mattress. Its scarlet head gleamed in the sunlight. Very slowly, Walde opened his hand and edged it closer to the bird, hoping it would perch on one of his fingers.

He flinched as a horn call sounded. Spooked by the sudden movement, the bird hopped back to the window and flew away.

Walde remained still, listening until the distant call was repeated by a nearby sentinel, then he loosed a tight breath and relaxed back onto the mattress. It was good news. The Harborlanders were finally trickling in.

He leaped up and began to dress. Excited voices filtered through the now empty window. In a short time, Walde was out the door and flying down the path toward the stairs.

He reached the boardwalk just as three boats docked. Cadar and six other Harborlanders disembarked in front of a small crowd of children. Elva and Idra hovered nearby, their eyes fixed on the packs Albin and Bran unloaded from the boats.

The Harborlanders looked dazed and weary. They'd probably never gone on such a long journey, and their first glimpse of the dilapidated First probably hadn't been encouraging.

Cadar strode over to Walde with a young, pale-haired woman hanging possessively on one arm. "This is Tress. Her father died in a fishing accident and her mum ... well, she's so afraid of the cursed children that she couldn't bring herself to come here."

"Good to meet you, Tress."

A bald man with a long gray beard strode up to Walde and fixed him with a raven-eyed stare. "Walde. Is it Walde?"

"I am," Walde said. He was rewarded with a firm handshake.

"I'm Cor, Cadar's sister's father-in-law." If Cor knew Walde was a Reacher, he showed no sign of nervousness. He stood so close that Walde could smell fish and spirits on his breath. "Cadar tells me you're chairman on the council here."

Walde said warily, "The vote went that way."

Cor gave a sharp nod. "I respect that. But I want you to know I didn't come here to play sentinel. I'm a builder. I used to repair huts and paths before the Mothertrees died and the Scats came in."

A curly-haired girl who'd been lurking behind him suddenly pushed herself between Cor and Walde. She was eight or nine years old and acted like it. "Me too. Look!" She held up her hands for Walde's inspection.

He pushed his finger into her palm. "Wow. You're getting calluses already."

She wasn't, but he guessed it was a cherished goal. She grinned at Walde's words and started jumping up and down. For some reason, she reminded him of the goldfinch.

Cor smiled appreciatively at Walde. "This is my granddaughter, Nic. She looks small, but she's a fine little worker."

And their good fortune, Walde thought. Cadar went on to introduce his older sister and her husband. And her husband's brother. So much extended family. And it was only the beginning. Cadar's aged parents had chosen not to come, but several other relatives were considering it.

Cor was determined to start on the First that very day. Bran and Elva were caught up in his enthusiasm. They'd begun to worry about the possibility their children would cease growing if they lived away from living Mothertrees much longer. Cor wasn't pushy about his opinions. He didn't need to be. Almost from the moment he arrived, he drew people into his whirlwind and took them along with him. He was constantly in motion. When he wasn't talking, he tugged restlessly on his beard and flung longing glances back at the First. Without saying it, he made everyone question why they were still living in a dead tree.

In the commotion, Carrac's disappearance was set aside. A search of his hut revealed that he'd taken a cooking pot and blanket with him, items he wouldn't have needed if he'd just gone hunting. Carrac's impulse to leave puzzled everyone. Even Walde remained mystified by Carrac's decision. But the intense sweep of activity didn't allow him to dwell on it. New groups of Harborlanders arrived daily, and most joined Cor in his efforts to make the First livable again. The momentum he created was overwhelming. It reminded Walde of how he felt while reaching. In the link, nothing else mattered but Thara's presence.

For a while, nothing else mattered but the First. The rotten steps came off, and sturdy ones were pilfered from neighboring Mothertrees. Cor's son and granddaughter taught others how to lay boards and drive pegs. And with the strong metal tools brought from the Harborlands, the work charged ahead without pause. From the stairs, Cor moved to the uppermost level and began disassembling the huts. Vertical chains of workers perched in branches or on roofs and handed down wood. Brite, still nervous of heights, remained on the ground and helped cart away the rotten boards and stack viable ones.

It was a wondrous time. The First's leaves had unfurled and were a shiny, glittering green in the sunlight. The sound of them rustling in the wind brought tears to Cor's eyes. For a whole morning, he did little more than stand and listen while wiping his face with the backs of his hands. It was a healing sound, and the constant presence of the link became a familiar song in Walde's mind, one that he missed when he was away from it.

Many chose not to be away at all. As night fell, the Harborlanders and not a few cursed children either slept in the weedy spaces between roots or braved the dilapidated huts. Few went back to the dead tree. Tir had built a steady cook fire by the river's edge, and its smoke chased back biting flies.

The work didn't always run smoothly. Two Harborlanders suffered injuries and had to be sewn up. And there were domestic disputes and panicked searches for lost children. Alcohol was another issue. Cor constantly sipped from a flask and let it be known he would want more when his store ran out. In response, Spit and Lina went in search of honey and juniper berries, anything that could be used to make alcohol.

The summer heat lingered long into the evenings. Night took its time closing in, and the sound of paddles dipping in the water mingled with the crackling fire. Tired folk gathered on the boardwalk to drink spirits brought from the Harborlands and to talk.

During these gatherings, Walde learned that the Harborlands had fallen into chaos after the First burned to the ground. Some homes in the wealthy quarter had been set ablaze. Animals had been loosed from pens. So many folk had been arrested that a warehouse had been refitted to hold prisoners. Most of these were young men who held the elders and seeders responsible not only for the loss of the First, but also for the deaths of all the Mothertrees in the Harborlands.

Harborlanders, Cor explained, fell into two categories: those who wanted to live like Lowlanders and those who did not. Folk who opposed a lowlander lifestyle were mainly made up of fishermen and former builders. But within this group, beliefs varied. Some held to the starseed story but felt that people should continue living in the dead Mothertrees. Others believed that the elders had intentionally poisoned the Mothertrees over a number of years and concocted the starseed story as a means to cover it up.

And there were a few who'd hit on the truth: that the Mothertrees' survival had depended on the Reachers. After the crack had opened in the First and took the Reachers, this last group had grown. And many of them were angry. They had no higher goal than vengeance.

Cor took a long pull from his flask and swept everyone with his glittering black eyes. A few Harborlanders looked aside from them. Had they been involved in the uprising? The thought had barely skimmed Walde's mind when Cor spoke again, his attention fixed on Fin and Cadar. "Coming back to get us was dangerous. Of course, you didn't know what was going on, but even so. Even so." He took another sip from his flask. "If you hadn't been as careful as you were, your secret might have leaked to more than just family. I don't know what would've happened then. Nothing good, that's for sure. Ah well. We're safe here for now. Maybe no one saw us leave in all the chaos. At the very least, we gained some time."

Walde stared pensively into the flames, his hand running slowly over Brite's arm. If he hadn't helped open the crack, the Harborlands would still be at peace. How many had died or been imprisoned because of that single act? And how would it end?

People make their own decisions, Thara had said. And she couldn't force them to make the right ones. Even if they destroyed themselves. Walde shook his head. But gradually, a faint smile touched his lips. So he had stirred the pot. Good. It was past time that someone did.

Brite gripped his wrist and looked at him.

"I'm fine," he whispered. "We'll all be fine."

***

On a warm midsummer night, a crowd of fifty people (a mix of Harborlanders, Lakelanders, and cursed children) sat in a semicircle around the First's trunk. Lamps hung here and there in the branches above them, washing their faces with warm light. Walde had butterflies in his stomach. But it was a good feeling, and he'd been trying to let out strong positive emotions lately, whether or not it drew eyes to his Reacher light.

They were about to have a real song rite.

Idra had suggested it after learning that Harborlanders were leaving offerings in the crack for Thara—flowers, carved figurines. The custom of making such offerings came from the Lowlands, where they worshiped Bergis, the god of wealth and prosperity. Nessa had bit her tongue when a Harborlands woman asked her what *she* would offer. Idra did not. "We need a song rite," she said to the council. "Let's show them how treefolk honor a Mothertree."

But how was a real song rite performed? All agreed that it included music and guidance from Thara. Reachers in the past had delivered that guidance by means of stories. But the only storyteller in the Woodlands was Brite. And even if she agreed to spin a story for them, there was no guarantee that a Reacher would be able to give her something to work with. Few Reachers retained the wisdom from Thara. Walde guessed that song rites in the past had been performed by Reachers with sufficient experience and talent. Would doing a song rite now be even more disrespectful than Lowlander offerings?

Walde didn't think so. But then, he didn't view Thara as everyone else did. He wasn't even certain that the being he reached for *was* a god.

In the end, they chose to treat the event much like a modern song rite, but with an important twist: a Reacher would sit in the crack and reach while a musician played. If the Reacher recalled the wisdom from Thara, they would bestow it to the crowd at the end of a song. If not, they would exchange places with another Reacher and the music would continue uninterrupted. Order of appearance would be decided by pulling strings.

It had seemed cool and logical when explained at the council meeting. But in the hushed darkness, it became something else entirely. Until now, Walde hadn't understood the significance of reaching during a song rite. The idea had seemed indulgent and attention-grabbing. Why reach before an audience when it could be done in private?

The answer was both simple and profound. Walde could sense the hum of the link, and with the trunk stretching above and the link below, the Reacher sat at a junction point. This made the act of reaching a powerful metaphor. His skin prickled as he considered how it must have looked a century ago—an old, wise Reacher sitting at the base of the tree and everyone waiting in anticipation for him to dredge up wisdom and spin it into a tale. How the elders must have hated it.

So many thoughts raced through his mind as Idra intoned the short chant given at song rites from time immemorial. The words were so old that no one save the elders understood them, but they were remembered nonetheless. Walde had heard the chant so many times that he could repeat it if asked to.

The reaching order was Garen, Shin, and Walde. Garen sat in the crack now, waiting for Walde to begin. The former guard had grown quiet and tense after Walde had helped Shin reach. He was not a happy person, and Walde had no idea how he would find the calm needed to reach. He had spared Walde a single glance before he'd entered the shadowy crack. His eyes had held a challenge. Did he hope to break through to Thara, as he'd promised Shin?

Walde fought the smile that leapt into his face at the thought of it. Well, if Garen wanted to try, then Walde would give him what he needed to get there. He lifted his eyes to the crowd, and the silence instantly deepened. Careful, he thought. He couldn't allow himself to grow expansive, no matter how strongly the music tugged at him. His eyes met Brite's as he drew his bow over the strings.

A song blossomed. It was a gentle flowering at first, but as the softness swelled, it lost its gentleness and became powerful. Dizzying. He kept himself back from it by a thread and let the music flow through him into the darkness.

It was a variant of his dream song. Walde had split the music into three parts: the first was a gathering thunder, the second the full storm, the third a mesmerizing descent into silence. He had spent two days teaching the lyra player—whose name was Abbe—how to play it. He'd admired her talent and quick mind. She was far more gifted than Walde had been at her age.

When the first part came to an end, there was no clapping. The crowd was spellbound. Even Brite gaped, her mouth curved in a half-smile. Walde glanced back at the crack and knew what held them all captive. Garen's Reacher light blazed, filling the crack and shooting an arrow up the trunk. For several moments, only the trickle of the river and distant hooting of an owl filled the silence. The former guard made a soft sound then.

Walde hardly breathed as Garen shifted, closed his blazing hands, and leaned away from the wall of the crack. He had certainly reached. His drunken movements couldn't be feigned. His gaze landed on Walde and quickly slid past him. Failure was clearly writ on his face. He had not been able to speak with Thara, nor could he remember her wisdom. Walde wondered if he'd have the audacity to make something up. Perhaps he considered it in the lengthening silence. Or perhaps he simply strove to remember.

At last, he got to his feet and stepped out of the crack. The crowd remembered to applaud then, but it was a stunned, chaotic sort of clapping. He bowed stiffly and strode past first Walde and then Shin without looking at either of them.

Shin was a nervous wreck. Her hands and shoulders trembled and her face glistened with sweat. Walde knew, even before she approached him, that she'd decided not to reach tonight. And since the others hadn't volunteered, that left Walde to reach through the last two segments of the song. He didn't allow his discomfort of that thought to show as he patted her arm and told her all would be well. She smiled and nodded as if she believed him. Probably, she did.

Walde handed Abbe the lyra and lowered himself down into the crack.

The flowers and figurines were gone, the lumpy floor leveled with dirt and topped by a kessa mat. He made himself comfortable on it, then closed his eyes and simply listened to Abbe play.

The tree enclosed him. Such an enormous, ancient being. He sensed its weight above him and the link thrumming through. It was all one thing. How could anyone see it otherwise? One could not exist without the other.

He let the thought slide away and lingered at the tunnel's edge. The music dimmed, and there was a brightness behind his eyes. It was a searing sensation, being conscious while feeling the duality of the tree and link. *Take a step*, he urged himself. *Let everything go.*

The music had dimmed, but he still heard it, so when it coughed to a sudden stop, he was jerked fully awake. He blinked, blinded by his Reacher light. A horn call was sounding, too distant yet to be understood, but its unusual length made his skin tighten. Something had happened or was in the midst of happening. Finally, the distant call drifted to silence, and another took it up. Before it had even finished, Abbe set her lyra in its case and turned to look at Walde. Her face was white, her eyes round as two moons.

An armed intruder had entered the Woodlands from the Harborlands side, and a sentinel was calling for aid.

CHAPTER 14

The night's peace crumbled.

Onlookers who still hadn't learned the horn calls sensed something was wrong and demanded answers. The council convened briefly at the trunk, then Albin ordered Abbe and Spitfire to hasten to the sentinel post. The post location had been in the signal. It wasn't far from where Walde and Brite had lain before entering the Woodlands. The two sentinels nearest the post would get there first, but Albin wanted backups in case these were overcome. He sent an additional two to man the abandoned posts.

As Walde crossed the courtyard to Brite, Cor stood up, swayed drunkenly, and wagged an accusing finger at him. "Why do you allow children to fight for you?" He looked around at the confused faces in the crowd. "Here are grown men and women, able to wield a knife or axe when called on—" he waved a hand at Garen—"even a former guard. And who goes to protect us? Children!"

An angry murmur washed through the crowd. In the midst of it, Albin mounted the stairs to the First's bottom level and scampered down a branch until he was directly above the heads of the Harborlanders. In the light of the hanging lamps, he looked more fay than human. "Quiet!" he shouted, and for a wonder, the Harborlanders obeyed him. "Understand this: the Woodlands belong to the cursed children. *We* haunt the dead Mothertrees and chase off all who enter here. We even have a dirty magic, which we use on anyone who comes near our home.

"That is what outsiders think. And it's what keeps us safe. If an intruder was greeted by an adult instead of by a cursed child, our story would be ruined and people would know the truth. So the council voted to post only children at the Woodlands' fringes."

Someone shouted, "Why not just kill the intruder?"

"Because that would be wrong. And even if it weren't, it would be stupid. If the intruder is a spy, then others would come to investigate his disappearance, and we'd never have peace."

Cor grunted and took a swig from his flask. "I don't like it. Don't like to see children hurt." Walde expected Albin to parry this comment, remind Cor that the cursed ones weren't as young as they appeared and had dealt with intruders before the adults arrived, but he said nothing at all.

The crowd began to disperse, some to the cook fire by the river, others to ramshackle huts on the eighth level. And those who had been trained to fight lingered on the paths like guards, waiting for orders.

Walde pushed a damp hand across his face. After the first council meeting, he had shied away from proposing any plan that involved killing. As a result, the village had fallen back on Albin's strategy of either forcing invaders out or hiding if there were too many. And then the Harborlanders had arrived and everyone had been swept up in the First's restoration. Weeks of peace had lulled them into a false sense of security.

And now this.

The village needed a better strategy, one that included safeguarding the First. Killing came with its own set of consequences, but if need be…

As if in answer to his thought, Albin approached with Walde's bow and quiver under his arm. The weapons had been stowed under the stairs. Walde accepted them with a murmured thanks.

"Be watchful," the youth said. Walde's head jerked in a nod, and Albin walked on.

Idra approached Walde. "It's good for them to see how vulnerable we are," she murmured, gesturing to the folk seated around the cook fire. She touched his shoulder. "It was a beautiful song. I wanted to know how it ended."

Walde tried to smile but only managed another stiff nod. Abbe had gone off to help the sentinel. He tried not to think about her getting hurt, but the fear edged back like water in an unsteady boat.

He found Brite at his side and hooked his arm around her.

The night moved painfully on. A final horn call informed everyone that the intruder had been expelled. Two children would follow to make sure he or she didn't come back. It said nothing about the condition of the sentinel who'd sounded the alarm. But around midnight, Abbe and Spitfire drew up to the dock by the First with a hunched Frey between them. Layers of cloth tightly wrapped her shoulder. The few who were up and about dropped what they were doing and huddled by her on the boardwalk. Brite begged alcohol from Cor, and Frey let her wash, stitch, and dress the knife injury in the light of the cook fire.

The stab wound had gone through the muscly flesh at the top of her arm. It had bled so profusely that she could no longer stand without aid. Albin hovered over her as Brite worked, his mouth a stiff line and his eyes blazing with anger. At one point, he became so frustrated with others pressing in around them that he shouted, "Keep back!"

His eyes widened then and his mouth gaped. His voice had cracked, and a deep sound had stepped out of it. Despite Frey's condition, she shrieked and reached for him with her good arm. "Albin! You're growing again!"

Grella, who had been washing something at the river, rose to her feet and stared. Albin lowered himself down beside his sister and allowed her to embrace him.

Walde was close to weeping as he watched them. Albin had been right all along. His proximity to a living Mothertree had been essential to his growth.

That night, Albin didn't return to the dead tree, not even to change his clothes. Frey was all but carried up the stairs to the meeting hall. The roof had leaked, but the structure was stable and not in danger of being struck by falling boards. She slept late into the morning and woke hungry and eager to talk about what had befallen her. She leaned against the wall that curved around the trunk, her small body wrapped in a blanket, her arm hanging in a makeshift sling. Albin, Walde, Fin, Bran, Nessa, and Idra—all in the council who weren't on sentinel duty—sat nearby and listened.

She spoke in a calm, low voice. "It happened when I was an hour into my shift. The sun had set and the clouds around the moon were bright. I heard a rustling, and then the thud of something falling into the dugout trap."

"Somethin'?" Tir said.

Her eyes lifted from the floor. "I didn't know what it was yet. Could've been a deer or a fox. I climbed down my tree and was about to light a belt lamp when light shone out of the dugout hole. I strung my bow and snuck down the path. As I got close to the hole, I saw the top of a man's head. I shouted for him to get down, that I had an arrow pointed at him and would loose it if he didn't obey. He looked straight at me and laughed." She frowned. "He was a young man of Walde's height and build. He carried a bow and wore a brown cape with a torn hood. His lamp was hooked onto his belt. My horn call startled him, but he went on struggling to climb out, so I came closer and shouted at him again. He dropped back down, and I thought it was over, that he'd wait until I said he could go. I promised he wouldn't be killed if he did what I said. He agreed but wanted to unhook his belt lamp. I told him no, but his hands were already on the lamp, then as quick as a snake he flung a knife at me."

Her good arm rose haltingly to her bandaged right shoulder. "I tried to pull it out, but there was so much blood that my hand slipped, and the knife fell onto the ground. When the man tried to grab it, I kicked it away and stomped on his wrist. Then I shot him in the left shoulder."

She dropped her arm and made a sickly smile. "He was shocked. He touched the arrow shaft, feeling where it'd gone in. I shouted for him to get down or be shot again. He did so, and quickly. I reminded him that he would live if he did as he was told. He agreed. But as time went on, he started to complain that he was bleeding and would die if his wound wasn't seen to. I told him to wait just a bit longer. My whole chest was wet with blood by then, and I felt sick and dizzy. He cursed me thoroughly." She lowered her voice in imitation of the man's. "May you die a traitor's death, may frogs chew off your ears and lips, may snakes enter all your orifices and—"

"Please," Albin muttered.

Frey shrugged. "It passed the time. Ned and Lina came while he was still cursing and completely disarmed him. They were worried about my injury, but I told them others would come and they needed to deal with the man. While they had him cornered, Lina poison-tipped her arrow and said he'd die if he didn't tell her who he was and why he'd come. I think she scared him, because his voice shook when he spoke. He said his name was Halvar and that he worked for the Twenty."

"The Twenty?" Walde cut in.

Fin explained, "The Harborlands' chairmen are called the Twenty. The other elders don't matter no more. They still sit at the meetin's, but they can't vote. So it's a council of twenty, with a single head over 'em all."

Walde felt a shiver of unease at this news. Until the formation of the Lowlands, no people had ever been ruled by a single body with a powerful head over all. The Harborlands really were morphing into the Lowlands.

Frey went on. "Halvar admitted he'd been sent to the Woodlands to find out who lived here and how many there were. He claimed to know nothing else, even after Ned threatened to cast a spell on him that would make his balls drop off. Lina was okay with his answer, so Ned found a rope in his pack and used it to help him out of the hole. While aiming at his back, they told him to walk down the slope. They were just a glimmer of light on the edge of the Woodlands when I last saw them."

She leaned her head back against the wall. They'd have to start work on a new trap, Walde thought grimly. Now that Halvar could map this trap's location, it was useless.

Frey continued, "I must have passed out. When I woke up, Spit and Abbe were there. You know the rest."

The hall went quiet. Frey's eyes closed, and she slept. Albin rose and laid her down on the floor. He grazed her cheek with the back of his hand. "She'll be all right, won't she?" he asked no one in particular.

"She will," Walde said. "Her bleeding has let up and the wound is clean."

Albin nodded to the answer Brite had already given him. He dragged a lock of greasy blond hair away from his eyes, revealing the dark shadows of a sleepless night.

Idra touched his shoulder. "Why don't you stay with her here and get some rest?"

"Ned and Lina aren't back yet. They might be in trouble."

"If they are," Idra said, "there's nothing we can do about it. Rest."

Albin nodded wearily and dropped his head into his hands. "We've never had a Harborlands spy here before. The elders must suspect something. Maybe they know about the runaway Reachers. Or maybe they tracked some of the Harborlanders who came here. Either way, we need to talk about what to do if a bunch of them attack us."

"We will," Walde assured him. "Here. Tonight." He looked at the others and received a chorus of nods. Tonight.

***

Lina and Ned returned that afternoon while Walde was on sentinel duty down the river. Their report held no surprises. They had escorted the intruder for miles and only turned back after he had descended a low hill. He went ahead of them unarmed, and despite his complaints about his injury, he fared well enough. Lina judged he would make it back to the Harborlands without needing aid.

Albin gave this news as part of a full report to the council. The members sat in a circle on the floor of the First's meeting hut. A couple of lamps stood in the middle of the circle, pushing back the darkness while illuminating their hands and faces. The intruder's bow, quiver of arrows, and throwing knife lay on the floor nearby. The night was quiet. The usual barks of laughter that drifted up from the bonfire had been quenched by news of the intruder and of Frey's injury.

185

Garen was speaking. Walde forced himself to pay attention. "...arrows are tinker-made, the same type that guards use in the Lakelands. His knife is also guard's stock, and it has two overlapping triangles engraved on the handle."

Tir said, "That's a guard's mark."

Garen nodded, his suspicion apparently confirmed. "So, it seems that Lina's 'interrogation' didn't go as well as she thought."

"She did her best," Albin retorted, his deepening voice cracking. "Does it matter that he's a guard as well as a spy?"

Garen said, "Yes. It does. A lone wolf has few friends. A guard, on the other hand, has several in his unit. Men and women he works with and drinks with. How will they feel when they find out what's happened to him?"

"Still doesn't matter," Bran said, running a hand across the back of his short neck. "The guards aren't going to go off on their own without orders. Besides, what kind of man is going to tell his comrades he was shot by a little girl and chased off by children?"

A stunned silence fell. Walde groaned and leaned into his palm. "Gods, why didn't I think of that? He won't tell them he met children, will he? He'll change them all to adults."

"No, he won't," Albin sighed. "He'll say what they already believe—that we used our enchantment on him."

Bran said, "There's nothing magical about an arrow."

"Albin's right." Idra's calm, confident voice drew all eyes to her. "Unless the man is a complete fool, he'll tell his superior what really happened. If he doesn't, he'll be found out when the next spy returns from the Woodlands. Of course, that won't stop him from embellishing his tale to his friends."

Walde's worry receded. Yes. That made sense.

Nessa asked tightly, "You think they'll send another spy?"

"Of course," Idra replied. "Halvor didn't do his job, so why wouldn't they send another?"

After a long pause, Walde leaned his elbows on his knees and tented his fingers. "I have a few proposals to make. The First is that all able-bodied Harborlanders should learn the locations of the posts and traps, the horn calls, and be taught to use a bow. I propose that the cursed children teach them these things." He paused when Idra chuckled.

"Clever," she remarked. "That would give the children a chance to show how skilled they are."

"If the Harborlanders agree to it," Garen said and was rewarded with a grim nod from both Tir and Fin. "Right now, we have no way to enforce any of the rules we make here. So if half refuse to obey, then the next time we set a rule, it'll be laughed at."

Walde tugged on his chin. Though he often disagreed with Garen, in this instance, he found himself nodding. The newcomers had carried more than goods with them from the Harborlands; many had brought drunkenness, anger, and disrespect for any semblance of authority. They were hard workers, and they didn't mind sleeping on the ground, but if the council didn't gain control of them, they'd become more of a liability than an asset. He threw a sideways glance at Albin. "How did you keep the children in line before we came?"

"I confined them to their huts for a few hours. And if that didn't work, I made them eat live worms, or mud if it was winter."

Tir guffawed. "My father used to make me eat worms. It's an old fisherman's punishment."

"It's suitable for children," Garen agreed, "but we'll need something stronger for adults. A public flogging perhaps, or a night in the corpse darkness." He looked at Walde pointedly. "Most people find that disturbing."

His words were met by silence. Those in the circle eyed each other uneasily. Garen sat back with crossed arms and a tight jaw.

When Walde asked if there were other suggestions, Shin made a sound.

"Go on," Walde encouraged when Garen flashed her a look. The two were not sitting together, and Garen's coldness to her lately seemed to be taking a toll on the already nervous woman.

Shin's thin lips disappeared, and she wrung her hands. "W-w-we could confine them to a large hut in the dead tree for a wh-wh-while. Under guard."

Several in the circle nodded thoughtfully.

"That," Bran said, "or have them clean out the First's cesspit. The newcomers are using the river right now as if it's their own private chamber pot. The river runs past the dead trees, so anyone who pulls in water down there is quite literally drinking someone's shit."

That drew a chuckle from some in the circle.

The night wore on. Walde's first proposal was agreed to by all but Garen, who believed that *he* should oversee the Harborlanders' training and discipline. After the vote, he got up and stalked out, complaining he had a headache. Walde was developing his own headache. Just as he considered postponing a discussion of what to do if attacked, Albin flashed him an impatient look.

You promised, his eyes said.

And so he had.

It was long and painful. No one wanted to contemplate the possibility of children being shot down, of Reachers being taken prisoner or killed outright. It was the stuff of nightmares, and the dark, quiet night made it seem inevitable. As if by mutual consent, they huddled closer together and lowered their voices until they all but whispered.

Negotiation was raised as an option. But they could think of nothing to use as leverage. Seed pods were valuable, but as squatters, they didn't have the right to sell them. Technically, the former Woodlanders still owned the Mothertrees' resources, whether they lived in them or not.

Just when it seemed that everyone had run out of ideas, Nessa perked up. "What if we negotiated with the former Woodlanders instead of the Harborlanders? Tir and Fin could go to the Lowlands and meet the elders as representatives. They wouldn't have to say anything about the Reachers, just that they left the Harborlands and were allowed entrance into the Woodlands. When they found out that the First was alive, they invited their families to live in it with them. But they're tired of all the secrecy and would like to exchange a promise of future seed pods for a signed approval to live in the First." She grinned. "So the next time a spy comes, we show him the document. Then the Harborlanders wouldn't have the right to touch us—any of us."

Before she'd even finished speaking, Albin was shaking his head. "I wish that would work, but it won't. Not with the former Woodlanders. These branches still belong to a village, and once they start producing again, those same villagers would have to vote on whether or not we can live on them. The elders can't make that decision for them, then sell the pods and pocket the coin."

Bran muttered, "They could do it secretly."

"Maybe," Albin said. "But if they did, they certainly wouldn't give us a signed document saying we can live here. That would be risking too much."

Nessa said, "We could let the villagers decide for themselves."

"We could," Albin conceded. "But I promise you this: they will never choose to allow the cursed children to live here.

Never. Instead, they'll offer to do the pod harvest themselves. And more, they'll demand that the elders send guards to flush us out. And if they ever learned about the Reachers..." His voice trailed.

There was another long, dark silence.

Walde doubted that anyone on the council truly believed they could remain in the Woodlands forever. It was a dream, but one that they couldn't afford to give up. They could only hope that their enemies would either leave them alone or that the tide of opinion would change once folk learned that Reachers had restored the First. Walde believed that the former option was possible, but its success depended on the strength of their defense.

Nessa whispered, "We can't just give up..."

"Give up?" Albin snorted and shook his head again. "Never. I'll never do that. We still hold this land. And people still fear us. If we have to fight, then we'll do it in a way to frighten them. We'll cover our faces with mud or paint. We'll poison our arrow tips. We'll lead them into a horror that they'll never want to meet again." His eyes gleamed in the lamplight.

Bran pounded a brightened fist on the old boards. "Yes."

Walde closed his eyes. He drew a breath and could almost feel a ghostly presence of his father in the darkness behind him, warning him that treefolk didn't mass together to kill. The council could still be swayed. Aside from Garen, they trusted him implicitly. He steadied himself and spoke.

"Killing isn't something to take lightly. I know. I know how it's affected me." His emotions were tightly chained as he met everyone's eyes in the circle. "So I would never suggest that we force others to do it. When the time comes, and an attack can't be avoided, each one must choose for themselves whether to hide or to fight. But those who choose to fight must be ready to kill or be killed. And they must follow orders. That is what I propose."

190

***

Walde and Brite lay in their hut in the dead tree. He'd just finished telling her what had happened at the meeting. She'd listened in tense silence, her breath catching every so often before easing out of her again. No lamp burned in the room. Moonlight through the open shutters limned the curve of her cheek, her bare shoulder. When he'd finished, she said simply, "Permission to kill."

"I suppose you could view it that way."

"Is there any other way to view it?"

He shifted closer to her. "Do you disagree with the—?"

"No. If it comes to it, we have to do what we have to do. How can I say otherwise? I killed the man who tried to rape me."

He hadn't wanted to be reminded of that.

Neither spoke for a while. The night was warm and still. Walde liked the dead tree's privacy. Few returned to spend the night in it now. Its bare branches and unlit trunk rendered it dark and uninviting. But something in that very starkness drew him and Brite closer together. Away from the others, they could sink back into that familiar place where it was just him and her and the world at their back.

She turned a little toward him. Her eyes were liquid black in the gloom.

"How are you?" he asked, and they both knew he wasn't asking about how she felt at that moment.

"I'm fine. I've been so busy these days that I haven't had time to think."

"So you don't...hate it here yet?"

She hissed out a sound that might have been a laugh or a sigh. "There's no perfect place, Walde."

He nodded slowly, then shifted onto his back and stared up at the shadowy ceiling. "No. But I think there used to be. Not perfect," he amended, "but a good place, a healthy place. Back before the purges." For a time, he was lost in a vision of purple blossoms, massive seed pods, flashes of Reacher light with no ensuing violence. And at night, stories and songs under a sea of treelights.

"Walde."

He turned onto his side again and looked at her.

Her mouth had curved in a gentle smile. She said, "I'm happy with you. This life isn't perfect. But it's what we have, and there's no use in asking for more."

"I know." He touched her face, tracing her lips, the soft angles of her cheekbones. He allowed his love for her to swell. Her smile, brightened by his Reacher light, was sweet. It subsided with his light. Her eyes closed, and he drew his hand away.

His thoughts were bleak as he listened to her deep breathing. Outside the window, a breeze blew up from the darkness. The smaller branches swayed, bare in the moonlight. If Zon had slipped through the forest undetected, then others could. The Harborlands elders would send stealthier spies. Hunters, if they could get them. He wondered how close they could get to the First...

The thought scattered, and he froze, listening. He was sure he'd heard the soft thud of a footstep. A falling Mothertree leaf might sound like that, but this tree had none. After a pause, he heard another, and it was close. Probably on the pathway outside the door. Walde's calm was icy as he slipped out of bed. Thankfully, Brite's deep breathing didn't change. He found his dagger and was about to rush for the door when a familiar knock landed on it. Three fast taps followed by a slower third.

Walde closed his eyes and slumped against the wall. A tremulous smile grew on his lips.

"Who is it?" Brite mumbled sleepily.

He swallowed a thickness in his throat. "My father. He's alive. He made it back alive."

CHAPTER 15

Walde flung the door open and embraced the shadowy figure, pounding his back with a blazing hand.

"You're wet," Walde exclaimed as he pulled away.

"I know. I didn't want to walk down those slippery boards to the bridge, so I swam across the river." He glanced over Walde's shoulder. "Sorry for waking you, Brite. I wasn't sure if either of you would be on sentinel duty tonight."

Brite yawned and turned over. "It's good to see you, Carrac."

Walde tugged on his father's damp shoulder. "Let's talk in your hut."

They felt their way carefully around the wall and up the paths until they reached Carrac's door. The string of chestnuts marking the hut as occupied rattled. Walde had seen to it that his father's few possessions remained undisturbed. He walked until he bumped into the clothes chest and then lowered himself down on it. His father dropped his pack and riffled through it. Moments later, there came a sound of flint striking metal. Light blossomed on a worn candle stub. Carrac said, "The tinder box I took from Albin's store is watertight." He set the candle in a holder and placed it on the cold woodstove. "It won't last long, and I don't fancy talking in the dark, so..." He sat down on the chest beside Walde.

Walde regarded him closely in the warm light. His skin had darkened to that of a fisherman's, and while he hadn't put on bulk, he held himself with an ease that spoke of strength and confidence. He was beginning to look like a healthy animal again. Walde flattened a smile that was growing on lips. "How did you slip past the sentinel tonight?"

"I didn't. I gave a birdcall, and Grella—she's the one on duty at the north fringe—answered it. She wanted me to come up and sit with her until the shift changed. That way I could take a boat across. I didn't want to wait, so she let me pass." His gaze drifted to the window. The shutters had been left open a crack to let in fresh air. "Where is everyone?"

Walde grinned. "Not yet. First tell me what happened to *you*."

He shrugged. "There's not much to tell. I was as careful as I said I'd be, walking at night and sleeping by the Nadi during the day. I had one close call when a man on horseback stopped to water his animal, but luckily he was far enough away that he didn't see me huddled against the embankment."

A chill seeped into Walde's heart. A rider. Could this have been an envoy from the Harborlands to the Lakelands? Walde said, "What did he look like?"

"He was short and stout, with dark hair and tanned skin. He wore brown hosen, possibly leather. A hooded kriksa robe. He carried some sort of blade on his belt and a pack on his back. He seemed like a capable sort of person. I don't know much about horses, but the beast looked well cared for." Carrac paused, running a finger over the bridge of his nose. "He was too far away for me to see much else."

"Was he going north or south?"

"North. But I hadn't passed the Lowlands yet, so I wasn't sure where he was heading."

"And I don't suppose you could have tracked him in the dark."

Carrac shook his head. "I couldn't have even in the daylight. It was too dry and windy, and the road was hard-packed."

"Of course." Walde nodded as he stared at the dancing candle flame. He drew a careful breath and set the matter aside. "Please go on."

Carrac leaned forward with his elbows on his knees. "I forded the twin rivers early one morning and slept in some bushes. But first, I got a good look at the Lakelands Mothertrees." He shook his head again. "Most of them look as bare and colorless as the Woodlands trees. I wanted so badly to go to them and reach. I can't even tell you.

"I crossed the wastes the next night and came to Killop Ravine before dawn. It was hard, leaving the hook at the cliff's edge, but I put rocks in front of it so no one would see it unless they walked right up to that spot. I was tired after I climbed down, but I couldn't rest until I found my tree." His mouth relaxed into a fond smile. "I couldn't believe how healthy she was. After seeing what happened to the others, I'd feared the worst."

"The link is all that matters, and your tree wasn't attacked by drugged Reachers fighting for their lives." Walde suspected that the attack on the Reachers had merely nudged the trees into a death they had already been courting. Only two had leafed. Those two might survive another year, but they wouldn't leaf again. Not without the help of Reachers.

Carrac gave a thoughtful nod.

Walde said, "So you stayed a week down there?"

"One week. The journey back went smoothly. I was delayed twice because of rain, but that's to be expected."

The candle sizzled, and a scent of animal fat thickened around them. Walde got up and paced around the room. "I've kept your secret. But it won't hold now that you're back. People will want to know where you've spent the last three weeks."

"That's my concern," Carrac said. Their eyes met in the shadows, and Walde almost smiled at the determined set of his jaw.

"Fine. And now I believe it's my turn to talk."

The last three weeks spilled out of him, beginning with the arrival of the Harborlanders and ending with the proposals passed at the last council meeting. Carrac was a contemplative statue through it all. His stillness reminded Walde of the times they had hunted together, lying on the backs of boulders while waiting for prey to come near. He was startled by a sudden flash of Reacher light.

As if embarrassed by the slip, Carrac rose and went to the window. He opened a shutter and leaned out. "I won't fight. Not to kill."

"I know."

"Do you?" He looked back at Walde.

Walde lowered his eyes. "You're too stubborn to change your mind."

Carrac closed the shutters, went to the mattress, and shook open a folded blanket. He talked as he made up the bed. His tone was casual, but Walde sensed a weight in his words. "None of us wants to be like Lowlanders. And there's a dozen reasons for that. But if you think of the most important ones, you'll realize there aren't many. In fact, there's only one that matters: the abuse of others. Take that away and what would you have? Some folks living near a bog with their animals. That's all. Nothing scary about that." He sat down and pulled off his boots.

After a long pause, Walde ventured, "What does that have to do with killing?"

Carrac set down the boots. Then, in a motion so fast it took Walde's breath away, he drew his knife and drove it into a floorboard.

He looked at Walde. "It's easy to *talk* about killing. But when Frey, Shin, and the others run their blades into men and women's chests and watch the life drain from their eyes, then they'll see how it really is. And when the dust settles, they'll feel it too. *If* they come away with their lives." He retrieved the knife. "There are many forms of abuse, lad."

Walde leaned hard against the wall behind his back. He cleared his throat, started to speak, and then stopped. Nothing he said would change either of their minds.

At last, he went to the door. "Welcome back, Father," he said gruffly as he lifted the latch. "I've missed you."

"And I, you. Sleep well."

***

The next morning, the Harborlanders gathered at the First for the community meeting. Idra had piled all the bows and arrows she had been busy making against the trunk. They made for a sobering backdrop as Walde related what was known about the intruder and how the council had chosen to respond. The Harborlanders took it all with remarkable equanimity. None grumbled about being forced to learn archery. Or about the prospect of fighting future intruders. Nevertheless, there was a tenseness in the crowd, a shifty sort of unease. Walde assumed that it was a fear of being attacked.

He was wrong. But the source of the tension didn't surface until three days later, on a cloudy afternoon at the archery range.

The range had been set up in a clearing not far from the First. The space had once been used for crops. Now it grew little more than weeds. Painted wooden targets rose from the ground on sturdy poles, each positioned at a different distance from the shooting line. Advanced students could climb a tree at the field's edge and practice shooting at targets on nearby trunks.

Cor was in a foul mood that day. Or so Walde had heard. Albin was the trainer on duty, and being alone, he was soon cornered by Cor and two of his drinking buddies. They pressured Albin to go to the Harborlands with a few others and do a gin run. The cursed children were good at sneaking about. They could steal with ease and be back home by the end of the week. Albin owed it to them. After all, he was growing again, and he wouldn't be if the Harborlanders hadn't done work on the First, allowing Albin to live there.

This went on and on until Carrac stepped out from the shadows of the tree line.

Walde's father had been accepted back into the community with surprising ease. Of course, many had demanded to know where he had gone. Garen had interrogated him for an entire morning, with nothing to show for it.

Through it all, Carrac had maintained that he'd simply needed some time alone. And he'd managed to win most people's sympathy. Like Zon, Carrac had been tortured for days longer than the other Reachers. No one knew all that he had endured, but several had witnessed the aftereffects—such as how he cowered at the sound of a horn call. They assumed he had sheltered in the mountains for a few weeks. His tanned skin supported this idea, and Carrac didn't deny it. So he'd slid back in, even rejoining the council, despite Garen's protests.

Carrac had been up in a tree with Tir that afternoon teaching him how to aim at low targets. His perch was near enough to Cor and Albin that he'd overheard their conversation.

Cor stiffened at the sight of him. Carrac's palms flared with Reacher light, and his eyes were hard as Lowland metal. So Albin said.

The other two Harborlanders stepped back and allowed Carrac to confront Cor alone.

"This is between me and Albin," Cor warned him.

Carrac glanced back at the young leader. Albin flushed, but he shook his head. Carrac said, "Seems you're wrong about that."

When Cor made no response, Carrac stepped closer and set a hand on Cor's shoulder. Albin strained to hear his quiet words. "Come, man, when you packed up and came here, you must have known you'd run dry. The children can't magic gin out of their asses. And they won't risk their lives to keep you wet. You'll just have to do without."

It struck Albin as odd that Cor disliked the idea of children as sentinels but would send them to the Harborlands to steal for him.

There was a tense silence. Cor's face had turned an angry red. He muttered something, his voice so low that Albin didn't catch it. Carrac's reply was just as low. For an instant, neither moved. Then Cor swung at Carrac's face. Carrac ducked low and grasped Cor's thighs. Cor's momentum carried him forward, allowing Carrac to overset him. The builder fell hard on his side, and Carrac was quick to pin him down.

In other circumstances, Albin would have been hard pressed not to laugh. Cor lay belly-down in the weeds. The unruly thatch of his beard had folded up so that it stuck to his wet lips and trembled with every puff of expelled air. He grumbled, "Get off me."

And Carrac did, stepping back quickly to give Cor space. Cor lurched to his feet and spat in Carrac's direction. His gaze raked the men around him, and then he turned and strode away toward the river.

And that was it. At least for that day.

The problem itself was far from over.

Cor refused to work, and someone overheard him muttering about returning to the Harborlands on his own to fetch drink. But another day went by, and no one left. Cor's drinking buddies took out their anger on each other and on the training field. Several trembled, and their gatherings at night were subdued. After another day without drink, Cor and his buddies were worse than useless—they were sick. Cor lay sprawled on the boardwalk, sweating, shaking, and muttering. Once, he frightened everyone by claiming he saw a strange man across the river. But after a thorough search, no sign of an intruder was found, and all concluded that he'd imagined it.

Evening came, and after a short council meeting, it was decided that no one would leave the First that night unless they were on sentinel duty. The five boats were drawn up onto shore and guarded (a sixth boat always remained at the dead tree). Relatives of the sick men crouched with them by the fire, dabbing their brows and trying to get them to eat. The children all but tiptoed around them, even the youngest speaking in hushed tones.

Walde had never seen the like of it, and he worried about how long the sickness would last.

The concern gnawed at him as he trudged up to the sixth level, a blanket under his arm, and found a hut to sleep in. Brite had chosen to stay up with the Harborlanders until her late-night shift started. The sixth level was safest at the moment. The two above it had been mostly dismantled, so there was little chance of being struck by rotting wood. Since the paths on the sixth hadn't been repaired yet, only the huts nearest the trunk were deemed safe for use.

The hut creaked as he stepped inside. It had been marked as safe, but he tested the boards anyway, nudging the ceiling beams with a finger. A board leaned on the windowsill to cover the window. The shutters had long ago fallen off and had been added to the growing pile of rotting wood that fed the cook fire. A quick scan of the hut turned up a squirrel and a grackle. He herded both out the door before setting down his bow and quiver. He unshouldered his pack and dug out a packet of dried green sticks. This was the daleroot Cadar had brought with him from the Harborlands. Walde hadn't tried it yet. Until tonight, he and Brite had slept in the dead tree.

Cadar had directed him to chew a finger-sized amount. Walde regarded the tiny sticks and wondered if he should forego it for one more night. He hadn't suffered from nightmares for many days. But he was in the living tree now. Knowing his luck, this would be the night they'd return. He chose a piece at random and popped it in his mouth. He winced as he chewed. The stuff was incredibly bitter. He forced himself to grind the stringy bits down, then uncapped his water bottle and rinsed them out of his teeth.

He wrapped himself in the blanket and lay on the floor. The air was still outside, but he didn't need the rustle of leaves to know he lay in a living Mothertree. The gentle hum of the link was a constant reminder. He smiled sleepily. He was in a good frame of mind to reach. Perhaps he should go to the trunk and try it. His heavy eyes closed. He would. Soon.

He woke with a startled shout.

The board on the window had slammed to the floor. Wind gusted through the opening, damp and cool, smelling of rain. He sat up and blinked, swaying. A glimmer of dawn light brightened the hut. How long had he slept? He rubbed his eyes and then jumped at the sound of an astonishingly loud thunderclap. He swore under his breath. Many of the Harborlanders would still be at the river. They would find no shelter there, but if they tried to cross to the trunk, they might be hit by wind-blown debris. Would they have the good sense to stay where they were?

He listened for voices, but the rustling leaves and creaking boards drowned out all else. Lightning flashed, brightening the branches outside. In the moment between the lighting and thunder, a familiar sound drove though the wind. He froze, enduring the thunder, and gradually heard it again.

The hair rose on his arms. It was a horn call. A desperate, pleading horn call that fought the wind and thunder to be heard. Lightning split the sky again. He threw off the blanket and pulled on his boots. Snatching up his things, he stumbled toward the door. The branch under him swayed in the wind. He steadied himself against the wall and found the door latch.

Despite the dampness, it wasn't raining yet. Or at least, rain hadn't reached the sixth level. He grasped the guard ropes as he fought to make his way back to the trunk. All the while, the horn call continued to sound. He glimpsed people on the stairs below him as he sped down, one hand trailing on tree bark. A crash of falling debris mingled with thunder. He reached the ground and ran.

Brite. Returning from her post, alone in the storm. Why couldn't it have been him? He forced his anxiety down and ran on.

"Walde!" Idra stood in the path ahead of him, desperately pointing up. Something, he guessed, was about to fall. He veered off the path and danced on the back of a huge root. Something crashed beside him. He didn't look at it but jogged along the root until he reached the boardwalk. Smoke gusted from the cook fire, stinging his eyes.

Albin found him in the smoke. He was wide-eyed and stiff with tension. "Listen!"

The wind had calmed. The world seemed balanced on an indrawn breath. Once more, the sentinel blasted a call through the forest. The message was simple: armed intruders had entered the Woodlands at the same location as before. No number was given.

The sky flashed again, followed almost at once by deafening thunder. Albin brought his horn to his mouth and asked the important question: how many? The call went out, slowed by the storm. All who were gathered on the boardwalk waited for the answer.

It seemed an eternity before the calls, moving from post to post, reached the sentinel nearest the First.

The answer was no answer. The sentinel who had sighted the intruders either would not or could not reply.

Albin gave a call warning the sentinels along the main path to keep quiet, then he turned to Walde, his eyes fever-bright. "I must talk to Frey."

CHAPTER 16

Armed intruders.

The Harborlanders who'd learned the horn calls spread the message to the few who hadn't, and in moments all had scrambled to their feet, even those still suffering from the drinking sickness. Cor looked like a madman as he lurched past the smoking cook fire, his callused hand outstretched and shaking. "Where's my bow and quiver? Who took them?"

His question was taken up by others who'd lain incapacitated the previous evening. Their relatives' efforts to calm them had little effect. While others stood around, stunned, Garen strolled around the crowd, pulling men and women away and arranging them into circles around the crazed Harborlands men. "Hold your lines," he barked. "Don't let them through!"

Walde had once witnessed Lakelands guards form this way around an angry man. When the man tried to break the circle, he found himself on the ground, threatened by the booted feet of several peacekeepers.

Walde struggled to keep calm. An unknown number of armed invaders was making its way through the forest, and instead of gathering to meet them, the village was fighting itself. Where was Brite? She ought to be returning from her post by now. He looked up and down the river but saw no sign of a boat full of weary sentinels.

Albin had ducked away and was speaking quietly with Frey at the river's edge.

"Walde." Idra jogged over to him. He didn't like the look in her eyes. "Brite is still at her post. Before you were here, we decided to call off the sentinel change. It's too dangerous."

Walde stared at her, stricken. Where was Brite posted? In the chaos caused by the sick men, he hadn't remembered to ask, and she hadn't told him. He dragged a brightened palm over his eyes. She was safe, he told himself. Adults weren't posted at the fringes. And if she were stationed at one of the two posts between the south fringe and the First, she would know to keep quiet and still.

As he fought for calm, the council gathered around him. Tir and Shin were on sentinel duty, leaving only Fin, Garen, Idra, Nessa, and Albin. Carrac stood back from the circle, indicating his wish not to participate.

Albin was speaking. "If they've taken the main path, they could reach the river within half an hour. We can't let them get there before us."

Idra said, "What if they didn't take the main path?"

"They almost certainly will. The main path is so bare that a trap would be easy for them to spot. The others are more overgrown. More dangerous. We need to get to that path and wait for them."

Walde cleared his throat. "And then?"

"And then we watch and listen."

"For what?" Walde asked.

Albin lowered his voice. "For a reason not to kill them. The old man who lived here told us we shouldn't kill. And we've held to that promise. Frey thinks we should err on the side of caution."

Walde suppressed a sigh. What had happened to the wild-eyed youth who'd spoken of face paint and poison and giving them "a horror that they'd never want to meet again"? He glanced at Frey, who hovered nearby, still nursing her injury.

She bore a satisfied look on her face. Walde said, "I don't know what you hope to see or hear. They're not going to talk to each other about their plans as they walk. And if they do, we couldn't trust what was said anyway. They know that a cursed child might be hiding in the trees, listening to their every word."

Albin folded his arms. "Not everything is conveyed with words."

Bran said grimly, "I think we already have an answer to your question, Albin. It's been a quarter of an hour since the sentinel spotted the intruders. By now, they would've moved on and it would be safe for the sentinel to make another call. But we hear nothing. There can only be one reason for that."

His words were met with a heavy silence. Walde glanced back at the Harborlanders. A terrible impatience gathered in him, brightening his hands. He said, "We're wasting time. We need to choose who to bring with us, and just go."

"We have no plan," Garen reminded him stiffly.

So Walde laid out what he had, and the council reluctantly agreed to it.

It was decided that they would select only those good with a bow. Some of the Harborlanders had begun training from the moment they'd arrived in the Woodlands. These, along with the Lakelanders and a few children old enough to fight, numbered seventeen souls. It was all they had. It would have to be enough.

In a loud voice, Walde informed the Harborlanders that the fight would be split into two groups: those who would meet the intruders, and those who would remain at the First to protect the village. He tried to make both tasks sound important. Even so, there was a murmur of discontent among the sick Harborlanders as he called out the names of those in the first group. His eyes found Carrac's and skittered away from them. Walde had not called his name. Would people wonder why?

It didn't matter.

Thunder growled again, but the storm had moved on. A light rain fell, the drops falling straight down like blood from a wound. Such a thought to have at such a time. While Idra fetched her store of arrows, Walde quietly reiterated the plan to the Harborlanders and children who would be joining them. He said nothing about what they would do if they were vastly outnumbered. And thankfully, no one asked. If something went wrong and everyone died, it would be Walde's fault. *He* had helped bring the Reachers and non-Reachers out of the crack. And *he* had proposed that they fight. Might there have been a better way?

As if in answer to his thought, he found his father at his side. Carrac said nothing. He simply pulled him into a rough hug.

"You're making me nervous," Walde muttered.

"Good. You ought to be." He drew back and gripped Walde's shoulders. Bald fear lurked in his eyes.

"Father—"

"No." His head shook roughly. "No goodbyes." He shoved Walde away from him and turned. When he strode off, it was with the heavy, uneven gait of someone far older than his years.

Idra stuffed the quivers and left the surplus arrows with the second group. She also had the state of mind to offer everyone dry bowstrings. Walde thanked her and was rewarded with a tired smile. She, Carrac, and old Caln were the only Reachers staying behind.

Dawn had fully broken by the time they set off. The slippery boardwalk soon ended and was replaced by weeds and scruffy saplings. Walde walked ahead, with Albin, Grella, Lina, and Spitfire trailing behind. The others had squeezed into four boats and were gaining on them. The children ghosted along the bank, their weight too light to break sticks and loosen stones. Walde couldn't duplicate their quiet tread.

It seemed a longer hike than it really was. The river's bend approached with excruciating slowness. Walde almost lost his footing as he scrambled between willow oaks and the sloping bank. The tree roots spread like knobby fingers toward the river. The rain had slickened them to ice, and the mossy stones at the water's edge were little better.

They were running out of time. Once they got to the beach, they still had to climb a rocky slope before reaching the main path through the forest. If the intruders appeared before they finished scaling the slope, they would be in a perilous situation, trapped on the slope with the intruders waiting above.

Walde's heart began to race. Desperately, he sought for calm. As he had not done in a long time, he pictured the medallion. Its four sides enclosed him. Each able to hold in the squall of his emotions. After a time, a familiar calm set in, and he stepped back from the image. The tightness in his chest eased.

He refocused on the ground ahead. They were nearing the little beach where he, Brite, and Albin had once picnicked. The boats had already been hauled up, and the remaining members of the group stood in a quiet huddle on the shore. Walde was dripping, as much with sweat as with rainwater, when he finally reached them and led the climb up the slope. He could do nothing about their noisy approach. The slope's loose, slippery stones made ghosting a challenge for Walde, never mind the Harborlanders who had never learned such a skill. He stared nervously at the brow of the slope. The path was nearly obscured by overhanging trees. It would be an ideal spot to lie in wait for an approaching enemy.

Don't think. Just move.

He glanced back at those nearest him. Albin and Nessa wore the same determined expressions. Bran—who had been named second in command—toyed with a bowstring. Garen walked a little away from the others, his heavily browed eyes unreadable. None of the Reachers leaked light. Yet.

Thunder rumbled again, and the wind stirred. Walde had no idea what they'd do if the storm came back around. One could not shoot arrows with accuracy in a strong wind, and unlike guards, they had no shortswords to fall back on. In the group, only Garen carried a sword, and Walde didn't know how well he could wield it. He practiced away from others, as if embarrassed to display his swordsmanship.

The stones changed to dirt, and they entered an area of scraggly trees and wiry plants. Their steps quieted, allowing the soft patter of rain to become audible. When they were within ten yards of the nearest mature trees, Walde signaled for them to stop. He scanned the forest in silence, his finger running over the fletching of an arrow in his quiver. He spoke in a low voice. "The way is clear. For now. But keep your eyes and ears open. If they took a different path, we might still hear them. Or they might be lying in wait for us on this one."

He strode on, motioning for Albin to walk beside him. The pattering of rain lightened as they passed under the sheltering boughs of an ancient oak.

Walde whispered, "Albin, where is Brite posted?" When the lad didn't reply, Walde slowed and looked him full in the face. "Where, please."

"I don't know. After Frey got hurt, she took over the scheduling."

Walde sighed. After a silence, he said, "I probably shouldn't be worried. After all, she wouldn't be posted at the fringe."

"That's true."

They came to a level space of land. A foothold trap lay just ahead. Walde followed Albin over to it. The trap was two feet deep and contained three layers of stake wheels that would grip a leg hard and dig into it if the intruder struggled. A slack loop of rope led away from it to the base of a nearby trunk. If the rope tightened around a leg, a wooden whistle would go off, and a nearby sentinel would be alerted.

The rope encircling the tree blended with vine, and the trap was concealed by leaves and other debris. "This is good," Albin said. "If a guard steps in it, his comrades will stop to help him."

Walde peered up into the canopy. Ancient trees grew on either side of the path, enclosing the area of the trap. Their branches, concealed in a haze of dripping green leaves, hung several feet above their heads.

He felt a building sense of urgency. If the intruders had chosen this path, then they could arrive at any moment. A rise in the land ahead would conceal their approach, and the rain and intermittent rumbles of thunder would dampen the sound of their footsteps. *No time.*

Swiftly, Walde divided the group into four smaller ones and sent them up into the branches. The Harborlanders struggled with the climb. They had spent too much of their life on the ground or in boats, and their feet slid on the wet, mossy bark as they struggled to find a purchase. Walde offered Fin his hand, but the red-faced fisherman refused it. At last, the branches stilled and birdsong resumed.

Walde and Albin stood on thick branches that overhung the path, their backs against the trunk. Their tree was farther ahead than the others. Walde had chosen it so that he and Albin could get a good look at the intruders as they approached. And he had placed himself within arm's reach of Albin in case he needed to stop the youth from doing something foolish.

Like jumping down and trying to talk to the intruders.

Walde broke off twigs, trying to get a better view. Leaves were both friends and enemies to hunters. While they provided cover, they also made aiming difficult. He was grateful that his father had spent the last few days training Harborlanders to "hunt" from up in trees.

Did Carrac regret that now?

This, and a hundred other questions skidded through his mind as he waited. And waited. The thunder ceased rumbling, and the wind stilled. Birdsong filled the wood. The rain was not heavy, but it fell relentlessly, dripping off his chin and weighing down his clothing. The uneven bark at his back jabbed him. He longed to draw his dagger and hack some chunks off, but he couldn't risk dulling his blade. What had happened to the intruders?

"No horn calls," Albin breathed after a time. "If the intruders went somewhere else, we should've heard about it by now."

Walde said, "They might've stopped to eat something." He refused to consider the possibility that they had silenced another sentinel.

"After that warning call was sounded?"

"Depends on how cocky they are."

Albin shook his head. "I'm starting to think they—"

"Shh." Walde stiffened, his gaze fixed on the path that snaked up the rise. The sound of marching feet filtered through the forest. Very slowly, he reached out and parted some leaves.

A stream of silver was spilling down the rise. As it neared, the parts of the stream separated into people. Each wore a metal apron on his chest and a smooth metal cap on his head. Walde counted eighteen guards before glancing back at Albin. The youth was staring, stricken, at the approaching force.

As it grew nearer, other details became visible. The apron was composed of two overlapping plates, one that covered the chest area and one the midsection. The two plates were bound together somehow, and the whole apron was secured with straps around the guards' backs and over their shoulders. The caps came to their brows and dipped down over their ears.

Walde had never seen the like of such armor. As he identified the places where the guards would still be vulnerable, he saw something that almost made him lose control of his Reacher light.

Fresh blood. The fat red drops soiled a man's pale sleeve. Not his blood, Walde thought. No, this had belonged to his victim. Cold anger moved through him. A cursed child had died this day. A cursed child would be avenged.

He glanced at Albin, wanting the youth to see what he saw.

He already had. His face was flushed, his mouth a thin line. His eyes were glowing sparks, promising vengeance and worse. Walde had never understood how people could think that the cursed children were enchanted, but Albin's countenance at that moment made it believable. The youth's hands trembled as he replaced his bowstring with a fresh one.

Walde followed his example. "Keep to the plan," he whispered.

When Albin didn't respond, Walde reached out and touched his shoulder. Albin gave a stiff nod. Walde doubted he would get anything more from him.

He refocused on the intruders, who were drawing ever closer to the trap. Two of the guards' metal plates were slightly askew, and one had removed his cap to scratch his head. Three might have been women, but the plates and caps made it hard for Walde to be sure. When they were only steps from the trap, the bloodied man shouted for everyone to halt. Did he feel the eyes on him? Would he look up into the branches? Very slowly, Walde selected an arrow and held it to his bow. One step along the branch, and he would be in position.

The man—probably the lead guard—found a stick and poked the ground. "Too many leaves here," he said. For some moments, he swept and poked, the stick moving methodically through the debris. Inevitably, it found the trap. "There she is.

Come closer and look. Tilma, Pen, eyes on the trees. Might be another cursed kid up there." Water dripped from the leaves onto the man's bloodied arm as guards huddled around him, baring their unprotected backs.

Walde made a birdcall.

At once, several arrows rained down. A couple of them bounced off the metal caps, making a loud pinging sound. Seven guards took arrows in their necks or backs. Walde's first arrow sank deep into a man's back, killing him instantly.

"Up and fight!" their leader shouted. Somehow, he'd come away unscathed.

Walde gave another birdcall and then scurried onto another branch. While guards still capable of drawing bows hurried to take aim at him, they were drenched in a yellow shower. Before leaving the village, Walde had ordered a few in the group to piss into flasks. He wasn't sure if the idea would work. But the rain had slowed, and the piss was still warm.

A stench rose like a sick smoke from the appalled guards. The tactic made it difficult for them to take aim while looking up at their targets. While they jerked away from the yellow streams, more arrows rained down. Three more guards dropped, leaving eight to go on fighting. But eight was still a dangerous number.

At last, the guards' arrows flew, tearing through leaves and thudding into branches. One zipped past Walde's ear as he rounded the trunk, pulling Albin along with him. They kept coming, arrows with sharp, metal heads and smooth bodies. He had no doubt that some would find human flesh. But he wasn't prepared for the loud thud of Fin's body dropping to the ground. There was a terrible cry from his cousin in the tree across the path. As the guards turned to the sound, Walde unshouldered his quiver and passed it and his bow to Albin.

"Don't," Albin mouthed to him. But it was too late. Walde edged around the trunk and then launched himself at the guards. Swinging on a branch, he kicked a guard in the face, then jumped to the ground and stabbed another in the back. Others dropped from the branches and joined the chaos. The six guards left standing, having no space in the narrow path to draw their swords, resorted to using their belt knives. Walde's fighting became frenzied. He stabbed, ducked, swung, and kicked. A guard stepped into the trap. He was an easy kill.

"Walde, she's getting away!"

He turned to find Albin pointing up the path at a loping guard. The youth was about to draw his bow when she scaled the slope and vanished into the trees.

Gradually, Walde became aware of his surroundings. Bodies carpeted the path. Bran stepped over them as he approached Walde. The others waited behind, their eyes hollow with shock. "Fin is dead," Bran reported, "and four others are injured."

Lina said flatly, "I can go on." Blood seeped through a cloth wrapped around her calf.

"Me too," Cadar said between clenched teeth. Two other Harborlanders chimed in, one with an ugly stripe across his chest, the other with a hastily bandaged forearm.

Albin handed Walde back his bow and quiver.

"Go where?" Walde asked.

Bran frowned. "To God's Eye. Didn't you hear the horn call? There's another force at God's Eye. Six armed intruders."

Walde wiped his bloodied blade on his tunic. His hands trembled with suppressed fear as he returned it to its sheath. How many such groups had infiltrated the forest? Could one have slipped past the sentinels and attacked the village? Despite his worries, his voice sounded flat. "I have to catch that fleeing guard."

"I'll join you," Garen offered, surprising him. "She has a sword and knows how to use it."

Walde shook his head. "She's injured. And the others need you more. Go."

Turning, he took off at a run.

CHAPTER 17

If it was midday, the sky didn't know it. If anything, the gloom had deepened. The air felt heavy and still. Walde would have preferred the rain. At least it would keep the biting flies at bay. His run had slowed to a weary jog. No point in rushing when the prey was near. Her blood trail had grown heavy and crooked. She'd paused a few times, perhaps unaware that she was being followed. He judged that she didn't have long to live.

A distant thud made him quicken his pace. He followed the path as it curved around a massive tree. The woman lay on the ground on the other side of it. As he approached, her chest gave one final heave before growing still.

His shoulders slumped. Dead already. He'd hoped to get the chance to speak to her, drag a few answers from her before she died.

He knelt beside her. She looked to be Brite's age. Black hair hung in a coiled knot at the nape of her neck. Her callused fingers were still clenched, as if they held something. Curious, he unfolded them. Metal spilled out. A tiny locket on a chain. He sprang the catch and was startled by the exquisite drawing of a man's face. Every detail had been rendered, right down to a wrinkle splayed across his forehead. He would have liked to give Brite such a gift.

He stared at the picture for longer than he should have, swallowing as the scent of blood filled the air. And in that space of stillness, something that had been raging inside him calmed; cold reality seeped in. When he looked up from the locket again, he saw a dead woman lying on the path. Not a faceless guard. Not prey. Just a woman who had once loved and been loved in return. His eyes closed, and he swallowed harshly. Sadness made a soft circle of light around him.

After an endless moment, he gathered her into his arms and stood awkwardly. Her neck wound had ceased bleeding, but her clothes were drenched, soaking the front of his tunic. He ought to leave her behind and go help the others. Someone else would collect her, along with the rest of the bodies. They would have to be stripped of valuables and burned.

He started walking.

Cheerful birdsong surrounded them, adding a surreal edge to the day. His mind kept sliding back to the Lakelands. To a young man who would have been horrified by him now. But it wasn't just him. The world had gone mad. How could he have known how he'd respond under such circumstances? A cornered man fights. *We have to do what we have to do.*

Several eternities passed before he saw the path of bodies in the distance. "Almost there," he murmured. Perhaps her lover lay in the path. If he was among the dead, then he had failed to protect her.

Probably better that he was dead.

Walde's arms ached when he finally lowered her to the ground. If he'd had time, he would have waded through the bodies to see if he could find the man wearing the face in the locket. But the living were more important. He edged around the path, drenching his legs with wet ferns. Somehow, he didn't hear Grella and Cadar's cousin, Hess, until they were standing in the path beside him.

"Walde!" Grella's eyes were huge. "What happened to you? Are you badly hurt?"

"No. The blood isn't mine."

"Thank the gods."

Hess loosened his belt and shrugged off his tunic. He offered it unabashedly to Walde. "Take it, please. If you go back looking like that, you'll scare people."

Walde stared at the tunic. "What happened? Where are you both going?"

"Oh." Grella tried for a smile. It didn't reach her eyes. She spoke in a nervous, hurried fashion, one hand endlessly rubbing her arm. "Sorry, I was supposed to tell you that we killed five of the six intruders, and the missing one is being tracked. Bran says he'll report to you when you get back. Hess and I are going to the downed sentinel. I'm to take over the post, and Hess is to bring the sentinel back."

Walde accepted Hess's tunic. The intruders dealt with. And no others sighted. Could the day's attacks really be over? He peeled the bloody tunic off and tossed it toward the bodies. "Are you all right, Grella?"

"Yes. Well, no. But I will be. It's been a horrible day." She gave a little hiccup that might have been a sob. Walde found himself staring at the ground. "I ate something," she added. "Albin told me to."

Walde said, "That's good. Good that you ate." He pulled on Hess's tunic. Mumbling a thank-you that sounded more like an apology, he left them both to their tasks.

He hugged himself as he made his way back to the river. Guilt and helplessness assailed him anew, and the day wasn't bright enough to conceal his Reacher light. Gritting his teeth, he forced it all back and focused on his hike down the slope.

The boats were gone. Others would eventually make their way up the river to do a sentinel exchange and to collect the bodies. He could either wait for them or negotiate the ragged west bank back to the First.

As he stood on the shore, unable to make a choice, his eyes were drawn to the curving river and the steepening rise of land on either side of it. What had happened at God's Eye? An intruder was missing. Grella had said he was being taken care of. But how? The more he thought about it, the more worried he became. He wanted to trust that a wise decision had been made. But the evidence suggested otherwise. The group had started out that morning with seventeen members. Remove Walde, Grella, Hess, and poor Fin, and the remainder was thirteen. Four of them wounded. Given such numbers, how many trackers could Bran have spared while still having enough left to properly man four boats?

The answer was one. Maybe two, if one of the injured had found the strength to row. But Walde had seen their injuries, and despite the bravado, their untended wounds would have weakened them a great deal by the time they returned to the boats.

It seemed that Bran hadn't sent enough trackers to deal with the intruder. Walde hoped he was wrong, but if he wasn't, and if the intruder killed the trackers and got away to report what he'd seen...

His lips compressed. He couldn't let that happen. So...

So he would go to God's Eye and help search for the missing guard.

Reassured by the decision, he regarded the river with a more careful eye. If he ran along the riverbank, he'd be in a weaker position. Better to head back up the slope and walk along its lip. From there, he'd have a view of both the slope and the shadowy forest.

Up he went, his bow strung and his eyes fixed on the line of trees above him. Though a single intruder wasn't as threatening as a whole force, it took only one well-aimed arrow to down a man.

He passed through the area of scraggly trees and turned off the path. It was an easy turn to make. Bran's group had carved a trail through the ferns that a child could follow. They had even left blood droplets. He tried to walk quietly, but his worn boots squeaked and sloshed. And to make matters worse, a hole was opening in one of the toes. After all this was over, he'd have to scavenge a pair from one of the dead guards. Maybe from the one who wore the face in the locket.

And just like that, his dark thoughts returned. He steeled his mind away and focused more fully on his surroundings.

As he neared the path that led to God's Eye, the group's trail veered away from the brow of the slope and into the denser trees. It ended at a large tree near the path. So, they had climbed the tree and waited for the intruders to appear. And then…? Sliding his bow over his shoulder, he swung up into the tree, climbing higher and higher until he could see not only the path, but also the wash that spilled down the slope like a dark finger.

The five intruders' bodies were strewn on the slope. It had happened just as he had imagined it might: an attack from the rise while trapped on the slope.

He descended the trunk and hiked down to the edge of the scraggly trees. The trail of blood drops continued on down the slope, indicating that the group had returned to the boats by means of the bank. Had Albin paused up here, wondering if he should call to the sentinel at God's Eye to see if the cursed child still lived? If he'd made such a call, Walde hadn't heard it.

His lips tightened. This had to end. The children who manned the fringe posts may be fifteen or sixteen in actual years, but that didn't mean that they should throw their lives away. Albin had been so set on the idea of posting cursed children on the fringes that no one on the council—not even Walde—had argued against it. Now he wished he had. No matter. He'd propose an end to it when he got back.

He eyed the fallen intruders appraisingly. Walde would be better protected if he scavenged some armor. But it would take time to remove it, and he didn't like the idea of lingering on the bare slope. Best just to go.

He removed his boots, upended them until they stopped dripping, and then attached them to his belt. His feet were wrinkled and sensitive from the long soaking they'd received, but at least he could walk now without squeaking. Feeling freer, he turned and padded up the path toward God's Eye.

The gray sky appeared as he passed through an area of younger trees, then the hoary arms of mature trees closed over him again. Jagged rocks rose crookedly between them, their mossy faces sometimes pebbled like that of an old hag. The birds had grown quiet. But he remembered that. This wasn't a place of birdsong.

He slowed after a time, feeling as though he were being watched. A soft thud made him wheel around, but when he looked toward the place where the sound had originated, there was nothing. Only deeper shadow. Sweat trickled down his spine, and he walked with an arrow to his bow. He had been among others the first time he'd come here, and the place had felt eerie then. Now it felt positively threatening. He forced himself to push on.

He hadn't traveled much farther before the forest opened and the shadowy wall of the cliff appeared, overhung by strings of vine. He kept well away from the mist-filled ditch that had formed at the cliff's base. For all he knew, it could be a fissure hundreds of feet deep. He scrambled over some jagged boulders and continued on until he reached the spot where the "ditch" yawned open in the shape of a giant eye. The thick white mist inside it had risen to the very edge of the ditch. A stench of rotting eggs permeated the air, making his nose wrinkle.

He turned away from it and studied the tangled wood. He saw no trail at first, but after walking a few more paces along the path, he spotted a crushed fern. This marked the beginning of a trail that cut a ragged path toward the sentinel tree. Walde ghosted through the brush on the pads of his feet, alert for any disturbance.

When he was only a few yards from the trunk, he stopped dead in his tracks. A man lay face-up on the ground, his hand still gripping a drawn sword. As Walde drew near, he spotted what had slain him: a single arrow through his neck. The shot must have killed him quickly, for there was very little blood on the ground.

Walde, afraid to see what had become of the sentinel— for this was a cursed child's arrow—unstrung his bow and lingered by the corpse. There was something odd about the scene. The felled guard had clearly worn a metal cap—his hair still bore a line showing where the cap's edge had pressed. Likewise, wrinkles in his tunic suggested he'd worn a metal apron. It could be that his fellows had pillaged these items, but if so, why hadn't they taken his sword?

And where was the tracker? Walde had met no one on the path heading back. Perhaps they'd taken the sentinel's place in the tree. But if so, they'd chosen not to greet Walde. He spied a small, shiny object on the ground near the body and squatted to examine it.

The movement saved his life.

A gust of displaced air by his head made him jerk back from the body and look up. He glimpsed a metal-plated chest before a sword slashed down toward him. Walde rolled away, picked up a large rotting stick, and hurled it at the swordsman. The tactic gave him only enough time to climb to his feet and identify the nearest tree he could climb. Then the stick shattered in the air, and the swordsman closed in. Walde caught a glimpse of the man's face before ducking to avoid another heavy slash.

A white shock filled him. "Garen!"

The name had no effect on the former guard. And at that moment, Walde knew he couldn't be reasoned with. He meant to kill Walde and then alter the intruder's wound to make it appear that Garen had stabbed him in an effort to protect Walde.

Walde's Reacher light flared before he retreated behind the walls of the medallion.

The brightness lit Garen's maddened face. "Filthy liar."

Walde had no time to reply. The sword didn't swing this time, but stabbed toward him. He twisted away from it and felt it catch for an instant in his clothing. Cold metal grazed his bare skin. He jerked away, tripped on a root, and fell backward. His hand curled around a muddy stone. As Garen came toward him, he hurled the stone at his face. It found its mark, slamming hard into the soft flesh of his cheek. Walde didn't wait to see how he responded. At once, he drew his dagger and lunged toward him, aiming for the tendons behind his knee. As dangerous as the situation was, Walde was loath to kill a Reacher. If he could hamstring even one leg, then he could get away.

He was within inches of success when the dagger was jerked out of his grasp. The sword came down so hard on Walde's blade that pain lanced up his wrist. He scrambled backward, stifling a groan. The sword sliced up, slashing a line across his forearm. He rolled away, crashed through a huge fern, and struggled to his feet again. If he could just get to the path, then he'd be free to run. He tore the dangling boots off his belt and backed toward the path.

Garen pursued him, a sickly smile on his bloodied face. "That's right. You're going the right way now."

Walde was quickly coming to grips with a terrible fact: a sword extended its wielder's reach by at least two feet. This meant that as fast as Walde retreated, the blade licked after him. He couldn't turn his back on it, and he couldn't retreat fast enough to evade it. In a desperate bid to move faster, he unshouldered his quiver and let it fall to the ground.

A mad gleam lit Garen's eyes as he charged through the undergrowth in pursuit, his sword slicing through leaves. He wasn't done speaking yet. "Brite wouldn't like to be in the pit alone. You should join her."

At the sound of her name, Walde's heart gave a little lurch. He shoved the weakness down and clambered over a mossy boulder. "Brite's at her post," Walde spat back, then added, "Who's the liar now?"

Garen snorted. "I take it you didn't question Grella then?"

Walde's palms slid on the boulder. Warm blood was streaming from his wound. His hand was a red glove. He needed to bind it but he had no time. When he didn't speak, Garen went on, "Brite met us after you left. She'd heard the horn call and wanted to help, so Bran let her join us. After we killed the five intruders, she offered to come out here with me and hunt down the sixth."

Walde didn't want to hear Garen's treacherous words. Yet they slid into him anyway, as foul as any poison. Walde retorted, "Brite's not a tracker."

"No? She said something about learning it from her uncle…"

Walde stumbled and almost fell into a shadowy space of green between two boulders. Brite would have said that. And if she'd been posted nearby, then she would've heard the battle. But would Bran have sent her along with Garen?

She would have been fresh. Uninjured. And unafraid of God's Eye. Yes, it was possible…

Garen must have glimpsed the worry in his eyes, for he spat out a scornful laugh. "You fool. Why do you think I'm still out here, waiting? I knew you'd find out she was with me and come after her."

Walde had reached the path, but at those last terrible words, his resolve weakened and darkness closed in. The metal apron and cap. Garen had donned them and waited. Why? He would've had no reason to think Walde would come unless Brite was here. Was it true then?

His gaze turned from Garen to the deep, swirling mist of the eye. He imagined Brite walking ahead, her attention focused on the forest as she searched for a trail. She wouldn't have expected an attack from behind. One sword thrust, and a push. Garen would've thought nothing of it. She was only a Lowlander, after all. Expendable.

A strangled sound escaped his throat.

Garen burst through the undergrowth and approached him with the confidence of a hunter who'd cornered his prey. Walde's Reacher light blazed on him. The medallion's walls were gone, and he had no will to find them again. He felt like he'd broken through ice into cold, dark water. Garen was herding him to the edge. *Join Brite,* a voice urged Walde. Yes, he should. He deserved to.

A gleam of victory in Garen's eyes made him want to be angry, to fight back, but the will was gone. Even his Reacher light had begun to dim. And he was weary, so weary. Perhaps he was bleeding to death.

The mist was warm as it grazed his bare ankles. He should just let himself fall, deny Garen the pleasure of finishing him.

The sword rose, and Walde stepped back, expecting empty air. When he found rock instead, he stumbled and almost fell at Garen's feet.

The sword. Why hadn't it caught him yet? His dizzied gaze rose, found Garen in the mist. But the former guard no longer looked at him. His eyes bulged, and he looked past Walde at something in the distance. Then, to Walde's utter amazement, he simply dropped, his body following the weight of his sword down. Walde jumped away to avoid being hit by his crumpling body. The weapon rang out against the stones and then vanished. Garen lay slumped on the pit's edge. The impact of his fall had chased the mist back for an instant, revealing an arrow in his back, before seeping over him again.

A silence fell, broken only by the droplets of Walde's blood hitting the stones. Movement in his peripheral vision made him look up. A wolf stood in the path, watching him.

No, not a wolf, but a man wearing a wolf's body. Walde's vision blurred, and he swayed.

A woman spoke. "He's going to fall. Catch him, Zon!"

Walde shook his head. "No. No, I have to go to her."

Someone grasped his uninjured arm and tugged him away from the edge. Walde fought the grip, but his efforts were weak and made him nauseous. "Let me go!" he pleaded.

Voices swam around him. One of them was his own, but the words were garbled. He needed something…a cloth to staunch the bleeding. He couldn't go after her if he bled to death.

So thirsty. His eyes closed, and he drifted.

CHAPTER 18

Walde woke slowly, his mind still clinging to some dark, senseless dream. He swallowed back a stickiness in his throat and tried to open his eyes. The familiar curve of a wooden beam told him he was in his hut in the lowest level of the dead tree. Late afternoon light danced on the ceiling, yet despite that warmth and the blanket draped over him, he felt chilled. He tried to collect his thoughts, but they danced away like fireflies in the darkness.

"You're awake." Brite leaned over him and touched his face. "How are you?"

"Thirsty," he managed.

A heartbeat later, a cup touched his lip, and he opened his mouth to let the water trickle in. He had swallowed twice before his eyes widened and he jerked away, spluttering. "Brite!" He tried to sit up, but dizziness and pain made him drop back down. Blackness swam at the edges of his vision.

Brite's hand flew to her mouth. "What is it?"

He couldn't speak. His eyes closed as the incident at God's Eye flooded back, red-rimmed and tasting of blood and death. Yet none of it mattered now. It ought to matter. Garen was dead, and Walde had come within a hairsbreadth of dying himself. All because he had allowed the former guard to deceive him into believing Brite was dead.

"You're alive." Stupid tears gathered in his eyes. "I thought Garen had killed you and pushed you into the pit."

Brite sat down heavily on the edge of the mattress. "Zon said something about you wanting to save someone, but no one was missing, so we all thought you were delirious from blood loss." She ran her finger over her shoulder blade. "You thought it was me. That I fell into the pit."

"Fell..."

"Or was pushed." A small wrinkle formed between her brows. "What happened out there? Zon said that Garen was about to kill you..."

He freed his uninjured arm from the blanket and wiped his damp eyes. Though he recalled the encounter with Garen vividly, parts of it made no sense to him now. He couldn't fathom why he'd believed the former guard so utterly. And, believing him, had chosen to die rather than run as he'd planned. He sighed and slid his arm back under the blanket. "I'd rather not talk about it now. So you're not hurt...?"

"No. I was posted on the other end of the river. I didn't even know there was a battle until the sentinel came to relieve me." She picked up the cup and pressed it to his mouth. He downed two cups of water before she spoke again. "How are you?"

"Fine. Just tired and a little dizzy."

"Do you remember me cleaning and stitching your arm?"

"No."

She shrugged without looking at him, and said, "You seemed to come to a few times." She set the cup on the chest and paused. A tentative smile tugged on her lips. "Remember that first time I stitched you up, when we were hiding by the Nadi?" She fingered the blanket at his side, finding the scar with ease.

"Yes. Of course."

"And the filthy bandage you wanted to keep?"

His lips twitched. "It would have been useful."

"So you said then." Her smile held a moment longer, then her head fell and she chewed her lip. An odd stillness grew between them. Walde's eyes drooped, but he wouldn't let himself sleep.

She gestured toward the door. "Zon's on the path outside, guarding the hut. I told him he didn't need to, that you're safe now and he doesn't owe you anymore—"

"Owe me?"

Her gaze flicked upward in annoyance. "For freeing him in the Harborlands."

He stifled an amused smile. "I doubt that's what's on his mind at all."

So Zon had saved his life. And now he saw himself as Walde's personal bodyguard. His eyes were closing.

"Walde..."

The odd note in her voice made his lids flash open. "Yes?"

She cocked her head at him, as if deciding something. Then the shy smile returned. "I'm with child."

Walde just stared at her. As the silence lengthened, his dizziness returned and he realized he'd forgotten to breathe. He managed a word. "Truly?"

"Truly. I've suspected it for a while. I should've said something, but I didn't know for sure until today when I spoke with Idra, and she said I had all the signs and should tell you." She turned away abruptly and rummaged through a pack on the floor. "Are you hungry? I have some smoked fish and a handful of berries..."

"Brite..." He tried to sit up, but the movement disturbed his injury, making it throb. His teeth clenched, and he lay back down. His heart was drumming hard. It was all too much, too fast. It didn't seem real.

But it was real. Brite was alive, and he was going to be a father.

The thudding in his chest had become painful. His heavy eyes closed, and he focused on his breathing.

A warmth grazed his face. Brite's lips brushed his cheek, then his brow. She whispered, "I'm sorry. I should've waited a bit longer to tell you. You aren't well now." She paused. Her breath smelled of blueberries and long kisses under moonlight. "Are you happy? Just nod if you are."

He tried. He thought his head moved, but he couldn't be sure. He felt the blanket lift off him and Brite gasp, probably at his blazing Reacher light, then the world blackened and dizziness rocked him into darkness.

***

When he woke again, the light on the ceiling had lengthened. He hoped it was still the same day. If it was, then the sky had cleared and the air had dried.

He turned his head and found not Brite, but his father in the chair next to him. Without a word, Carrac filled the cup and brought it to Walde's mouth.

"Brite has gone to check on the injured. She's a good nurse, that one. Makes people feel safe and cared for."

And she's going to be a mother. Walde longed to tell his father the news, but he didn't know if Brite wanted to keep her pregnancy secret for a while longer.

"How are you?" Carrac said.

Walde was growing irritated by the question. "As you see."

"I see a pale young man on a mattress."

"There you are."

Carrac snorted. "You seem to be in good spirits, considering how close you came to death." He took the cup back from Walde and gripped it hard for a moment. A glimmer of light came and went around the edges of his palms. "Thank the gods for Zon. If he hadn't come just then..." His jaw tightened and the light faded.

After a long pause, Walde asked, "Is he still wearing that wolf pelt?"

"You remember that, eh? Yes, the old thing still sits on his shoulders, even in the summer's heat. He's an odd fish, that one. Bran asked if he would help bring the bodies back, but he refused to leave your side." He refilled the cup. "Nor would he talk about his journey to the mountains. All he said was that he had to fetch his family."

"His family?"

"His brother's wife and son. That's all he has left, after the purge. His brother's wife told us that some of the Reachers were on hunting trips in the mountains when the purge happened. She escaped to warn them, and after that, they just stayed there. Some were caught later; others died in hunting accidents. Zon was the only Reacher left when he was seized and hauled back to the Harborlands. His nephew is a cursed child. Looks to be about twelve, which would make him nearly seventeen. Albin's eyes bulged when he saw him. Not only were they neighbors, but the boy's mother is Albin's aunt."

"I suppose Albin asked about his parents, then."

Carrac gave a slow nod. "His aunt said they were caught in the purge, which means they're dead. She's a blunt woman, that one. Reminds me of a battered leather shoe. Tanned and weather-beaten, with eyes that have stared too long at cold, lonely hills."

His voice trailed. Walde was grateful that his father hadn't asked about God's Eye.

"Can you sit up?" Carrac asked.

Walde pushed the blanket off and struggled to rise. The pain in his left arm had receded, but his weakness had not. Even an act as simple as sitting up made his heart pound and his breathing quicken.

Carrac helped him lean against the wall. "You lost a lot of blood," he said quietly. "The injury isn't bad. If you'd trussed it sooner—"

"I didn't have time." The words came out harsher than he'd meant. He closed his eyes and drew a long breath. "Where are they burning the bodies?"

"At the training field, by the river. Everyone's helping to bring wood over. It's a good thing they kept some dry, or it'd all be drenched."

Walde cringed at the thought of burning the guard's bodies, but they had no other option. They couldn't haul them outside the Woodlands and leave them to rot. Nor could they float them down river to the Nadi. If the Harborlands elders had been keeping their assault on the Woodlands secret, the sudden appearance of twenty-four carcasses in the harbor would put an end to that and force the elders to retaliate. No, it was best to burn the dead guards and hope the loss would make their enemies reluctant to attack again.

It wasn't an altogether foolish hope. The elders couldn't afford to keep throwing guards at the Woodlands—not while having to deal with their own unrest at home. Of course, that didn't mean that the dead guards' relatives wouldn't come to seek their own vengeance...

He thrust the locket and its wearer out of his mind.

Carrac went on, "You should be there, if you can. Zon and I can carry you down..."

Walde loosed a soft snort, imagining that. "All right."

He ate what food Brite had left for him, then Carrac went outside to fetch Zon. Brite had removed Walde's bloodied clothes and replaced them with ones he was almost certain had belonged to poor Fin. He held his grief over the man's death away from him. Too much had happened for him to dwell on it just then.

Carrac hauled him to his feet and asked him to lay his uninjured arm across his shoulders. "Can you walk like this?"

Walde didn't answer at first. The change in position from almost flat to upright made his head spin and his stomach sicken. He nearly begged to be returned to the bed. Instead, he clenched his teeth, swallowed his pride, and said no. He would need to be carried. He bit back his pain as he draped his injured arm over Zon's furry shoulder and allowed the man to heft him up. Carrac and Zon dragged Walde through the door, down the walkway to the path, and then more awkwardly around the winding stairs. Happily, the ground wasn't far. By the time they'd reached the bottom, Walde had regained a measure of strength and could move his legs in a semblance of walking as they made their way to the dock.

They lowered him awkwardly into a boat before clambering into it themselves and pushing off.

Zon sat at the prow, his wolf pelt flowing down his back like a cape. Its great head leaned over one shoulder, ears erect, fur ruffling in the breeze. Walde had glimpsed such a pelt once or twice at a tinker's stall in the Lakelands. It was strange to see the expensive item tossed like a blanket over a man's back.

The sun was sinking over the forest. Walde sensed the familiar tug of the First's link as they drifted past the massive tree. The cook fire by the boardwalk was dead and abandoned, and no lamps glowed either at the tree's base or in its branches. Everyone was gathered in the field farther up, where a great pyre was already burning. Carrac guided the boat into dock and climbed out to secure it.

No one noticed their arrival until they were past the boardwalk and approaching the fire.

Walde had never seen a pyre so large. The mound of broken or rotting boards stood in a cleared area of the field. Much of it hadn't caught yet, but when it did become fully engulfed, he judged it would burn quickly.

The shadowy pile of bodies lay in a heap upwind of the flames. Normally, the corpses would have been placed on the pyre before the fire was kindled, but there were simply too many for this to be possible. Once the pyre was lit, a vigil— usually carried out by the dead's relatives—would begin and continue all night long. In a day or two, the cooled bone fragments would be sifted from the ash and carried to the corpse darkness to be interred.

This was the old way and nothing new to the Lakelanders. Walde still wasn't sure how the Harborlanders disposed of their dead, but they didn't appear uncomfortable with the ceremony.

Many nodded to Walde as he approached the assembled crowd. Of the council, only Idra, Carrac, Tir, and Albin were present. The rest were likely on sentinel duty. The children wept openly for the lost sentinels. Even Albin, though he didn't wail as the younger ones did. Tir stood like a statue of himself, his face pale and stiff, his eyes hollow with shock. Walde met his gaze and opened his hand over his father's shoulder. Reacher light flared, a small thing next to the rising flames, but Tir saw it and tipped his head in acknowledgement that Walde grieved with him.

No one would mourn Garen. Shin was either on sentinel duty or off somewhere on her own. Walde was grateful not to have to face her.

Brite slipped out of the crowd and strode over to him. The warm light of the setting sun burnished the copper in her braided hair and cast a silken glow over her cheekbones. She looked beautiful and exhausted. She shouldn't take posts anymore, he decided. A wash of protectiveness swept through him, followed at once by shame and self-loathing. Even if he were healthy, how could he protect her when he had failed to protect himself? Oh, he'd had his moment while fighting the guards. But if one had managed to draw a sword, it might've all been over. Garen had shown him that.

Brite said, "I'm glad you were well enough to come."

Walde would have shrugged if his arms weren't stretched over Carrac and Zon's shoulders. He jerked his chin at the piled corpses. "Who were the sentinels?"

"They were Ned and Cara."

He tried to picture them. Ned had been frozen at age nine, Cara at ten. Walde hadn't got to know either of them well. Now it was too late. He said, "I suppose Albin gave a speech."

She nodded, and their gazes lingered. Walde longed to hold her and tell her he was happy that she was with child, but the moment for that had come and gone. After a long silence, Carrac cleared his throat, and Brite looked swiftly away.

The sun had set over the tree line. It was time to start the burning.

Abbe walked to the pyre, a heavy drum secured by shoulder straps to her chest, a beater in each hand. As the villagers looked on, she lifted the beaters above her head and slammed them down hard on the skin. The sound that reverberated from the drum lifted the hairs on Walde's arms. Again, the drum sounded. The fire seemed to listen, its flames leaping up to meet a body that wasn't there.

On the third beat, a corpse, stripped of all but its underclothes, was swung up onto the pyre. Rather than linger to watch it burn, folk gathered around the mound and tossed bodies up into the flames.

It was a burning like no other. Walde would never forget the stench that hung in the air, nor the deep pounding of the drum. He stood for as long as he could before tiredness and pain made him ask to sit down. By then, all twenty-eight corpses had gone onto the pyre, the drumming had ceased, and everyone had edged back to avoid the heat. A circle of stones held the flames in, but not the sparks. Thankfully, the dampness from the day's rain prevented the field weeds from catching.

It was a warm night, and the fire kept the insects at bay. Walde lay back on the soft earth and stared up at the sea of stars. Sparks rose to join them, like treelight meeting starlight. The two merging.

We are children in a great womb.

The thought came to him unbidden. It was the first piece of knowledge Thara had given him and an answer to the question of whether or not she was starseed. *We are all one thing*, the words seemed to say, and there was a power in that. Unity and power were connected somehow. But reaching for them was like grasping after thistledown in the wind. Unity didn't exist in the fragmented womb of the world.

His hand found Brite's, and he drifted off.

He wandered into a strange and terrible nightmare. In it, he marched through a dark forest. The trees were guards, the branches arms, reaching for him. He swung a great sword and felled them. But the forest was endless, and he was tired, so tired. He felt something small and hard in his hand and opened it. The locket. His heart lurched sideways in his chest. The forest disappeared, and the catch snapped open. The female guard lay inside it, her pleading face upturned. Her mouth moved, but she made no sound...

"Walde. What is it? Your Reacher light..."

He woke, blinking at Brite's shadowy face, then without meaning to, sank back into a deeper sleep.

***

The next day was abuzz with activity.

Grella, Elva, and Buzz scrubbed the dead's clothing at the river's edge. After the clothes dried, Grella fetched a stoppered bottle containing the juice of boiled black walnut hulls and dyed the clothes that were still lightly stained. It didn't matter to her that the fabric was kriksa instead of kessa or that the tunics were cut longer than she was used to. The villagers needed spare clothing, and it could all be altered and worn.

Meanwhile, Albin rounded up all the Harborlanders who hadn't yet gotten to know the posts and traps and took them through the forest. He also taught them the horn calls. Those with the drinking sickness seemed to have fully recovered, and many Harborlanders were eager to join what they now called "the rebellion." The death of the two dozen guards had fired them with enthusiasm. They saw the fight as a victory and downplayed the losses. They refused to understand the moodiness of those who had killed guards. A victory was a victory, and it ought to be celebrated. If only they had gin.

Brite sighed and shook her head. She and Walde sat on some blankets on the floor of the First's meeting hut, their backs to the wall. After the storm, Cor had deemed the sixth level's huts too dangerous to shelter in. And Walde had refused to be taken back to the dead tree. Now that he knew of Brite's pregnancy, he wanted her to spend as much time as possible in the arms of a living Mothertree. The growth of their unborn child might depend on it.

Since arriving at the hut, he had remained abed, rising only to relieve himself in a nearby chamber pot. He told himself he was improving. He could lift himself off the floor and take a few unsteady steps. His chill was gone, and Brite had commented that he looked less pale.

But the truth was that he had never felt so weak in his life. He asked her, "What about the bones?"

"The fire's not cool yet. Tir thinks they'll be ready by tomorrow afternoon, but it's going to take hours to haul them all over to the corpse darkness. There's so much of the stuff that Idra thinks it should be piled onto a hand cart."

"She's forgetting how worn and rickety our only handcart is."

He sighed and leaned against the wall beside Brite. His hand strayed to the faint bump of her belly.

After a long silence, she asked, "What are you thinking?"

"That there's a good chance our child will be a Reacher someday. My father was, and *his* father before him. We don't have the certainty Albin and Frey have, since *both* their parents were Reachers, but..."

"There's still a chance." She ran her fingers over his. "That's why you wanted us to sleep here instead of in the dead tree, isn't it?" She tilted her head to look into his face.

Walde slid his hand out from under her stiffened fingers. "I could be wrong, but if I'm not, we need to take precautions."

"What kind of precautions?" She folded her arms. "I don't want to be imprisoned here."

"You won't have to be. My mother spent time at the community garden during her pregnancy, and there was nothing abnormal about my birth."

Brite's arms relaxed a little. "That's good to know." After a few moments, she nodded to herself and smiled.

Walde had opened his mouth to speak when she suddenly reached over and grasped his hands tightly in hers. "Are you happy?"

He didn't have to ask what she meant. "Of course." He smiled a little at their entwined hands. "You can't say you owe me anything now. This covers it all."

She considered that for the length of a breath before answering, "Yes. I think I'll accept that."

***

Evening came, and the familiar din of voices by the cook fire floated up to him. Brite had supplied him with hot food and drink before scurrying off to a nearby sentinel post. Walde had bitten his tongue and not argued with her about going. Even if she'd consented—and he doubted that she would—she'd still have to find a last-minute replacement.

He would tackle the problem his own way. And hope she didn't try to kill him afterward. He wished he hadn't said anything about his mother's gardening.

A groan of old boards reminded him that Zon leaned against the door outside. Walde called to him. When he didn't answer, Walde struggled to his feet and shuffled to the door. He was chagrined to find that he couldn't open it. He spoke through the crack.

"Zon, you should go down and eat with the others. I'll be fine up here on my own."

"There's no sentinel." He growled the words in his deep, throaty voice.

"What?"

"There's no sentinel here."

"There's no need for one. All those people down there watch the tree."

"Not for the tree. For *you.*"

Walde blinked, not sure whether to be amused or offended. "I don't need one." When the hunter didn't reply, he added, "No one's trying to kill me now."

"How do you know that?"

It was useless to try to reason with him. Walde slid to the floor and edged away from the door in case someone tried to open it. "Zon?"

"Yeah."

"You need to eat."

"I did. Brite gave me fish."

Relief vied with frustration, but his own weariness quickly overcame both. Walde muttered, "That's good," and closed his eyes.

He woke to the creak of the door opening. Lamplight flooded the darkened space. "Walde?" Idra's voice. He swallowed back a stickiness in his throat and answered, "I'm here, by the door."

"The council wants to meet, but only if you're well enough to talk."

Walde hated the sympathy in her voice. He said, "I'm fine. Just a little tired."

She opened the door wider and ran the light over him.

"Come in," he offered before she could comment on how he looked. "I'm awake. We can talk."

She pressed her lips together worriedly and then set the lamp by his foot and ducked out, closing the door behind her. Walde strained to hear the whispering voices that followed, but the door was built to prevent eavesdropping. He struggled to his feet and crossed the room to his pathetic shelter of blankets and water. His arm injury wakened like a stirred fire, making him grit his teeth. He pissed in the chamber pot and then forced himself to drain a skin of water. He felt better afterward and even managed a welcoming smile when the door creaked opened again and the council poured in. The meeting hut brightened as several lamps joined Idra's on the floor.

Walde said, aiming for levity, "We should move some furniture in here."

There was a general murmur of agreement, followed by silence. Walde scanned the familiar faces. Out of the eight members, only Zon, Idra, and Carrac looked unchanged from their usual selves. The rest were hollow-eyed and withdrawn. Shin had returned from wherever she'd been hiding but would not lift her face from the floor. Her nails were beyond bitten. Angry red wounds had formed over the nail beds so that it was hard to tell if any nails still remained. Bran sat with his arm around her, but something in the way he embraced her made Walde think he was comforting himself as much as his sister. Nessa and Albin shared eerily similar looks of discomfort and unease, like they were dissatisfied with their own skins. Killing did that to you, Walde thought with a twinge of guilt.

Walde's head bumped the wall behind him, and he straightened, hoping no one had noticed. He said, "I'm sorry, I'm a little tired and my head's full of pod seed. Where should we start?"

Idra clasped her leathery hands together. "There's a lot to talk about. But much of it can wait until tomorrow." She paused. Her eyes flicked to Walde's and then away. "We'd like to know what happened at God's Eye."

Of course they did. And it was the last thing he wanted to talk about, with Shin sitting across from him, ready to tear off the ends of her fingers at his first mention of Garen. He guessed that hurting herself kept her from fully feeling the emotion she desperately stifled.

But she was here, prepared to listen to his story. He moistened his suddenly dry lips. "Right. Where should I start?"

He began at the beginning—from the moment he had left them to chase after the runaway guard—and left nothing out. Even when his own actions embarrassed him.

When he'd finally finished, it wasn't Idra but Bran who spoke into the silence. "It's my fault. Garen asked to go on his own. He said he'd move freer and quieter that way. I knew that guards were trained trackers, and I had the wounded to care for, so I let him go. He was supposed to capture the intruder, bind him, and interrogate him. After that, he was to signal whether the sentinel at God's Eye was dead or alive and stay there until help came." He had spoken all this with his eyes cast down. Now he lifted his head and met Walde's gaze. "I'm sorry. It was a mistake, and it almost cost you your life."

Walde shook his head firmly. "It wasn't your fault that Garen attacked me. He had a chance, and he took it. If you hadn't given him that chance, he would've waited for another."

"Why?" Idra whispered.

Walde ran his hand tiredly across his face. He hadn't expected an interrogation, but perhaps he should have. Idra had known nothing about Garen's hatred of him. The former guard had been unpleasant and surly with everyone, and if Walde had been browbeaten more than others, it could be put down to a touch of envy over Walde's position. He said, "I don't know myself. Not for sure. When he attacked me, he called me a liar. He believed that I lied to you about the content of my conversation with Thara. Lied in order to gain power."

Albin asked, "Why would he think that?"

Walde shrugged. "Perhaps because that's what *he* would've done, had he been in my place."

The others shifted uncomfortably. No one liked to speak ill of the dead. All the more so when the dead's bones hadn't been interred yet.

Albin said, "That doesn't explain why he wanted to kill you."

While Walde was still assembling his thoughts, Bran muttered, "Because *he* wanted power."

Shin made a soft sound of protest, but a black anger glinted in her brother's eyes. A thought struck Walde then. While Bran had stood back and allowed his older sister to fall under Garen's spell, that didn't mean he hadn't been watching.

Bran's Reacher light glimmered briefly before he got control of himself again. "Think about it: the dead guards left us two dozen swords. Enough to arm every Harborlander in the village if they learned how to use them. Garen would've become their sword master. And in that position of power, it wouldn't have taken much to create a mutiny. With Walde dead, the council would've been weakened enough for him to take control."

Walde's mouth slackened. *Of course.* What else could Garen have wanted but his own company of guards to command? And with Shin at his side, he could have pushed out the other Reachers and taken the First as his own fortress.

Bran added, "That's only a guess, of course. I might be dead wrong."

Walde said, "No, I don't think you are." He picked up the water skin, shook it, and set it back down.

Carrac offered him his flask. "This one didn't have piss in it."

The comment roused a few tense chuckles. Walde accepted the flask gratefully and downed what was left. With an effort, he pushed Garen and the swords from his mind. Doubtlessly, they'd return to haunt him later.

Carrac stretched his arms out behind him. "Whatever his reason was, it does us no good to dwell on it now."

Idra gave a reluctant nod, then reached over and laid her hand on Walde's shoulder. "I believe you. I wasn't suggesting that..."

"I know."

She straightened and looked around the circle. "If anyone else bears a secret grudge, you had better resolve it. We can't afford conflict at a time like this." When no one spoke, she looked again at Walde. "Do you wish to end the meeting now, or..."

"No. I can stay awake a little longer." While he had their attention, he introduced the idea of removing cursed children from the fringes. Harborlanders could take those posts while wearing the guards' metal armor.

He had expected someone to argue with him. Albin at the very least. But to his surprise, his proposal passed without debate. Perhaps everyone was sick of seeing dead or injured children. Or they suspected, as Walde did, that their cover was blown. The Harborlands elders probably wouldn't accept that a few wild children could overcome twenty-four armed guards. Cursed or not.

Afterward, Idra wanted to talk about what they should do if the Harborlands enlisted the help of the former Woodlanders in an attack. It was a possibility Walde had shied away from, but now it had to be faced. Carrac and Albin were enthusiastic about creating a detailed escape plan. Walde went along with it while doubting it would work. The Harborlanders were eager to fight and didn't take well to direction they considered cowardly. Walde suspected they would reject the idea of hiding during "the rebellion," especially if it meant leaving the First unguarded. Tir objected most strongly, saying it was the job of all treefolk to defend the Reachers and the Mothertrees. Walde judged that his urge to fight stemmed from a desire to avenge his brother's death, but he kept his silence.

In truth, Walde disliked the idea of abandoning the First. If their enemies took control of it, the Reachers would never win it back. Walde couldn't bear to think about what would happen then…

"Walde."

His father's voice made him jerk awake. The hut was dark and empty. Only Carrac remained, crouched beside him with a lit candle stub. The light flickered on his father's gray beard and sun-darkened face. Carrac said, "I took out the pot and brought you more water. How do you feel?"

Walde ground a fist into his eyes. "I didn't mean to doze like that."

"It doesn't matter. Everyone knows you're not well." He patted Walde's good arm and then rose to his feet. "I'm glad we have a better escape plan. It gives us a chance if things turn ugly."

Though he said *if*, Walde heard *when* in his voice. He offered a tight nod and closed his eyes. "Goodnight, Father. Thanks for the water."

He heard Carrac's footsteps recede and the door close.

In the dark, empty room, Walde was left wondering who should have died at God's Eye, Walde or a man who could've produced two dozen swordsmen to guard the First.

CHAPTER 19

Shortly after noon the next day, the villagers gathered around the musty hole of the corpse darkness to watch the last of the bone fragments spill inside. Tir, Carrac, and a handful of others had sifted the ashes all morning using a basket weave. Two strong men had half-carried the cartloads over to the weedy gap between roots. Walde hadn't been there when the door was worked open, but Carrac—now well powdered with ash—told him it had taken some doing.

A small hill of hacked vines now lay off to one side. Walde leaned on a makeshift cane Idra had formed for him and tried not to cough on the dusty air. It was a bright, warm day, and the First shaded them well from the blazing sun. The Harborlanders not on sentinel duty had left off training at the range or working on the First to observe the ceremony.

A burial was a solemn affair. Usually, a short speech was offered by the family of the deceased, followed by the traditional four lines of the Bana—a poem or prayer, depending on how one looked at it, which bid the dead to find rest in the Mothertree's stillness. Walde had learned the translation of the poem from the old tongue years ago but could only recall bits and pieces of it now.

At a nod from Carrac, the two Harborlanders tipped the cart and the last haul of bones spilled in. Some were tiny, blackened things that could've as easily been wood as bone, others—such as the skulls—would have sat well in the fabled bone man's sack. While the cart was still emptying, an old, tremulous voice began to intone the first line of the Bana in the old tongue.

Walde glanced back at his solitary great-uncle in surprise. Old Caln sat cross-legged on the hill of hacked vines. His eyes were closed and his arms open as if he were physically pushing the words out. The sight stirred the hair on Walde's arms. Brite gripped his brightened hand, and they stood motionless, listening until the aged man's voice wavered out.

He had recited all four lines.

Before Walde knew whether it was appropriate or not, he clapped. Others joined him in slow, firm clapping. Caln bowed his head and appeared to nod off.

The handcart was empty. The two Harborlanders closed the door, and there was an awkward silence.

On impulse, Walde took a step forward, cleared his throat, and spoke. "I didn't hear Albin's speech the other day, but I want to say something about the loss of Fin, Ned, and Cara." As he paused to gather his thoughts, he found his eyes drawn to the field beside the First. From his vantage near the elevated trunk, he could see past the blackened smear left by the pyre to the shadowy trees beyond.

What stood between the village and their enemies? A few sentinels, some traps that could be uncovered by determined guards. Or dogs sent ahead of them.

His courage faltered.

In an instant of clarity, he saw how utterly vulnerable they all were. This freedom wouldn't last long. One day it would come to an end. But what could be done about that? They couldn't just give up and walk away.

As the silence lengthened, a deep sense of purpose filled him. His jaw set and Reacher light glimmered again from his tightening hands. "They didn't die for nothing. Because of them, we stand here alive and free, better armed, better prepared. We shouldn't let their deaths go to waste. This is the last sound, mature Mothertree, and these are the last Reachers. If we fail, everything does. So there can be no failure."

The speech hadn't been planned, and he was startled by the power in his voice as he gave it. Perhaps his great-uncle had inspired him. Whatever it was, it had a remarkable effect on the Harborlanders. Fire lit their eyes, and they roared. And after they roared, they chanted, "The rebellion." Walde struggled to stay upright as they jostled him, slapping his back, gripping his shoulder. Even ones who used to be nervous around Reachers greeted him like a long-lost brother.

Walde managed a tight smile and jerked his head down again and again nodding to them. Yes. For what else could this be called but a rebellion?

As the commotion calmed and folk separated into smaller groups to talk quietly, Walde found Albin at his elbow. The youth said, "Idra thinks we should delay the village meeting until tomorrow. Talk about an escape plan wouldn't go over well after…well, after that speech you gave. I've already talked to Frey about changing the schedule. The new one will start up tomorrow."

He scarcely met Walde's eyes as he spoke, and while there was no censure in his voice, Walde sensed that a distance had grown between them. He sighed and gave a stiff nod. So he had offended some people today. He hadn't meant to. Some things just happened.

And maybe it was time they did. It made no sense for the council to be at odds with the Harborlanders, especially when they had the same goals.

Albin whisked Brite away to tend to one of the injured cursed children, leaving Walde alone with the ever-present Zon. He glimpsed Frey in the distance and recalled his plan to remove Brite from sentinel duty. Now was a good a time as any.

Frey leaned against the trunk, her injured arm still in a sling. The paint on her face made it difficult to judge her state of health.

"I'm not in pain," she assured him when he asked. "But I don't think I'll be using a bow for a while." She tapped a bit of leaf against her chin. The faintest thread of a smile came and went from her painted lips. "Did you come to ask me about changing Brite's schedule?"

Walde eyes widened. "How did you know?"

"Because Brite told me you would. She came by earlier this morning to ask for fewer posts." Her painted smile softened, and she glanced down shyly. "Congratulations, by the way."

Flustered, he offered a quiet thank-you. "So what did she say?"

She shrugged her uninjured shoulder. "She warned me you would come by. And she said I should tell you that it's early days yet, and she's still able-bodied. So if you want her off the schedule, you'll have to take it up with the council."

Walde was at a loss for words. Frey watched him from the top of her eyes with a mixture of amusement and worry. Suddenly he snorted and turned aside to hide a rueful grin. Brite had cleanly won this round. He wasn't about to "take it up with the council." And he doubted he could persuade her not to take posts, if she'd already reduced her schedule.

Frey offered, "I'll fix it so she won't be on the fringes."

It was a small comfort.

A string of warm, dry days followed. Freed of the fringe posts, the children split their time between training the eager Harborlanders at the archery range and repairing the First. Cor showered them with tasks. The builder worked feverishly on the tree from morning until night and urged his workers to do the same. He focused first on the huts affixed to the trunk, a couple of pubs, a school, and meeting hut. These spaces all had wood stoves and could be lived in without fear of falling debris. Once these were repaired, he declared he would move on to the huts nearest the trunk on the sixth level. Walde wished they had more hands. The bottom five levels needed to be completely stripped of rotting boards. A token effort had been made to identify and remove the wood most at risk of falling, but another storm could loosen soft boards and send them hurtling to the ground. The villagers seemed to sense that and avoided sleeping under the First's heavy boughs. Some slept on the sixth level, others by the cook fire. No one slept at the dead tree.

Walde's health was slow to improve, or at least it seemed so to him. He yearned to help Brite remove the old wood and thatch Cor sent down the tree or simply to go hunting. He pleaded with Zon to leave him. The hunter refused to take sentinel posts until Walde was up to the task. He was wasted as a bodyguard, unable to perform any errand that would involve leaving Walde's side.

While Walde searched for a way to keep them both occupied, Frey suggested they start up a tannery. "Albin stretched some deer hides," she said, "but never got around to doing more. But now that winter's coming, you'll need warm clothes. We still have what we wore last winter, and the Harborlanders brought their own, but that still leaves a dozen people without winter things."

There was something comforting about preparing for winter. It forced Walde to step beyond the mere hope that he could remain in the Woodlands and actually act on it.

Albin offered him chairs, a workbench, a large cook pot, some sturdy planks, and a few stretched hides to use as a shelter. He and Zon set up their tent by the old pyre, which was full of the wood ash needed to create the soaking solution for the hides. Zon didn't mind sharing the tools he had carried with him from the mountains.

In a short time, they had a rock deer to work on.

The experience of being in a tannery again—smelling the old smells, hearing the scraping, feeling the texture of the skin—was almost overwhelming to Walde at first. Several times, he paused over a hide and lowered his head over his brightened hands. Home breathed over him, forcing him to look at himself once more and see just how much he had changed. His father's presence would've made it worse, but Carrac had disappeared again, this time without warning and before Walde got the chance to tell him he'd be a grandfather.

Walde hadn't spoken to him since he'd stalked off after the speech. He'd glimpsed him briefly at the village meeting the following day. Carrac had stayed long enough to witness the Harborlanders' indifference to the escape plan. Walde told himself he wasn't to blame for that. But perhaps his father felt differently.

As the tannery became known in the village, younger cursed children came by to help or to simply sit on the ground nearby. A couple of them played with lengths of river cane, shoving hot coals through them with sticks. It was a strange game.

A girl asked Zon one day, "How did you come by the wolf?"

Zon's scraping slowed. "Name is Stake. And he was my ma's."

A boy Walde recognized as Buzz lowered his stick and stared at the rugged hunter. "Your ma named her kill?"

"No." Zon turned to face the children. "He was my ma's animal."

This stunned Buzz to silence, and even Walde set down the pelt he'd been working on and leaned back in amazement. Zon ran one of his clean fingers over the wolf's snout. There was a grumble as he cleared his throat. "My ma shot a wolf for its pelt. Didn't realize she had a pup. She felt so bad she took the pup home with us. Course, then the purge happened. But we were out hunting again so we didn't get caught. Stake stayed by us to the end of his life. Poor pup."

Walde stared as he stroked the wolf's snout, bemused not only by Zon's sudden talkativeness but also by his obvious affection for the beast.

"Why was he called Stake?" Buzz said.

"It's short for *Mis*take." He rinsed his hands in a pail and shook them out.

"I'd like to touch him."

Zon drew the wolf off his shoulders and waved the boy over.

While Buzz examined the pelt, Walde picked up the length of river cane he'd set on the work table and turned it thoughtfully.

Buzz said, "It's going to be a blowpipe. My da taught me how to use them."

Walde's eyes lifted. "A blowpipe."

The boy smiled absently while his small hand stroked the fur. "Blowpipes kill."

***

"It's a blowpipe." Walde held up the cane Buzz had lent him for the council members to see.

Tir and Shin were on sentinel duty, leaving Idra, Albin, Bran, Zon, Nessa, and Walde. They sat in their usual circle on the floor in the First's meeting hut, most of them bleary-eyed from the day's activity. Walde said, "Buzz told me he can down a deer using a single poisoned-tipped dart. His father trained him on it—without the poison, of course. Buzz can hit a target from six yards away, farther if he shoots a ground target while up in a tree. And the poison works fast—Buzz says he's seen it work in under a minute."

Idra yawned and rubbed her face. "A poisoned-tipped arrow is more deadly. It has better range. Why does this interest you?"

"Because it's not easy to loose an arrow while standing on a branch. A couple of the Harborlanders who were with us at the last fight couldn't manage it at all. And even if they had, it would've left them fully exposed while taking aim. Better to lie flat on a branch or behind a trunk. With a blowpipe, you can do that."

Idra said, "A lot can happen in a minute's time. But I see your point."

There were a few uneasy nods. After a short discussion, Idra agreed to produce the pipes and darts on the condition that the source of the poison be kept secret from the Harborlanders. It could be dispensed when needed. Once the weapons were created, the villagers would practice using them without poison.

The proposal passed.

***

A string of soft, peaceful days followed. Late summer brightened the field next to the First with meadowsweet and yarrow. Bran and Elva's children ran and tumbled in it while Elva shouted for them to mind the bees. Walde watched them, wondering what kind of child he and Brite would have. At one point, they'd tried to play with him, but he couldn't find the interest to do so. The old Walde would have.

Worried he might be neglecting Brite, he placed a nosegay of meadowsweet into her work-worn hands one evening. His own were stained and sore, but experience told him the discomfort would pass. He was regaining muscles he'd lost after months of being away from his father's work tent. His injury was nearly healed as well, and he could walk without the assistance of a cane. Even run, though only over a short distance. He would have offered to take sentinel posts if he had spare time. When he wasn't scraping hides at the tannery, he was at target practice with the pipes. The weapon looked simple but was maddeningly hard to master. The flimsy darts didn't fly like arrows when blown. After a dozen feet or so, they began to nose down, and the wind easily pulled them off course. The poison was another discouraging factor. The darts were so sharp, and the poison so lethal, that he doubted the weapon could be used safely. Walde had practiced with honey, and even while being cautious, had nicked himself once. Still, he and a few others were determined to master the weapon. They went up trees and practiced on small targets. They learned to move quietly while keeping their pipe from knocking against twigs and branches. Zon had had some experience with the weapon and seemed to enjoy his time away from the tannery to practice with Walde. He even went so far as to remove the wolf pelt so he could move more freely in the branches. The hunter was remarkably agile for a man of his bulk.

Brite said, "Have you taken it yet? You're awfully quiet."

Walde fingered the bit of daleroot in his palm. "No." He usually waited until her breathing deepened before popping it into his mouth, just in case she wanted to talk.

They lay on some bedding on the floor of a repaired hut on the sixth level. Zon, stubborn as always, slept across the doorway outside. The cool night air slid through the shutters, smelling faintly of wood smoke. The scent mingled with the meadowsweet that stood in a cup on the nearby chest.

He glanced at her still face. "How are you doing? You've been working hard…"

"I'm fine." She turned onto her side and fingered his smooth chin. She had filched Garen's razor a few days after his death, and Walde hadn't had the energy to refuse it. "I've been worrying about *you*, actually. You haven't been yourself for the past few weeks. At first, I thought it was because of your health, but you're better now and still the same."

Walde rubbed at his forehead. "How am I *not myself*?"

She gave a little shrug and spoke to the ceiling. "You used to be full of life. Once I compared you to a fall day, bright and dark and breezy. Now…it's not that you don't have energy, but you're just…flat. Sort of empty. You don't talk about reaching anymore, and you rarely smile. I haven't seen you blaze since the day I told you I was pregnant."

He propped himself on an elbow and cupped her cheek. "I'm happy you're pregnant, Brite. It has nothing to do with that."

She sighed. "I know. I didn't think it did."

"Then—"

"Grella told me you chased down a runaway guard after the fight. A woman. And carried her dead body…"

Walde stopped breathing as the dead woman's face filled his mind. As it had every day since she had died. Swallowing, he lay back on the mattress. His voice was flat when he spoke. "She died from a knife wound she took while fighting. I might've been the one to stab her…or not. I don't know because I don't remember. I went somewhere else for a while…"

After a long space of silence, Brite asked, "Do you want to talk about it?"

"No. I'd rather not."

He popped the daleroot into his mouth and chewed. The bitter herb ground slowly between his teeth, making his eyes water. They lay still for a long time.

As the effects of the drug began to work in him, he whispered, "Sleep well, my love."

***

He was shaken awake by both Brite and Zon. Walde jerked upright and looked around. The door was open, revealing a glow of early dawn light. Walde asked sharply, "What is it?" He could scarcely make out their faces in the gloom.

They both spoke at once. Walde caught the words "invaders" and "main path off the cart road," before Zon stopped and let Brite go on. Walde rose and dressed while she spoke. A glimmer of Reacher light slipped from his unsteady hands. He closed his eyes briefly and pictured the medallion. His anxiety eased.

"—call sounded faint before Albin repeated it. Zon and I both heard it. Twelve armed invaders sighted on the main—"

"Only twelve?" Walde dropped his belt and stared at them.

"Twelve," Zon confirmed.

Walde rubbed the space between his brows. There would likely be other groups, then. He hated not knowing where they would emerge, and when. He snatched up his belt and fumbled with the clasp. "How long ago?"

Brite said, "Just before we woke you."

He slid his blowpipe through a sheath attached to his cross strap and fixed the quiver and dart pouch to his belt. The dagger sat on the opposite side of his hip, its blade freshly sharpened on the whetstone.

Brite made a soft sound in her throat. Then she blurted, "Walde, you shouldn't go this time. You're still recovering from your injury." When he didn't answer, she snatched up her bow and quiver and strode out the door.

"Brite!"

He caught up with her before she'd reached the stairs. Grasping her arm, he turned her toward him. "Please, don't," he said breathlessly, blinking in the gloom. The daleroot was still working on him, making him slow and dizzy.

"Why? If I can do the posts, then I can fight too. Stop trying to imprison me."

His mouth opened, then closed. Suddenly he drew her fiercely into his arms. "I never meant for you to feel that way."

"I know. You never do."

"And you're right. You *can* fight. But I'm asking you not to. Please. Just this once. I don't think I could stand seeing you and…and the baby in danger." He gripped her harder, wanting to tuck away both her and their unborn child somewhere in his heart where they'd both be safe.

He felt her breath catch, then her shoulders slumped and she loosed a heavy sigh.

"I have to go," he said after a long silence. "I'll wear the metal armor, if it makes you feel better."

She nodded against his shoulder, then unslung her quiver and handed it to him. "See that someone gets the arrows."

"I will. Brite—" He jogged after her as she made for the stairs. Zon's familiar step thudded behind.

The gathering at the boardwalk was quite different from the one Walde had encountered on the morning of the last attack. The Harborlanders stood together with quiet impatience, their hair slicked back and bound, their weapons readied. They followed Walde with their eyes as he quietly conferred with Albin, Tir, Shin, and Idra—all on the council who weren't on sentinel duty that morning.

Idra said in a low voice, "This feels like a trap. They know we can take on a dozen guards. And that the sentinels will alert us to invaders."

"I know." Walde ran a hand over his jaw. "But I don't see what we can do about it. We can't just let them come here. They'll be well armed, maybe better than they were before."

Idra lifted her arms in a gesture of defeat. There was no clear solution, and they didn't have time to consider the problem deeply.

Tir shifted restlessly from one foot to the other. He said, "I don't think Reachers should go this time. Best to just send Harborlanders."

Walde disagreed. "We need our best archers and pipers out there, no matter who they are. Cor and his friends lost training time while they were sick, and they never took much of an interest in the pipes..."

Tir's jaw tightened, but in the end he was outvoted. Walde smoothed his injured pride by placing him in charge of the ones staying behind.

It took some convincing to make Cor and his friends agree to remain at the First. They had missed the last fight, and it seemed profoundly unjust that they should miss another. Walde reminded them of what had happened during the last attack. "Another group might turn up, and we can't fight them if we're all in one place. We need a back-up force in the center in case there's an invasion at the other side of the forest. So be ready. Tir will command you." He found Tir at his side and snared his gaze. "Remember the escape plan."

Tir gave a stiff nod. "Of course."

Walde drew a heavy breath and turned away. Idra would be here to advise the Harborlander. And she was no pushover.

While Walde was speaking, Brite, Idra, Albin, and several cursed children retrieved the metal armor from its storage in a spare hut. Someone had coated it with a brown substance in an attempt to camouflage it. Brite helped the adults don the chest plates, securing the bloodstained leather straps. Her fingers lingered on Walde's back. At once, he turned and kissed her with the passion she had accused him of lacking.

She broke away first, her finger grazing his palm. His Reacher light glimmered but didn't blaze. Walde looked away from her searching eyes. He whispered, "It's not you."

"I know." She brought his hand up to her cheek and held it there. "Come back alive." He gave a wordless nod, and she strode away.

I'll make things right, he promised. *Just as soon as I get back.*

"That's all that will fit," Idra declared, speaking of the armor.

Walde studied his band of misfits. Albin, Abbe, and Grella stood alongside Shin and Zon. No one had expected timid Shin to become an expert on the blowpipe, but she had taken to it at once and her climbing skills were as good as Walde's. He hoped he hadn't made a mistake by including her in the company. Nine Harborlanders stood ready beside Walde; all had become proficient with the blowpipe and had become better climbers as a result. Among them were Cadar, Lerin, and Hess—three of the five who had come through the crack in the First. Walde pursed his lips, wondering if it had been wise to deprive the village of its best fighters.

He chased the thought away. Chances were this same team would confront the next group of guards.

Idra pressed a small wooden box into his hand. "The poison," she explained and then moved on to Albin and Abbe. Frey was also making her way through the group, anointing everyone with green and brown paint from a little wooden jar. Walde leaned down to let her cool fingers run over his face and neck, leaving wet trails behind them. She promised, "It'll dry quickly."

Unable to see his own face, he glanced curiously at the others. The green mimicked leaves, the brown shadows.

As the group began boarding boats, he looked back at the village. It took him a moment to realize who he was searching for: his father.

He sighed and turned away. It was probably for the best that Carrac was in the wastes. Walde couldn't endure his disapproving looks any more. Or the distance that had grown between them.

This time there were enough boats to accommodate everyone. Walde paddled with Zon. The hunter had removed his pelt, and with the cap and face paint, Walde scarcely recognized him.

They paddled swiftly through the early morning gloom. The armor looked heavy, but it was actually quite light. The metal chest plates had been hammered thin and shifted as he moved, giving him a measure of comfort. They were also quieter than he'd expected.

He paused to scratch his scalp where the edge of the cap sat. A shiver of foreboding ran through him as he did. What new toys would the guards have now? He had assumed that the small number of intruders meant more would appear, but it could also be that they were more dangerous. If that were the case, Walde should have gathered a larger company to meet them.

Too late now.

The oar slipped, and he grasped it more firmly, but not before Zon got an eyeful of his glimmering hands.

"Stop thinking," the hunter grumbled, then returned his stern gaze to the river.

The beach came up swiftly, and they drew the boats up on shore. Without a word, they formed a line and began their hike up the slope. The air was sticky, the stones damp with morning dew. An eerie glow from the rising sun lay on the stand of stunted trees. The forest was quiet. Perhaps a little *too* quiet.

The slope plateaued. Walde was about to pause and do a careful scan of the trees when Abbe tugged on his arm and pointed. Walde jerked to a sudden stop. A man knelt in the path, perhaps fifteen yards ahead. He wore metal armor and a shortsword. His quiver lay on the ground beside him. As he sighted Walde, he raised his hands over his head and shouted for mercy.

Abbe said, "He's caught in the foothold trap."

Walde didn't respond. His eyes were locked on the man's face. Even with the distance and shadow, he recognized it. How could he forget the image from the dead guard's locket?

Walde took a slow step back. "Whistle to the sentinel," he murmured to Albin, who was just behind Zon.

The youth obeyed at once.

He received no answer.

The man was still now, his eyes fixed on Walde. Walde moistened his lips and spoke softly, without looking back. "Into the trees. Now."

The moment they dove for the trunks, arrows rained down, a couple of them pinging off armor. As Walde suspected, the guards had hid in the trees on either side of the foothold trap. He climbed swiftly, higher and higher, until the leaves all but concealed the path below. The man in the foothold trap roared in anger, and there came a muttering of voices. *The guards,* Walde thought, *frantically regrouping.* A grim smile touched his lips. He glanced around him at the others. Zon was at his side, Albin and Abbe just below, but climbing fast. Leaves rustled in the oak across the path, and he glimpsed Shin's dark braid through the branches. Cadar's beaky nose peeked through leaves just behind her.

Walde made a birdcall: *Higher.*

On they climbed. And their enemies waited, trapped in the trees. If either group climbed down now, they would be at the mercy of those in the branches. It was either attack or retreat and be attacked later. Walde chose attack.

The time came when the leaves ceased quivering and the branches swaying. Walde loosed another birdcall: *Advance*.

The big old oaks had grown together, tangling their branches. Even so, there weren't many safe places to cross from one tree to the next, and Walde was acutely aware of the heavy man behind him. A branch that bore Walde's weight might not bear both his and Zon's. So he chose his path carefully, keeping his eyes peeled for movement in the branches ahead.

Having crossed to the next tree, he didn't pause at the trunk but identified the thickest branch that extended toward the guards' tree and mounted it. He crept forward like a spider approaching its prey. Despite Zon's bulk, the hunter was equally quiet. Albin, Abbe, Cadar, and a handful of other Harborlanders followed in the surrounding branches.

The near silence was eerie. The guards waited by the trunk as their quarry approached from above, probably sure of victory. After all, Walde's company had abandoned the lower horizontal branches that were necessary for archery and now seemed tangled somewhere in the upper ones. If they'd guessed the truth, he doubted they would've allowed their enemies to get so close.

Walde edged closer until the six guards were just visible in patches through the leaves. A murmur of low voices trickled up to him. None of it made sense until Walde heard the unmistakable words: "Fire at will."

His eyes closed briefly, and he drew a shaky breath. Fear had fled, leaving behind a rising excitement that was edged with something darker. He shoved it down ruthlessly and focused on the task ahead. He made a birdcall: *Now*.

While clenching the branch with his legs, he selected a dart from the pouch secured to his belt and held it between his teeth. The dart was only four inches long from blackened point to feathered tail. His hands were gratifyingly steady as he removed a tiny poison box and opened it. A sticky brownish substance coated the bottom. He dipped the dart and held its tail in one hand while stowing the box in the pouch with his other. All of this took only a few heartbeats.

An arrow thudded into a branch near his head. Another disturbed leaves just below him.

Stop thinking.

Zon's words were a calming litany. Walde slid the brown pipe out of its leather sheath and used it to gently part the leaves.

A man's face came into view through a web of branches. It was a good, open target. He made one last birdcall: *Fire.* Then he loaded the dart and set the pipe to his mouth.

CHAPTER 20

Too many things happened at once.

Just as the poison darts rained down, some hitting their targets, others flicking off metal armor, a horn call sounded. Walde had no time to lie still in shock as the message sank in, leaching its own terrible poison. He stowed his pipe and poison box and spidered back toward the trunk of the neighboring tree. The guards' enraged shouts were soon followed by another volley of whizzing arrows. One landed dangerously close to Albin's neck as the lad retreated down a slender branch.

The distant horn call blasted again, and Walde, now safe around the other side of a trunk, dragged a hand across his face. Three dozen invaders sighted at the northern fringe. Three dozen.

He shoved down a black despair. The former Woodlanders must have united with the Harborlands' elders to create this trap. And they had done it with ease. Thirty-six guards were at the very edge of what the village could handle all at once.

But the number wasn't three dozen. When one included the twelve Walde was currently engaging, it was forty-eight. The council had settled on forty as the upper limit of what they could successfully defeat. At forty-eight, Idra would demand that Tir initiate the escape plan.

But he wouldn't. Of course he wouldn't. How could Walde have thought otherwise? Vengeance still burned in Tir, and no one, not even level-headed Idra, would be able to dissuade him from fighting.

He cursed himself for encouraging the Harborlanders' passions.

What would happen to Brite? Would she and the younger children flee, or would they be compelled by the Harborlanders to stay back and fight?

The crashing sound of falling bodies forced his mind back to the present. Some of the guards must already have succumbed to the poison. A hand fell on his wrist, and he looked up to meet Albin's anguished gaze. "Do you think the Harborlanders will follow the escape plan?"

"No. I don't." Walde slid his bow out of his quiver and went about stringing it. "So we have to make an end of these guards and get back."

Albin gave a jerky nod. Zon, who leaned on a branch next to him, growled, "My nephew is back there."

Walde said, "I know. But we can't head back while these guards are on our heels. String your bows!" he shouted to Shin and the others, then started down the trunk. Another body crashed to the ground, followed by a howl of rage.

The moment he reached a sturdy lower branch, an arrow pinged against his chest. His attacker was the man who had been caught in the foothold trap. The guard had slipped free and was now firing at whomever he could glimpse in the leaves.

Walde dispatched him with a single arrow to the neck.

He was no longer even trying to quell his emotions. Doing so would dampen the onrush of heat that now tore through his veins. He would kill them all.

Zon pushed in front of him and scrambled up the heavy branch toward the guards' tree. The two guards still standing at the trunk jumped down and fled up the path. Two in the opposite tree did the same. With a roar, Zon leapt to the ground and tore after them. He downed one before the rest of the group joined him in a frenzied charge. Shin, Walde, and Albin each took down one, and then it was over. More heaps of bodies to clutter the path. And a terrible fight still ahead.

Shin nudged the female guard she had killed. Her thin lips tightened, and she looked quickly aside.

Hess bent down to tighten a makeshift bandage on his leg. He must have caught an arrow in the fighting.

Albin kicked the ground with his heel. "I wish I hadn't left my horn with Frey."

Cadar seized Walde's shoulder. "My girl is back there..."

"I know. Mine too." His Reacher light still burned as he looked around at the anxious faces. "Frey was supposed to signal if they chose the escape plan. But she didn't." He glanced down the path toward the river. "We have to go back."

Even as he spoke, a distant clamor carried over the river toward them. The hair stood up on the backs of Walde's arms and his legs weakened. But the surge of fear was swiftly replaced by anger. How dare the Woodlanders attack treefolk who were just trying to live in peace? The Reachers were restoring a dying Mothertree, and what did they get in return? Ruination.

No. It couldn't happen.

Just as when he had chased his father's raft down the Nadi, he found his legs moving. Footsteps thudded behind him as the others struggled to catch up. But only Zon reached his side and paced him.

Walde said, "You shouldn't have come back to this place."

Zon made no reply. They broke through the scrubby trees and started down the slope, half-sliding down the scree. The others weren't far behind.

An angry purple smudge now hung over the mountains, deepened by the rising sun. Walde prayed it wouldn't come any closer. "We'll tie up at the edge of the field and take stock of the situation from there," he said as the others clambered into the boats. A distant scream from the direction of the village made his teeth slam together. He pushed the boat into the water and leapt in.

Their quiet paddling could not drown out the distant cries. *Don't think,* Walde pleaded to himself. Anger was fine, but another onslaught of fear would render him useless. He glanced back at the others and was pleased to see determination on their faces rather than dread.

They pulled up alongside a willow oak and carried the boats up onto the rocky shore. Then they paused in a tight huddle and looked at Walde.

The screams had died down, leaving only a distant murmur of voices.

"It's too open," Albin whispered. "We can't approach from the field. They'll see us."

"Not," Walde said, "if we hide in the river."

Albin's violet eyes widened. "Of course. We can creep along the dock."

Cadar poked his long nose between them. "And then what?"

Albin said, "We keep going until we're far enough past the First that they won't see us get out. Then we sneak back, climb the First, and get them with blow darts."

The others were nodding along to this plan. Walde's anger had turned cold. He sensed it burning in his eyes now rather than in his hands. He removed his armor and set it quietly on the shore. "We can't let the slightest sound give us away. And the weight will drag us down." He added his bow and quiver to the pile, then eyed the blowpipe worriedly. It wouldn't do to get it wet. Or the darts.

Albin said, "We'll have to carry it between our teeth."

Shin chewed her lip. "W-w-what about the darts?"

Zon removed his cap and wrapped a bowstring twice around his head, securing it tightly at his temple. He unhooked the dart pouch and latched it over the bowstring. The pouch now hung sideways over his ear. Albin snickered at it. Walde's mouth remained a tight line. The very real possibility that Brite had been captured made him impatient to move on. One by one, they all copied Zon until each had a brown goat's ear hanging from their head.

"Keep your head up," Walde warned them. "And be careful not to splash."

He winced as he waded into the icy water, the pipe an awkward weight between his teeth. The river spilled down from the mountains, carrying with it the summer's melted ice. He wondered how long they could be immersed in it before losing feeling in their limbs. It was just another thing to worry about. He set it aside and pushed off. The river's floor dropped quickly, but near the shore it was only a few feet deep. The others waded quietly behind him. Fortunately, they were moving with the current, and before long they reached the outer edge of the dock. The thick wooden wall rose three feet above water, concealing them from view.

It was going to work. No one had spied them yet, and Walde was growing accustomed to the cold. If they all kept quiet, they would pass right by the guards and on toward the children's dead tree. From there, they could cross to the forested slope behind the Mothertrees and double back to the First. He gripped the dock's softening wood and pulled himself along. The others waded in a line behind him, pipes swaying a little between their teeth. The tips of the First's branches hung over them now, yet he heard no voices. Perhaps the guards were eating.

Heavy footfalls fell on the boardwalk. Walde sank a little lower but didn't stop moving.

Then a voice thundered over the water. "We see you. Stop and hand up your weapons. Now!"

Walde went still. His nails, full of dock slime and bits of wood, slid on the rotting boards. Denial washed through him. This couldn't be it. It couldn't be over this easily. Perhaps the man was bluffing. Perhaps there would be only a few guards, easily overcome.

He drew a steadying breath, gripped the edge of the dock, and pushed up.

A terrible sight met his eyes. The ground was littered with bodies. Villagers and guards, sprawled over roots and paths, bloodied and still. Perhaps twenty guards remained, but each was equipped with a bow, a sword, and armor. Worst of all, they held Idra hostage. The usually stout-hearted woman was on her knees on a path, her chest heaving, her hands brightened in fear. Blood dripped from a wound on her arm. Her captor had rested his sword blade on her shoulder. In a single movement, he could slit her throat.

But of course, he wouldn't. The guards meant to hold Idra hostage until their prisoners were fully restrained.

Walde had no energy to move, but the arrow aimed at his neck gave him no choice. Clinging with one hand to the dock, he removed his blowpipe, pouch, and dagger and tossed it all up to the waiting guards. The others did the same until the boardwalk was littered with weapons. A couple of guards gathered them up and tossed them into a space between two roots. The way they glanced at each other while handling the blowpipes made Walde doubt they knew what the weapons were.

The first guard barked again. "Out of the water. Now."

Shin loosed a strangled cry, and Walde turned to find her draped over the edge of the dock, trembling violently and blazing light. Walde had managed to keep calm until now, but a wisp of light escaped him as he observed her.

"Now," the guard repeated, his sharp eyes on Walde's hands.

Somehow, he found the energy to drag himself up out of the water. If only he'd kept some of the poison on his body. Behind his ear or in his hair. Why hadn't he thought of it?

As he struggled to his feet, a morbid desire to locate Brite's body overtook him, but the guards gave him no opportunity to look. After being frisked, he was escorted along with the others to the repaired path that led from the boardwalk to the First's trunk. Cadar muttered something under his breath and was rewarded with a sound whack from the flat of a sword. Walde, Zon, and Shin were placed in a row beside Idra. Albin, Grella, and Abbe were lined up next to them, followed by the Harborlanders, a long line along the path with guards placed behind each prisoner. A tall female guard carrying lengths of rope strode leisurely to the end of the line and wrenched Cadar's hands behind him. Walde jerked his head straight at the touch of cold metal on his neck. A guard must be behind him on the lip of the path.

A gray-haired man wearing a red tunic under his armor walked down the path alongside the prisoners. When he spoke, his voice was tighter than a bowstring. "If you move or speak without my consent, you die. Understand?" After a pause, he added, "Answer me."

The blade grazed Walde's neck again. "Understood," he said quickly and heard his words echoed by others.

"Good." The man strode past. Walde couldn't turn his head to watch him march to the end of the line, but the heavy thudding of his boots made him aware of his location at all times.

He must have turned on his heel and started back, for the sound increased again. Walde ached to kill him. The desire was potent enough to stir his Reacher light.

Albin, standing next to Walde, made a small sound in his throat as the man stopped in front of him.

"That's him, Cap'n," Albin's captor spat as his superior leaned in to study the boy. "Hasn't changed much either."

A female guard from the boardwalk muttered, "They never do."

So these guards *were* former Woodlanders. They'd have to be to recognize Albin, who'd once lived in their community.

The captain unbuckled his sack and dug out a sentinel horn. At the sight of it, Albin's face turned white. Walde knew what scorched thought must be passing through his mind: Frey had carried that horn. Where was she now?

The man thrust it at Albin. "Call the sentinels back here. All of them. Now." He leaned in and added, "And be sure to make the right call. If they don't return, these girls beside you will die."

The horn fell heavily into the youth's arms. Albin's head drooped, then in an unbearably tender gesture, he brought it to his chest and cradled it. After an impatient bark from the captain, he brought it to his lips and made the call. "It'll take time," he croaked afterward, his voice roughened from the tears that must have gathered behind his throat, "for them to come back,"

"I'll give them an hour."

The captain probably assumed that the sentinels were the missing cursed children. Despite the death threat, Grella and Abbe remained silent and still. Their strength inspired Walde to dredge up his own. If there was even a chance of escape— and the returning sentinels might provide that chance—he had to remain calm and ready.

The captain retrieved the horn and returned it to the sack.

His boots thudded twice more before pausing again. Walde felt the weight of his eyes but would not meet them. He fixed his gaze instead on what he could spy of the bodies. All in his line of sight were either fallen guards or Harborlanders. Tir. Cor...

The captain's tight bark jerked his attention back to the path. "Are there other Reachers here besides you four?" The guard stood in front of Zon, but his head swiveled to include Shin, Walde, and Idra. "I will know, either now or later. But if you tell me now, I'll remember that and treat you accordingly. Understand?"

Silence.

The blade bit, ever so slightly, into Walde's neck. Blood dribbled down, pausing to pool in his collarbone before finding its way to his chest.

"Very well." The captain flicked his hand, and the blade relaxed. Turning on his heel, he marched back down the line. "Throw the leaves in," he said over his shoulder.

A terrible premonition swept through Walde. He braved the blade at his neck and turned his head toward the cook fire. A female guard was emptying a box of something into a pot. The captain strode on, booted feet pounding like a beater on a funeral drum. *Thud thud thud.* The cauldron steamed. *Thud thud thud.*

A breeze stirred the air, carrying with it a sickly sweet scent. Walde's stomach twisted at the smell, and his palms brightened. He didn't know the herb's name, but he knew what it could do—drug his mind so he couldn't control his emotions. Make him dazed but still able to sense the damage his pain would inflict on the tree.

Suddenly, Zon roared and grabbed the blade at his neck with bare, blazing hands. The guard who had been busy binding the prisoners' wrists came to help Zon's captor restrain him, but the hunter's strength overwhelmed them both. At a shout from the captain, a third slammed the hunter down over the path and held him while others bound his bloodied wrists.

Do something, Walde thought desperately. Four Reachers might be enough to damage the tree if they were forced to drink the infusion. He could already feel the familiar hum of the link weakening as if battered by an angry wind. Zon and Idra were both maddened by fear. Sandwiched between the two, Shin moaned and whimpered, her Reacher light blazing.

We're all going to die anyway. The terrible thought scudded through him, numbing him with dread. Without the Reachers, there would be no Mothertrees.

Walde almost jumped as his captor swore under his breath.

Albin's captor asked, "Are they biting you too?"

"Lin, see what's sucking my neck. I'm sure something's there."

"I'm busy bandaging this freak's hands. Deal with it."

The captain tilted his head up. "Brin, did you find anyone up there?"

"No, Cap'n," a woman called down breathlessly from somewhere above. "The tree's empty."

"Good. Find a look-out spot and watch for the returning sentinels."

The woman made no reply.

"Brin?" the captain queried.

There was a rustle of leaves, then a crash like something heavy tumbling through branches. Walde braved the blade at his neck once more to look up. He scarcely had time to leap away before a body crashed onto the path where he'd been standing. The female guard collapsed on top of Walde and Albin's captors. Before Walde could draw another breath, several more of the captors simply dropped, their bodies falling backward onto roots, their swords clattering on the path.

The commotion was punctuated by a distant childish giggle. Walde was stunned for the length of a heartbeat, then his fists clenched and his chest swelled with air. "Fight!" he roared.

He and two others who still had free hands dove for the guards' weapons. Walde unsheathed a guard's dagger, turned and threw it at the captain, who had drawn his sword on a Harborlander. Brite's training paid off. The blade sank into the man's unprotected back. He made a coughing sound, then fell forward and went still.

Another crazed giggle fell into the space of silence that followed. The remaining guards' eyes darted at the branches. Sweat dripped down their temples and pebbled across their brows. Their superstitious dread of the cursed children had clearly returned full force.

Several more guards had dropped since the first ones, leaving only three on the path and one on the boardwalk. After losing their leader, the guard on the boardwalk leapt into the river. Surrounded, the other three had no choice but to fight. Walde raced over to the small hill of confiscated weapons and retrieved a strung bow and quiver. After missing twice, he managed to incapacitate one guard and kill another. Cadar cut down the third, but not without taking injuries. By the time it was over, only Cadar, the cursed children, and the Reachers still lived. There was no sign of the escaped guard.

Walde's nose wrinkled at the sickly sweet smell that now permeated the air. With an angry kick, he knocked the pot off the coals and upended it on the ground.

A boy's wavering reflection looked up at him from the retreating liquid.

CHAPTER 21

The storm over the mountains had lingered, grumbling distantly like some hungry beast.

Walde knelt beside Buzz so that they could talk eye to eye. The boy clutched a small blowpipe with white-knuckled fingers. His eyes were wild, the pack across his back grubby with dirt. Walde had showered him with praise and promised that he was safe, but still the boy could not focus. Idra was the only other person who could've provided details on what had happened, but she had passed out, either from stress or blood loss. Possibly both. Grella tended to her wounds.

Walde reviewed in his mind the few facts Buzz had given him.

The Harborlanders had refused to leave the village and even pressured the cursed children to stay with them and fight. Idra had argued with them, but they hadn't listened.

Walde gripped the boy's shoulders and shook him gently. "Buzz. Look at me."

"I'm lookin'."

"Good. I want you tell me what happened to the other cursed children."

"The others..."

"Yes. Everyone who didn't stay here."

The boy looked down, as if it hurt to hold Walde's gaze. "After all the arguing, they didn't have time to do the escape plan. So they ran over there..." He swung his free hand down the boardwalk at the neighboring Mothertree.

Walde jolted to his feet.

Behind him, Cadar demanded, "They're hiding in that tree?"

"No." Buzz dropped his arm. "They're hiding in its corpse darkness. With all the bones." His mouth twitched, and a nervous bubble of laughter burst out. He coughed as if to hide it and turned away.

Walde's sympathy for him was overwhelmed by an urgent need to find Brite. Muttering hasty thanks, he took off at a run. Cadar and Albin weren't far behind. The three raced down the boardwalk until the repaired section came to an end, then picked their way over roots toward the neighboring tree's trunk.

"It's over here," Albin called from the back of a particularly large root.

Walde rushed over to the shadowy gap at the root's base and sighed with relief at the cut vines. "Wait!" he hissed as Cadar scrambled down. "They don't know it's us yet. All they've heard is muffled voices. If you open the door now, you might get attacked."

Cadar straightened abruptly and stepped aside. Walde stared at the door for several moments before dropping to a crouch and placing his face near the tiny gap under the door's handle. Wetting his lips, he whistled the tune to his dream song.

A muffled cry broke into the melody. Loosing a groan, Walde flung open the door and dragged a dusty Brite out of the darkness and onto the weedy ground nearby. He clung to her, smelling ash and mushrooms, holding her clenched, trembling hands while she wept.

***

A couple of long, hard days followed.

The villagers had neither the wood nor the energy to burn the bodies, so they hauled them to the neighboring trees' corpse darknesses and tossed them in unburned. The action would have shocked the villagers a few months ago; now it was just another decision that had to be made.

Two full days passed before Walde was able to piece together all that had happened.

Idra, unable to dissuade the Harborlanders from fighting, decided to stay with them rather than hide with the others. The invaders approached from the neighboring tree, and from the dryness of their clothes, Idra suspected that they'd crossed at a bridge. She killed three guards before being injured herself. But because she leaked Reacher light, the captain spared her life. How the man had guessed that Walde and the others were in the water remained a mystery.

Sadly, Albin's aunt was killed alongside the Harborlanders. Her son and Frey wisely hid with a few other cursed children in a corpse darkness two trees down from the First. They planned to wait there until nightfall so they could steal out and follow the escape plan. They tried to get Buzz to hide with them, but the boy broke away, saying he'd hide elsewhere. Instead, he raced back to the First and crouched in its lower branches. There, he observed the entire fight, awaiting the moment when the guards were still enough for him to fire off his tiny darts.

Once Walde got him talking, Buzz revealed an important piece of news: that he'd shot a dart at the guard on the boardwalk before she'd escaped into the river.

This relieved some of the tension that gripped the village. But not enough. On the morning after the bodies were interred, a newly widowed mother gathered her young children and set off for the Harborlands to live with her parents, promising not to breathe a word to anyone about her time in the Woodlands.

Her husband's death had been a shock to her. She'd believed him to be safe at a sentinel post. Sadly, he and two other Harborlanders at the north fringe had abandoned their posts to join in the fight. It was through them, and not Frey, that the captain had come into possession of the horn.

Only twelve adult non-Reachers remained in the village now. The reduced number meant that they had to readjust their priorities. Work on the First ceased, and the villagers divided their time between sentinel duty, daily chores, and gathering food. There was little joy in their movements, and the empty training field stood like a monument to the stillborn dream of their fight against the elders. Everyone knew that if there were another attack, they would simply flee. And that made the First more of a hideout than a home.

It was even less than that for the Reachers. Their supply of daleroot had finally run dry, and at the worst possible time. Several began spending their sleeping hours at the dead tree. Even Zon, who'd managed without daleroot until the fit that had damaged his hands. Walde didn't know how much he'd miss the ever-present hunter until he was gone. "Can't protect you with these hands," he'd said simply and wandered off.

A deep, unquenchable loneliness took hold of Walde, worsened by the unresolved issues that hung between him and Brite. Much of it probably had to do with just how hard he worked at blocking things out. He couldn't let himself dwell on what had happened, or worse, what might still happen, without stirring emotions he desperately needed to keep in check. Grief. Guilt. Anger. Fear. So he retreated to a lonely space in his mind and relentlessly pushed back the darkness.

All the while, the First's link called to him, as it must have been calling to all the Reachers—with a desperate pulsing. A damaged link was worse than a crooked frame on a wall. One could walk away from the frame and forget it for a time. Not so with a link. Day and night, it plucked at him. And he *wanted* to repair it. The desire to plunge himself into the tunnel—into that place of forgetting—had crept on him again. At times, when he lay in bed beside Brite in the darkness, he imagined getting up, going to the trunk, and just reaching. But it never happened. He couldn't explain why, even to himself. The last time he'd tried to reach, he had failed. Perhaps he worried that he would fail again, and if so, what that would mean. His father had once told him that he was strong. Walde had to admit that he had been proud of that. His power had become part of who he was. How he saw himself. How would it be then if he lost the ability to reach altogether?

But choosing not to reach amounted to the same thing. And he wasn't permitted to make that choice. Not when the life of his child depended on a healthy link.

***

Four days after the attack, Carrac returned from the wastes. The fact that he didn't go to Walde the moment he came back spoke to how tense their relationship had become. It didn't get any better after Albin explained what had happened during his absence.

Walde sat at the cook fire, smoking strips of meat and furtively watching his father and Albin as they spoke in low tones on the path. Carrac had been nodding along without much expression until Albin said something that caused his face to fall. Walde didn't doubt it was news that Uncle Caln was dead. The old Reacher's heart had given out on him in the arguing that had followed the horn call.

Walde told himself that Caln might have died anyway, regardless of what happened. However, that didn't ease his guilt over the other deaths. If Walde hadn't stoked the Harborlanders' desire to fight, they might've gone right along with the escape plan instead of arguing with Idra. Lives might've been spared.

Mouth tightening, Walde turned away.

Carrac requested that the council hold a meeting that very evening. None had been held since the attack. Idra and Zon were still recovering from their injuries, and the rest had taken more frequent sentinel posts. But all managed to be present that evening in the dead tree's meeting hut. They sat on chairs around the table, Idra and Zon still pale but neatly bandaged, Shin curled into herself, hiding her chewed fingers, Bran tight-lipped and tense beside her, Nessa and Albin staring morosely off at the open window. Walde sat at his old place at the end of the table, his finger tracing a raised knot in the wood. After a long silence, Carrac, who sat calmly at his side, asked, "Why are we here, in *this* tree?"

Idra straightened from her slump. Her mouth opened and closed twice before she blurted, "Why are *you* here? You take off for weeks at a time without telling anyone where you're going or why, then you come back and expect everyone to jump at your demands and answer your questions." Her lips quivered as her words ran out.

Bran's already tense face had reddened with anger during this speech, and Reacher light leaked from his clenched fists. The moment Idra stopped, he stood up and demanded to know where Carrac had been.

Carrac's eyes widened, and as he looked from Bran and Idra to the other council members, some sort of understanding passed over his face. He stood slowly, pushed in his chair, and walked out the door.

Walde sat with his head in his hands for several moments before loosing a sour laugh. "That'll show him."

Bran's chair scraped the floor as he dropped back into it.

Idra touched Walde's arm. "I'm sorry. I'm not myself. Maybe you should go after him."

"And say what?"

She shrugged and looked down. "I don't know. He hasn't been here for the past two weeks, so he doesn't understand… why things are the way they are."

She meant *we*, Walde thought. The way *we* are.

Nessa said, "I wonder what he wanted to talk about."

Albin yawned and blinked his shadowy eyes. "I already told him everything that happened."

Bran said in a subdued voice, "Whatever it was couldn't have been important, or he wouldn't have left."

No one spoke for a time. Walde traced the knot again, then drew a long breath through his nostrils and forced himself to say what he must. "He probably wanted to discuss the failing link."

No one stirred at those words but Albin. The youth jerked back as if awaking from some dream and regarded Walde in confusion. "The link is failing?"

Walde gave a tight nod. "It was damaged on the day of the attack, and unless it's repaired, the First will go back to the way it was before. And it won't take years to do so. The tree hadn't completely recovered *after* I repaired the link. Now that it's damaged, its fall will be swift. Its—"

"Then repair it!" Albin interjected. "Why sit here and talk about this while the tree is dying?"

Walde brought his folded hands to his chin. "Reaching isn't like lighting a lamp, Albin. One has to be in the right frame of mind and feel free to let go. That hasn't been easy for any of us lately." Several heads nodded in assent to these words. Walde smiled tightly. There it was. He wasn't alone.

Nessa said, "Carrac could do it. He hasn't been around through all the killing."

Walde sighed, and his smile fell. "I'm afraid he couldn't. Carrac can maintain an already healthy link, but not one that's damaged. Someone has to enter a link to repair it, and my father has never done that." He felt a twinge of guilt at sharing this secret, but he didn't think his father would care.

Shin whispered, "Couldn't you teach him?" She spoke so seldom that everyone straightened at her question.

"No. I've spoken to him about it, and he's happy with how he is." Walde tried to keep the sour tone from his voice, but it crept in anyway. "To be honest, I'm not even sure that he could."

Albin looked around at the others with wide eyes. "What are we saying, then? That we're just going to give up and let it die?"

"Of course not," Walde said. "We'll have to have another song rite. Tomorrow." He paused, waiting for a reaction from the others, but only Albin nodded. Walde asked, "Is this something we need to vote on?"

"No," Idra said when no one else responded. "But you might have trouble finding Reachers to participate."

After asking around, Walde learned that she was right. The other Reachers agreed to attend if Walde did the reaching but would not attempt it themselves, *could not* in their present state of mind.

Anxiety bubbled up in him as he considered that. If he failed again, then the other Reachers would lose confidence in his power and maybe even in their own. He ought to wait, but that was one thing he couldn't do. The link couldn't wait. "I'll do it," he said.

CHAPTER 22

Walde couldn't have asked for a more beautiful evening. The air was soft and still; warmth from the day's heat was gradually dissipating as the azure sky darkened to black. He had watched it change from rose to violet as he waited for the villagers to gather around the trunk. Frey had removed a couple of expendable posts so that all Reachers could attend. By chance, Brite was on sentinel duty that evening. She could have swapped her shift with one of the Reachers but she hadn't asked to. Perhaps she'd suspected that Walde would fail and didn't have the heart to watch it happen.

A familiar figure on the boardwalk banished Brite from his mind. Carrac unshouldered his quiver and a heavy pack by the cook fire and ambled up the path toward the trunk. Walde tried to catch his gaze as he lowered himself down by the other Reachers, but Carrac seemed determined not to look at him.

So be it. He was not here to please his father. The only thing that mattered was the link.

He felt it now in rolling waves. One moment, it was so faint he could barely sense it, the next, it swept over him like a storm surge. He could block it out if he focused on the task. That was probably what the other Reachers were doing. All six sat on the courtyard that surrounded the trunk—Bran, Shin, Nessa, and Carrac near the front, Zon and Idra at the back. A handful of Harborlanders and more than a dozen cursed children filled in the center. Abbe stood with her lyra before the crowd, small hands waiting to work their magic. Lamps hanging on the branches above lit her pale face and tightly braided hair. Walde laid a hand lightly on her shoulder, then lowered himself into the crack and closed his eyes. Idra hadn't volunteered to intone the ancient chant, and Walde didn't trust himself to recall the words properly, so he would go on without them.

His dream song awoke from Abbe's fingers, soft at first, but hinting at the climb to come. Walde pulled his attention away from it and focused on the brilliant sliver of the horned moon rising over the forest. Its light was strong and silvery, like his own, and so far removed from the world below that Walde could imagine there was no world. Only the darkness and light in that far-off place.

The moon blurred then, and the expansiveness hit him. As if the link sensed it and responded, its rolling presence crashed over, sweeping him along with it. But much as he wanted to, he couldn't enter it. Instead, he hung like something snared at its entrance.

He didn't know how long he remained that way, desperate to let go but unable to do so. It was an exquisite form of torture.

Perhaps it was the lyra's silence that brought him back. He blinked his eyes open and looked around.

The villagers were all still there, their hopeful faces lit by the hanging lamps. Walde couldn't speak. Without thought, he climbed out of the crack and drew the lyra out of Abbe's startled hands. An urge to know if any part of him from the Lakelands had survived overcame him. He snatched up the bow from the box and set it to the lyra.

He drew out a song rite tune, choosing one at random, only to realize halfway through that it was the last song he'd performed with his friend, Jak. He relived the instant when Jak's playing had faltered and Walde had guided them into a new song, one he had dreamed. Sweat dribbled down his brow. As the dream song woke from his fingers, something desperate, full of longing, emerged. His eyes closed, and he grimaced as memories clambered, unexpectedly, into his mind.

They weren't from the Lakelands.

Once more, he saw Fin fall to his death, felt the soft cheek of the dead guard. His teeth clenched and the bow shrieked as the Harborlanders perished, Tir, Cor; their screams echoed up the river. Zon gripped a sword with his bare hands, Buzz blew death from the low branch of a Mothertree.

All of it ripped out of him, raw and fire-bright, until with a cry he dropped the bow and crumpled to the ground.

No one had moved. His head shook as he lifted his eyes to their haunted faces. These were not treefolk anymore. It wasn't their home that made them who they were; it was them. And Walde had destroyed that, along with himself. He had drawn them all into his death song and played them out like so many notes. And now, it was too late. Leaves dropped around him, pale in his silver light. He sensed the frail link still, but the tree was badly damaged.

He stood shakily and found his voice. "Garen was right," he croaked. "I didn't tell you the whole truth. In fact, I withheld the most important thing. The only real piece of advice Thara ever gave me." He dragged his sleeve roughly across his wet eyes. "She said 'stay true to who you are and what you are. If you do not, you will fail.'" At these words, Carrac's face dropped into his hand. Walde plunged on ruthlessly. "Do you know what that means?" He looked around. "What am I? What are we all?"

"Treefolk," Bran murmured.

"Yes. And treefolk don't mass together to kill. I knew that. But I proposed we fight anyway, even though most of us knew nothing about killing. So now this is what we get. Loss of life. A dying tree. Reachers who can't reach. I'm sorry. I'm so very sorry."

A long silence fell and then Bran spoke. "I don't think there's anything wrong with defending one's home from invaders. But it's not something treefolk have had to do before, and we're not trained guards so we weren't prepared for it."

"It's not about being prepared," Walde said gently. "Every time we kill, we anger our enemies, so it becomes an endless cycle of killing, and waiting, and then killing again. How can Reachers find peace in such a storm when there's fear and sorrow all around us? We can't. And maybe we shouldn't." He lowered himself to the ground and leaned into an arm. A soft wind blew. He felt a hand on his shoulder, warm, but not warm enough. When would this misery end? Never. Not until they were all dead and the tree with them. But his child and the cursed children needed a Mothertree to grow.

"Walde. Son."

He lifted his head and found his father's calm face, only inches from his own.

At that moment, a vision entered his mind, drawn from that peaceful place in his father's eyes. Walde loosed a shaky breath and gripped his father's arm. "It's time to tell them," he whispered. "Tonight."

***

Carrac said, "She's a third the size of an adult tree, and her lowest branches have already started to level." He spoke eagerly to the council, his arms extending as he illustrated his beloved tree's structure. The others, having recovered from their initial anger that this secret had been kept from them, listened thoughtfully.

At first, Carrac had been reluctant to part from his secret, but once Walde told him about Brite's pregnancy, his attitude changed. Now he was determined to resettle her and others in a lonely ravine in the wastes. It wasn't a permanent solution, but it was what they needed now.

He went on, "They're not ready to build on yet, but until then, the roots can be lived on. When I was last there, I hiked down to the west end of Killop Ravine where it turns into a low, wet cave. After a bit of exploring, I found storm-felled Mothertree driftwood driven up against the cave walls. Some pieces are big enough to build a sizable shelter. And there's more than enough wood to last through the winter. With the right tools, I'm sure I can build a large enough shelter to winter in." He paused to take a breath.

Idra was shaking her head again. She'd been doing that a lot since she learned of Carrac's tree. She had once been a wastes hunter and was surprised that Carrac had even ventured down into that lonely crack in the land, never mind planted a Mothertree there. The dream Carrac spun of a healthy tree springing up from a meadow, hedged on one side by a curving ravine wall and on the other by a fish-filled river, was astonishing. All the more so for the deserted area in the wastes it inhabited.

It was a small bubble of hope in a dark world.

Carrac continued, "It'll be a long and dangerous hike to get to it though. A week, at least. That's a long time for Brite to be away from a Mothertree."

Walde dragged a hand across his eyes. She would have to risk it. They had no other choice. Even if he *had* restored the link, that wouldn't have resolved the village's other problems.

Albin leaned forward, his face alight with some new thought. "There's another way to get there. The old man told us that if we ever needed to cross the Nadi, we could do it where the Woodlands River runs into it. He said that the river lightens the Nadi's current just enough to allow a crossing."

Walde's heart leapt at the idea. Approaching Killop Ravine from the opposite side of the Nadi would take days off their travel time, not to mention make travel safer.

Albin went on, "But once we cross, we can't go back. There's no river pouring into the Nadi on that side to help us along. We'll have to drag the boats up over the bank and hide them." He chewed his lip. "And we only have five boats. Well, eight if you include the three in storage that need repairs. Still, that's not enough for everyone."

The Reachers glanced awkwardly at one another, then at Walde. At last, Walde drew a breath and told Albin what everyone in the room seemed to know but him. "Some of the Reachers won't be going, at least not yet. So there will be enough room. We'll just put two or three small children in the middle of each boat, and we should be fine."

Albin's jaw slackened. "Why won't some of you be going?"

After a long pause, Idra opened her hands over the table. "We've been hurt, Albin. We've either burned or buried dozens of bodies, some of them men and women who died at our own hands, others friends. Some of us were captured and had to relive memories of our torment in the Harborlands." She glanced at Walde, who had sunk into his chair. "I don't blame you for any of this, Walde. We all made our own choices. Didn't we?"

The other Reachers mumbled their assent. Walde swallowed sharply and clutched his blazing palms in his lap.

Albin's lips compressed. "So you don't want to damage Carrac's tree. That's fine. Just set up a shelter somewhere else along the river."

Carrac said, "The banks outside the gap aren't wide enough, and the tree's roots extend almost to the ravine wall. I'm afraid it's the tree or nothing, lad."

Albin looked around as if in panic. "What will you do then? Where will you go?"

Idra's chair creaked. "Somewhere peaceful and safe. A place where we can heal for a while." Her gaze flicked to Walde's, and he suddenly knew what she wanted—to be back inside the crack with Thara. A wistful glance from Zon and Nessa told Walde they yearned for the same thing. Perhaps they hoped that if Walde kept trying to reach, he would eventually succeed and rekindle the light in the crack so they could step back in. They knew nothing about the terrible risk the task posed to him. He had kept that piece of knowledge a secret, even from Brite.

Walde lowered his head and dragged a hand through his hair. He offered, in scarcely more than a whisper, "It might be possible." He refused to give them more.

Albin stared at them for a long moment before sighing and hunching into his arms.

Idra assured him, "This works out for the best. Not all of us can cross in the boats. Some must stay back and go the long way around. And we will. Eventually."

Walde found himself relieved by her words. He needed time to think about what to do, and having a ready excuse for Brite would help if he chose to remain behind and help the Reachers. He cleared his throat. "This will take a lot of preparation." His gaze moved from Carrac to Albin. "We'll need to bring a good store of dried meat and preserves. And seeds for a garden in the spring. Tools for building, and winter things. Whatever we can carry on our backs." He focused on Carrac. "How deep is the Killop River, anyway? Can it be forded?"

"An adult can cross it, but not a small child. The young ones will have to be carried."

After a space of silence, Albin straightened and looked around. "This is really happening, then? We're really leaving this place?"

Walde's answering smile was touched with relief. No matter what decision the council reached, Albin had enough power over the children that he could forbid them from going if he'd wanted to. But he was a wiser leader than that.

Walde lingered in the meeting hut as everyone filed out. Usually, someone wanted to talk to him privately. He'd expected that person to be his father, so he was surprised when Bran closed the door and strode toward him.

The lines on his forehead had deepened since he'd stepped out of the crack months before, and dark circles haunted his eyes. He halted close to Walde and set a hand on his forearm. "I think you'll be able to light that crack. After Carrac and the children are safely away from this place, we'll all be in a better frame of mind."

When Walde didn't reply, Bran dropped his arm and paced across the room. "I could do with a few days in that peaceful place myself. Thara is aware of what goes on around her links, isn't she? She'd know if invaders were near and let us know so we could leave the crack and escape?"

"Yes. I believe she would."

Bran's eyes closed briefly, and he gave a sound nod. "I suppose you'll go in too. Only for a few days of course, with Brite pregnant and all." He leaned against the wall affixed to the trunk and stared at the floor. Once more, Walde didn't reply. A window shutter creaked in the night breeze. Bran lifted his eyes to it and spoke again. "It'd be few days for you and me, but not for the others. Idra made Albin think she'll be coming out. But I doubt she will. And I wouldn't bet on Shin, Zon, and Nessa coming out anytime soon either."

"I know," Walde said.

"I thought you might, but I just wanted to be sure." He drew a noisy breath from his nostrils, then strode heavily back across the room to the door and left without another word.

Walde fled to his bed to think.

***

Several days passed in a blur of activity. The three extra boats were dragged out of the storage hut in the dead tree and patched. Goods left by the dead Harborlanders and guards were sorted through and the most useful tightly packed into large carry packs. And all the while, the First's leaves fell in a heavy rain on the tree's roots. The relentless sound drove most people back to the dead tree, where they prepared to depart.

The council chose not to reveal the young tree's location until everyone was committed to relocating there. This turned out to be wise, for within a day, two Harborlanders decided to return to the Harborlands and seek out members of the rebellion. Had they known the young tree's location, they might have divulged it under interrogation by the Twenty. Now, all they would know is that the villagers traveled by boat.

Throughout all the activity, Walde kept a stranglehold on his thoughts and emotions. He slipped up only once.

Shortly after the village meeting at which the relocation plan had been revealed, he and Brite sat in their hut sorting through their belongings, deciding which to bring.

"I hope you won't be gone long," she sighed, for the second time that afternoon. "I know you need time to heal, but it's hard to think of us so far away from each other."

Walde rubbed at his eyes. His mouth opened, and then closed. He yearned to promise that they'd be together again soon, but he couldn't find it in himself to lie.

She lifted the bone man and passed a finger over his wooden bag. "Walde, what was your mother's name? I think you told me, but I don't remember."

He straightened from his slump. "Her name was Emry."

"Emry." She laid a hand on her belly. "That's a good name. If it's a girl, I think I'll call her that."

Walde swallowed hard, then got up from the chest and crossed to the window. His Reacher light flared as he leaned on the sill.

He heard Brite's step, then felt her warm body press into his back. She said, "I'm sorry, I shouldn't have reminded you about your mother. We can find another name."

"No." He found her hands and gripped them. "Emry is perfect."

***

A few days later, on a bright but chilly morning, the villagers gathered on the boardwalk with their heavy packs and prepared to leave the Woodlands forever. Walde had never seen all the cursed children together in one place before. The sentinel posts had all been abandoned—something that had not occurred since the previous autumn. Albin's unease at the lack of protection made him loud and jittery. He hopped from place to place, urging the children to move quicker. Carrac's gentle attempts to calm him had no effect.

While Walde stood on the boardwalk, trying not to watch Bran and Elva's farewell, Carrac came to him and offered a rueful smile. "I really made a mess of things between us, didn't I?"

Walde shook his head. "It was a bad situation. And I refused to listen when you warned us about killing."

"True. But I didn't help you either. I just went off and did my own thing." Carrac sighed, then pulled Walde into a tight embrace. Walde leaned his face into Carrac's shoulder. For an instant, he was a child again, basking in his father's affection.

Carrac's deep voice rumbled through him. "My boy, you came so far to find me. Did I ever thank you for that?"

"You didn't need to. You would've done the same for me."

"Yes. I certainly would." Carrac cleared his throat and stepped back. "Well, you'd best be going on ahead of us now. We'll be setting off soon."

There were a few more farewells before Walde and Bran started their trek along the boardwalk toward the Nadi, where they would watch the eight boats cross. Walde clasped hands with Albin, Cadar, Spitfire, Buzz, Frey, Grella, Lina, and Abbe. And there were some he couldn't see off, Tir, Fin, Caln... Guilt threatened to pummel him again, but before it could, he found Brite in his arms.

She trembled against his stiff body, her face wet against his neck. "Please be careful on your way to us. If they catch you—"

"They won't." He smoothed her hair behind her head and then drew her in for one last kiss. His hand grazed her belly where a tiny life grew, closed over by warm, soft flesh. So much more fragile and precious than pod seed. "My love," he whispered.

They couldn't delay any longer. Walde slung his quiver over his shoulder and followed Bran down the boardwalk. As luck would have it, it hadn't rained for some days, so the rotting boards weren't slippery, merely soft and crumbly. Still, they walked well away from the water and the small but dangerous traps that Albin had left, like parting gifts, for whomever dared to invade the Woodlands in the future. They paused to drink and eat twice along the way. It was half a day's walk to the river, and they paced themselves so they would not grow weary.

The ground dipped down as they left the Mothertrees behind and the boardwalk disappeared. The line of boats passed them before they'd reached the Nadi. As planned, Hess and Cadar rowed in the first boat with two cursed children tucked in the middle between them. Albin and Elva followed in the second boat with Elva's two children; Brite and Carrac were third.

The boats rounded a deep curve in the river and disappeared from view. Walde increased his pace, and before long, a worn stone bridge came into view. The bridge allowed travelers on the cart road to cross over the Woodlands River. The eight boats were tied up behind the bridge. The river's current had strengthened as it neared the Nadi, tugging on the boats. The old man's assertion about crossing the big river would soon be put to the test. If it failed, then Hess and Cadar would have a challenge ahead of them as they struggled, perhaps for miles, to reach the opposite shore. The rest of the villagers would have to abandon their boats and take the long way to the ravine.

Walde crept to the edge of the road and looked south. It was empty. For now. He shouted, "South side is clear."

"And the north," added Bran, who had mounted the arched bridge to get a better view. Walde strung his bow and held it ready in case travelers appeared and threatened the crossers. He didn't want to hurt anyone else, but he would if he were forced to.

Hess and Cadar pushed off. The Woodlands River's current plucked them up, and their fierce paddling only added to their momentum as they passed under the bridge and charged into the Nadi. For a time, it looked as though they would fly right across the river like a loosed arrow, but as they reached the middle, they began to veer off course. They paddled frantically but couldn't keep the boat straight. Walde held his breath as they struggled, the current dragging them as they inched forward.

And then the fight was over. The current released them, and they sliced into the reedy shoreline. The children helped the exhausted adults haul the boat up onto land, where it disappeared from view behind some long grass.

The nail-biting sight repeated seven more times. Two boats pulled up farther down river than the others, but not so far that Walde couldn't watch the passengers disembark. Once all the boats had been dragged up and concealed, the crossers huddled on the bank and waved at Walde and Bran. Walde fixed his eyes on Brite's distant shape, as if a rope strung them together across the water. He imagined he would be jerked into the water if she moved away. But when she finally did, he remained fixed where he was.

Only the sound of Bran's tired voice calling to him made Walde turn and hike back into the Woodlands.

CHAPTER 23

Neither of them spoke as they trudged back to the dead tree.

They paused by the cook fire and scavenged what remained of the village's breakfast and then, as one, continued on to the First. The forest felt strange in its emptiness. Walde looked past the Mothertrees to the forested slope that rose behind them. The color seemed brighter somehow. He drew in a breath and scented the river, the familiar sweetness of a flowering vine that grew over the Mothertrees' roots, a drift of pine needles. A sun-warmed breeze brushed his cheek, and he briefly closed his eyes, reliving the softness of Brite's lips.

Why was it that the world burned brighter when one knew their time in it might soon be cut short?

They arrived at the old cook fire in front of the First and joined the others around it.

Bran said, "The crossing went well."

A few pleased words were spoken in response, then silence resumed. Gradually, everyone's eyes drifted to Walde.

In that moment of discomfort, the link's presence swelled and washed over him. He lifted his head and had to physically stop himself from getting up and walking straight up the path to the trunk.

He knew he could reach.

Soon after his confession at the song rite, he had felt a physical change. Some sort of self-imposed block had been lifted from him, making his sleep deeper and his waking hours brighter. He'd begun to feel more himself, and with that change had come an odd sort of clarity. He stood back from everything that had happened. Clouds parted, and light shone on the bare, cold landscape of this reality he now inhabited. But hope glimmered, and he had fixed on it through the long days that had led up to the villagers' relocation.

The link's presence receded. Nervousness fluttered in his core as he tried to decide what to say, how he could convince the others to his way of thinking.

He flinched when Zon snorted. "Whatever you've been chewing must be hard as a bone by now. Just spit it out."

Walde's mouth twitched, but he didn't raise his eyes to the hunter's. He gave a slight shrug. "I've been thinking about the term 'Reacher.'"

"Why?" Nessa mumbled.

Another shrug. "Well, it's an odd word, when you think of it. When someone reaches for something, they don't mean to just brush it with their fingers. They intend to grasp it and even move it from its place. But that's not what we do now, is it?" He paused, tugging on his chin and hoping someone would take the bait and chase the argument to its conclusion. No one did. He drew a long breath and said bluntly, "I think we should try a different sort of reaching today. One that involves all of us. *Together.*"

Bran ran a hand tiredly over his face. "Even if we *could* reach...the way you want to, only one person can enter a link at a time, can't they?"

"No," Idra said. The others had straightened and appeared more alert as they followed the conversation. "My great-grandmother once told me that Reachers sometimes entered a link by accident during song rites, and they got no harm from it."

What more had Idra's great-grandmother told her? Suddenly it seemed absurd that so many Reachers had lived together for months without exchanging much knowledge. They had been too focused on surviving.

"Doesn't matter," Zon said, hunching into his pelt. "You can't drag up a god."

Walde considered revealing his doubt that Thara *was* a god but set it aside. They didn't need another reason not to trust him. "It wouldn't be against her will. We would simply offer her the opportunity to rise."

"Rise," Bran repeated softly, his eyes narrowed in thought. "What would that do, anyway?"

Walde said, "I'm hoping it will make a visible change. One that people can't set aside as easily as they did the crack in the Harborlands' First."

Nessa tossed a blackened stick onto the dead coals. "You keep saying *we*. What makes you think *we* can reach at all right now?"

He shrugged. "Why not? What have you got to lose?"

She went still and thoughtful at the question.

Walde rose to his feet and paced around the fire pit. "We've *got* to try something. You know as well as I do that sending the children to that ravine hasn't solved anything. One day, they'll be found out, maybe sooner than later with all the new activity down there. It was a quick fix when we desperately needed one, and no one wanted to think beyond that. But now we *have* to. We have *got* to make a change. If this idea doesn't work, then we'll try something else. That's our task. Not to hide somewhere for a while and lick our wounds."

His voice lowered as he went on, "I've done some things I regret, things that changed me. I've accepted that now and moved on. How would my children feel if they knew I could have changed things but didn't even try because I saw myself as damaged? That's not good enough. If the future depends on what I do now, then I'll do what I have to do and be what I have to be to change things, even if it kills me."

Bran's back had straightened, and he was staring at Walde with wide eyes.

Idra chewed her weathered bottom lip. "Say we do succeed in entering a link," she mused, "and we all reach her together. You're the only one who can cling to Thara."

"I realize that. But I have an idea I think will work." He tried for a hopeful smile. Inside, he was far from confident, but he couldn't let them see that, couldn't suggest anything that might hamper their ability to reach. Death was worrisome enough, and he had only hinted at it.

Guarded anticipation flickered in the Reachers' faces. After all, this was what a Reacher always wanted but could never have: not merely to reach, but to clasp and raise up. Or at least, that was something Walde had always wanted.

Bran and Shin eyed each other as if in silent communication, then they both shot to their feet at once. Shin clasped Walde's hand. "W-we'll do it."

"We'll try," Bran amended.

Nessa stood with a shrug and a dry smile. "It's as you say, I have nothing to lose."

Idra and Zon were last to rise. Out of all the Reachers, Walde had the least confidence in these two. Idra had been injured recently, both physically and mentally, and Zon was still a mystery. Walde wasn't even sure that the hunter *could* enter a link. Nevertheless, they both agreed to try.

They took the main walkway to the trunk in single file, Zon and Idra staying well away from the faint bloodstains that now marred the boards. Walde didn't stop at the trunk but led them straight on toward the roots at the backside of the tree.

Bran made an appreciative sound as Walde ushered them down into a deep, weedy space between roots. It was where he had learned to enter a link.

They shoved their packs into the narrowing end of the root and spent some minutes trying to get comfortable. In the end, it was decided that they would lie on their backs in pairs. Walde and Zon lay nearest the trunk, followed by Shin and Bran and Idra and Nessa.

Nessa sighed. "If this doesn't work, we're going to have to spend the night in the tree and try again tomorrow."

"Stop whining," Idra muttered.

Walde edged away from a hard vine and tried to loosen his stiff muscles. To *not* think about the possibility that he'd never see Brite again. The urge to reach had become so overpowering that it was its own emotion, brightening his hands before the link's swelling presence even hit him.

He hummed his dream song, knowing it would help the Reachers let go, and stared up at the gap of blue sky through the branches. The leaves didn't fall so heavily now. More than half were already gone; the rest would likely cling on until the cold air changed their colors. He watched one lift lightly on a breeze.

The wave came then, and his heart followed it into the blackness of the void.

At once, all concerns fled from his mind. The invisible walls of the tunnel pressed him, thrusting him toward Thara's retreating presence. With an effort, he stifled the urge to arrow forward. He had wanted to do something. It had been important. It had involved waiting—

The sudden crash of another presence against his own shocked him. But in that instant, he recalled everything. At once, he seized the presence and tangled himself with it. Shin. He recognized her timid, feral mind. He fought her as she struggled to writhe away. Fear of losing herself added strength to her efforts, but Walde was stronger still, and soon she was unable to move. He had knitted himself so closely with her that neither could've separated had they wanted to.

When a second presence collided with him, he was ready. Bran wasn't as strong as his sister, but he was more stubborn. Walde was still struggling to hold him when Zon arrived.

Zon was a surprise. Instead of jerking away, he sank willingly into Walde's desperate hold and allowed Walde to knit them all together. Zon's was a surprisingly mild presence, but Walde suspected he had hidden reserves of strength. Twitchy, nervous Nessa was next to join the tangle, and then there was a long space of nothing. No Idra. Meanwhile, the tunnel continued to heave them on. But time was running out. They had passed through what Walde thought was the healthy stretch of the link and entered a decayed section. A sensation of being frayed assailed him now, and it would only get worse.

Too late for Idra now. Nessa, who was weaker than the rest, had already lost consciousness. She was with him still but not aware. Bran went next, and then Shin. Walde clung to the last Reacher that still shared his awareness. It was as he expected. Zon had hidden reserves of strength.

Walde needed every bit of it when, to his shock, Idra finally arrived. She was barely there when Walde and Zon weaved her into the tangle. Zon's efforts weakened before they were through, and then he too drifted out of consciousness.

Walde knew nothing more until his mind screamed awake; a pain like that inflicted by fire ripped through it. The others flinched from the pain in horror, but Walde couldn't let go, no matter what it cost him to cling on.

He understood their outrage. A Reacher was used to approaching Thara while aware. Colliding with her overwhelmed the mind, causing extreme discomfort. And if his own wasn't enough, the others' amplified it five-fold.

The point came when it was too late to escape, had he even wanted to. He had formed a rictus against her, and the others with him. Would they ever forgive him for making them endure this?

An instant later, the answer didn't matter. All at once, the pressure lifted as if it had never been, and he floated with the tangle in a formless, lightless space.

He didn't know how long they drifted. He felt nothing from Thara. Perhaps she would not speak to him again. After all, he had ignored her advice and pushed on with his own ideas. But he wasn't the only one here. No, she wouldn't avoid them all for Walde's misdeed.

He set aside his spinning thoughts and let his mind go still.

Thara spoke his name.

"I'm here," he said. A surge of excitement emanated from the tangle, but their thought voices were muted. Either they chose not to speak or could not. Walde waited with a mix of anticipation and dread for her next words.

None came. Did she wait for him to speak?

At last, he blurted, "I'm sorry. I didn't follow your advice, and people got hurt because of it. But now I've—now we've— come to make things right." Rather than explain what he wanted, he showed her with his mind.

A faint thread of amusement reached him. "I am afraid that is not possible."

Walde's disappointment was echoed by several others. He was about to beg her to think of some other way to make a change when she went on, "You have astonished me, Walde. I had never imagined that a Reacher would bring others through the way you have. It is almost beyond belief. And yet you are here with me. You are all here." Her presence intensified as she wrapped them in the warmth of her regard.

Walde would have wept if he could. She had forgiven him. Just like that. He didn't deserve it.

"You want to make a change," she went on. "And so you will. But know this: if you live through it, you will also be changed. Utterly and irrevocably."

"So be it," Walde said and heard his thought voice echoed by the others. Bran had grown nervous, but his resolve didn't waver. After another pause, Walde asked timidly, "Will this change work?"

"It will tug your people back from the dangerous path they are on. More than that, I cannot say. Life is never perfect, Walde. It never was before, and it will not be after. If you live past this, remember what you learned while you were in the Woodlands."

"Wait," he blurted as she receded from him. Was this really happening now? "What is the change, and how can we prepare for it?" If anything could help them survive, he would do it.

Her thoughts came to him at a great distance, "I am changing the Woodlands First into a Worldtree, and you—all of you—will emerge from its pods. Brace yourselves. This change will happen quickly."

As the others stiffened with fear, an image of Brite entered Walde's mind. *I love you,* he thought, knowing she couldn't hear him but wanting to think that somehow, someway, she would feel it.

Then something slammed into him, separating him from the others and sending him flailing into a void. Something like stars stretched away from him. A vastness of space. *We are all children in a great womb,* he thought. Then the stars blinked out, and he knew no more.

CHAPTER 24

*In the mists of time, the Worldtree seeded us from her womb pods.
The summer sun warmed her, the rain wetted her roots, and when she
grew heavy with life, she loosed us into the world.*
—A fragment of the Seed Pod legend, translated from
the old tongue

*If you think you've strayed from the path, trace your steps back to
the beginning.*
—Hunter's wisdom

A large crack of light opened above the man, waking him
from some long and dreamless sleep. He squinted against it
until his eyes adjusted, and warmth flooded his sticky skin.
He breathed in deeply and then wriggled around in whatever
encased him until he was unstuck from the walls and floor.
The enclosure was only a little longer than his body, and it
swung a little as he grasped its open edges and hefted himself
out of it onto some sort of uneven surface outside. He got to his
feet and looked around.

He was in a Mothertree. Leaves flapped around him, and
the seed pod he'd climbed out of lay at his feet. The air felt cool
in his throat and against his wet body. He was about to take a
step toward the distant trunk when he swayed, and something

akin to double vision beset him. In some other world, some other time, leaves were not the size of his body, and seed pods were never larger than his forearm. Yet he'd fit inside this one, and with room to spare. He wiped at his sticky eyes and then stared at his fingers. They looked paler than...than they had been at some other time.

An urge to keep moving swept the strange images from his mind. He hiked along the top of a massive branch and then down another, pushing past huge leaves. The bark was rough, full of bumps and fissures, but the bare pads of his feet were tough and he seemed to know how to step to avoid tripping. He came to the mountain of a trunk at last and peered down it.

The double vision returned, and he dug his fingers convulsively into the bark. He stood on the tree's lowest branch, yet the ground looked to be a hundred yards down; in some other time and place, it shouldn't be more than ten.

He shook his head and started down the sheer face of the trunk. His arms were strong and his feet dug into the mossy grooves, finding footholds with ease. His mind wandered as he descended. He must have lived before. Who had he been? He tried to recall a name. Was it World? No, World wasn't a name. World was the tree. A Worldtree. And he was climbing down from its lowest level.

Level. That was another word to remember. A word from before.

Motion at the corner of his eyes made him look down and to the side. Another naked person was climbing far below him.

Naked? He glanced down at himself and snorted. Yes, he was naked. The tree had bark, but he was bare. He'd need to remedy that. As his gaze drifted from his body to the bulging roots far below, he glimpsed something else... The space between the roots was full of people. Hundreds of them, perhaps even thousands, stretching on and on for as far as he could see. Many appeared to be kneeling instead of standing.

The naked person reached them and was drawn into their huddle so that it disappeared from view. He drew an uneven breath. Should he be afraid of all those people? He didn't know, and so he decided not to care. Instinct urged him to keep moving. He needed to eat and drink and then sleep some more. A glimpse of much smaller Mothertrees nearby comforted him, promising he was a normal size.

At long last, he reached the roots. Voices rose in a cacophony around him. A woman passed a wailing baby to someone next to her and raised her arms up to him. Glancing at her shining eyes and tear-streaked face, he suddenly felt his heart turn over. A brightness gathered in him and radiated out. Bright. *Brite.*

"Walde!" she screamed.

His eyes blurred with tears. "Yes. I'm coming."

BOOKS BY W.K. GREYLING

THE AURE DUOLOGY

*Beneath the Roots

*White Bird

THE MOTHERTREE DUOLOGY

*Silver Light

ABOUT THE AUTHOR

Canadian novelist W.K. Greyling lives in the maritime province of Nova Scotia. When she's not writing, she spends her time curating the music library for Ancient FM, an online medieval and Renaissance radio station.

Printed in Great Britain
by Amazon

27871747R00182